Don't Ever Work In Childcare!
A cautionary tale

Arika Brittany

Dedication

In loving memory of my sweet, determined friend, Maakara Khepra, who never let a cancer diagnosis stop her from living a full life. If she could complete college with all the physical changes her body went through, then surely I could write a novel.

Prologue

"Why couldn't I just have been born rich? I don't want another job. I'm sick of this," Serena griped as she stomped into Bessie Coleman Library shaking snow off her boots. "I don't ever want to work again. I need a break from men. I need a break from humans in general. What job involves total isolation and earns obscene amounts of money?" Serena vowed to find out.

"Good afternoon, welcome to Bessie Coleman!" The chipper librarian's greeting assaulted Serena as she entered the lobby.

"Can I use the restroom?" Right to the point. Serena had no desire for small talk.

"You sure can." The helpful employee pressed the button behind the circulation desk unlocking the door immediately to Serena's right.

While washing her hands at the sink, Serena tugged at the bags under her eyes. Her skin had definitely seen better days. Normally it was a rich caramel color, but it had become dull and dry. "I really need to invest in a moisturizer." She unzipped her coat, and observed the extra pounds that stress eating had added to her figure. "I have to get it together."

"Is there anything I can help you with today?" The librarian asked in a sickeningly sweet tone as soon as Serena exited the bathroom.

"No. I'm fine," Serena retorted irritably and made a beeline for the computers in the adult section, bypassing the prominent African American history displays. There were nine vacant desks and two occupied with patrons. Serena sat as far away from them as possible. No distractions.

"Excuse me! Miss? You have to reserve a computer first." Serena turned around to see the overzealous librarian waving in her direction. She rolled her eyes and ignored her. Seconds later, there was a tap on Serena's shoulder. "Miss, members have to reserve a computer before logging in."

"Even if most of the computers are available?" Serena asked looking up into the librarian's stereotypical reading glasses with the chain around her neck.

"Yes, we find it makes things run smoothly for everyone. There's no confusion on time limits this way." The employee gave Serena a warm smile that almost helped melt her chilly exterior.

"Okay what do I need to do?" Serena asked resigned to the fact that she was going to have to leave her seat before handling business.

"Just follow me. It will only take a second." The persistent woman ushered Serena back passed the posters of Jennifer Hudson and Michelle Obama to a different computer by the printers. "This is where we make reservations. Just enter your library card number and take it from there. Do you think you need any help?"

"No ma'am. Thank you."

"You're welcome. I'm Ms. Jones. Just call me if you need me." The lady ambled back to the front desk. If Serena was in a better mood, she'd probably find her grandmotherly appeal pleasant.

Once she finished her reservation, Serena noticed the machine had assigned her a specific computer; it was not the one she had her heart set on. Trying not to let it deter her any further, she searched for cubicle #3. Once found, she plopped down, tossing her purse on the floor. As soon as she logged in, she heard someone say her name.

"Serena?" The confused female voice called from beside her.

Serena took a deep steadying breath before glancing over. The young woman in the cubicle looked familiar. "Maakara?" Recognition spread across her face. "Hey girl!" Serena grinned in spite of her shitty mood.

"Wow, how long has it been? 10 years?" Maakara grinned back and hugged Serena without lifting her butt from the chair.

"The last time I saw you was eighth grade graduation, so yeah 10 years. How have you been?" Serena took in Maakara's short cinnamon colored afro and dainty nose piercing.

"I've been great. You look the same as you did in grammar school, more mature now though. Damn, we're getting old!" Maakara laughed. "Your hair looks healthy too," she added taking in Serena's long silk press peeking from beneath her winter hat.

"And I love your 'fro. It really fits your face. Your skin looks great too. I was just saying I need a new moisturizer." Serena touched her face insecurely. Her complexion paled in comparison to Maakara's glowing copper one.

"I'm not going to put any heat on my hair for a year and see what happens to it." Maakara stretched one of her tight coils. "You might have to refer me to your beautician eventually though because your silk press is everything!" Maakara admired openly.

"Thank you." Serena blushed. "You can follow her on Instagram to see her work."

"What are you doing here?" Maakara turned her body completely in Serena's direction.

"I'm about to start looking for jobs." Serena sighed thinking of her past job experiences. "I've had such bad luck finding a good fit. I figure I can focus better if I'm not at home so here I am."

"What line of work were you in?" Maakara inquired.

"Childcare. You would not believe the drama. I thought childcare would be safe!"

"Shoot, I would think so too. You got to hang with a bunch of cute kids all day. What was the issue?"

"The kids were cool but the employers? Hot mess! Don't get me started. I'm still traumatized," Serena half-joked.

"You definitely have to tell me about it now." Maakara laughed and leaned forward with interest.

"Where should I start?" Serena was unable to resist the perfect opportunity to vent.

"Start with whatever your first job was."

"That was the home daycare. Let me think…"

Morning Glory

Woodlawn, Chicago

A wave of excitement rushed over me as I approached the gate of my new job. Eager to learn everything there was to know about childcare, I rang the bell well before my shift was scheduled to start.

"Who is it?" the intercom piped.

"Serena Davis." The woman immediately buzzed me in, unlocking the gate.

"Good Morning! Welcome back to Morning Glory!" Jessica Hall greeted me at the front door. "It's nice to finally have you join us! Come on in." She gestured me inside with a nod of the head. She was pretty and reminded me of the way Vivica Fox looked before the plastic surgery.

"Good morning Jess. How are you?" I asked stepping over the threshold.

"I'm great. And you?" Her voice was soothing, helpful in her line of work.

"I'm happy to be here. Thanks again for the opportunity." I glanced around the house as she closed the door behind me. Morning Glory home daycare was situated in Jess' ranch style home. It was just as clean and organized that day as it was when I first met her.

"Feel free to store your shoes and coat here." Jess tapped a closet door. "The kids' belongings go in the basement. On the back of the front door is the sign-in sheet for you and the parents. Just fill out the clipboard each day. Name and time of arrival and departure. I'll give you a quick tour before we head down to meet the kids." She stepped further into the house.

"This is the living room, mostly my territory, but sometimes the kids relax up here too. To our left are my two bedrooms and the bathroom. You can either wash your hands here in the mornings or in the bathroom downstairs. It is imperative that you do not track germs inside," Jess said firmly.

"Yes ma'am," I said finding her tone intimidating. She continued as if she didn't hear me.

"This is the dining area. As you can see, we have the kids' highchairs stacked here for mealtimes. We clean them off after every meal. Continuing towards the back of the house, we have the kitchen. Everything you need for meals is here. Easy to find." Pointing towards a door at the back of the kitchen she exclaimed, "Now let's go see the kids!"

The basement stairs creaked beneath our footsteps. Before I reached the bottom, I could see that the room was gray. I immediately made a mental note to cover the dark walls with posters and artwork from the kids. Once our descension was complete, I saw that the space was rectangular with two doors off the left and right walls. The tile floors were covered with alphabet rugs. On the wall to my right, there were wooden cubbies labeled with the kids' names. The back wall had a full bookcase next to a TV. There was a radio on the floor that I knew I would use for dancing and singing with the little ones. I couldn't wait to play with the toys stored in containers lining the walls next to bright blue cots. Except for the dark bare walls, the place was perfect for toddlers. The kids were in the middle of story time, sitting in a semi-circle surrounding a teacher in a rocking chair.

"Looks like we have a visitor! Let's say hello," encouraged the young teacher who stood up to greet me, revealing a heavily pregnant belly. Out of breath, she sat back down and settled for a wave. The kids, happy to have a reason to start wiggling, turned around and vigorously mimicked their teachers' action.

"Hey, guys! I'm Serena." I smiled as I took in their adorable faces.

"Serena is going to be joining us as your new teacher," Jess interjected. "Serena, this is their other teacher, Amanda Ruiz."

"Hey, Amanda. Nice to meet you." I returned her wave.

"Nice to meet you too." She swept a loose piece of her long dark hair out of her face.

"I was just giving Serena a tour. We'll only be a minute," Jess announced.

"Okay." Amanda grinned clearly happy for the distraction.

"Serena, as you can see," Jess continued. "We have plenty of toys and books for the kids. We have MAGNA-TILES, Legos, paint, Play-Doh. To our left is the bathroom, and the washer and dryer. Behind the door to the right is the nursery for the babies under two. Kids under two sleep in Pack N Plays because they struggle to stay still. It's safer for them. Any questions?"

"So far, no. I'm just taking everything in." I glanced around the large room once more.

"Good. Let's head back upstairs to chat then you can hang out with the kids and Amanda for the rest of the day." As we went up the stairs, I felt a bunch of little eyes following me.

Seated at her kitchen table drinking a homemade smoothie, Jess continued her run-down. "Cleaning supplies are stored in the bathroom closet downstairs and under the kitchen sink upstairs. You get to make breakfast, lunch, and snacks for our eight kids. You are responsible for teaching them their colors, shapes, numbers, and letters. You will also lead them in art projects, outside play time, and naptime. On Fridays, I need you to sanitize the toys. There may be some minor details we have to hammer out, but I think that's enough for now. If any of that seems overwhelming just let me know. You sure you don't have any questions?"

"It sounds like a lot, but I guess it'll get easier as I go," I said not feeling confident in my abilities.

"Let's stop the boring talk. Go enjoy the kids. I'll see you later. Have fun." Jess shooed me away.

"Jess," I paused at the top of the stairs. "Thanks again for this opportunity. I'm sure you could have hired someone with more experience. I appreciate it."

"No problem. You seem like a sweet girl. It was an easy decision."

-

"How do you like it here so far?" Amanda asked as soon as I got to the bottom of the stairs.

"I wanted to ask you the same thing. Jess seems great. Very professional. I like her."

"Yeah, she's okay. I've never had a major problem with her," Amanda responded as if she was trying to be polite.

"Tell me about yourself," I said while observing how the kids played with one another.

"Well, I've been working here for three years. I'm 29. I've been married for six years, and I have a five-year-old son. I have a BA in early childhood education. What about you?"

"I'm 18. This is my first job since I graduated from high school in June. I really like working with kids so here I am." I shrugged and paused before asking, "When are you due?" I pointed towards Amanda's belly.

"I'm nine months. Due in two weeks. I'm having a girl. I'm glad my water didn't break while I was working!" She made a nervous face.

"I can't believe you're still working. That had to be tough!"

"Yeah, honestly it's been hard on me. Luckily I'll be able to stay home now that you're here."

"You're not coming back after you have the baby?" I asked, panic taking over.

"Jess didn't tell you? You're replacing me. My last day is Friday." Amanda looked at me with pity in her eyes. "I want to stay at home for a while. My husband can take care of us."

"Good for you, but now I'm scared." I immediately started nibbling at my nails.

"I'll help you. I'm sure you can do it," she responded positively.

"I'd really appreciate it."

"I think you will catch on quickly. Just keep the kids busy and safe. Stay on top of letting the parents know when it's their turn to bring wipes for the week. Keep the kids happy. Perfect multitasking. Jess spends most of her time upstairs. Be prepared to work alone. Once you get used to it, it'll come natural to you. We have four days before I leave. I'll walk you through it." Amanda's voice was filled with encouragement.

"Okay," I said weakly, my nerves getting the best of me.

"You want to join the kids now?" Amanda asked trying to lighten the mood.

"Absolutely!" I shouted.

"Hey, guys! Come over and give Ms. Serena hugs."

The preschoolers who could walk rushed right over. The crawlers turned their heads curiously and slowly made their way in my direction. A blonde boy about a year old hugged me first.

"Towwa!" he said pointing towards the blocks and taking my hand.

"He wants you to make a tower with him." Amanda laughed.

"Sure, little guy. What's your name?" I asked squatting down to his level.

"He's Otto," Amanda cut in. "He's a year and a half. Cool kid. That little crawler over there is Amari. She's 10 months." She pointed towards a tiny light-skinned baby with a little afro. "This is Christopher: age two. He looks exactly like his dad. Wait until you meet him. These two are Cici and Elijah, best friends." She gestured to the little ones holding hands. "They're both the same age as Otto. You'd think they were twins since they're so close and have the same dark curly hair. They're both quiet, never give me a hard time. Aiden is over there. He's three and pretty easy going. Our other infant is Jada. She's six months old. She's the youngest. And last but certainly not least, this sweet little girl with the big pretty eyes is Morgan; she's three too," Amanda concluded with a look of pride on her face.

"Such a diverse group of kids. You all are so cute! Can I play with you?" I looked around the room.

The toddlers smiled and resumed their activities as Otto guided me towards his blocks.

"Her name is Serena, Otto. Can you say Serena?" Amanda leaned over in her chair to talk to him.

"Na, towwa!" he said sitting on the floor.

"I think he tried to say your name. You will now be referred to as 'Na'. He calls me 'Da'," Amanda said with a giggle that reddened her cheeks.

"Na it is," I grinned.

My new friend Otto and I made towers until lunchtime.

-

"Wait, so your new boss didn't think to tell you that you'd be working alone?" Maakara cut into the story for the first time. "Why would she introduce y'all like you would be working together? That's shady already," she said folding her arms with attitude.

"And that's not even the half of it. I can't believe I stayed there as long as I did." Serena shook her head in shame.

"What else happened?"

-

Reservations about the future aside, my first day went well. Everything from the cleanliness of the house to the kids' personalities made me feel comfortable enough to stay at Morning Glory. Amanda did a great job of filling me in on everything I needed to know. After snack time, Jess joined us in the basement.

"Serena, how are you feeling about Morning Glory so far?" she asked with a hopeful smile on her face.

"It's a lot to take in. I feel myself getting tired now that I've finally slowed down, but otherwise everything is great. I have to adjust quickly since I'll be doing this alone next week," I stated pointedly.

"I'm glad you're feeling confident. How do you like the kids?" Jess asked not taking the bait.

"They're amazing! Otto seems to like me. As soon as he saw me, he took my hand and asked me to make a tower with him. Little Amari is adorable too. They all are," I replied earnestly.

"Great. I hope we're a good fit for each other. Maybe we can work together long term."

-

The end of my first week was Amanda's last day. "Serena," she looked over her shoulder then whispered, "don't stay as long as I did. The pay sucks considering the amount of work you have to do. There's not any room to grow."

"It'll be fine. I appreciate the help. Good luck to you. Congrats on the baby." I hugged her.

"Good luck to you too. You'll need it." Amanda left without another word.

On My Own

My first week without Amanda was hard! I burned the chicken nuggets, forgot to warm up a bottle of breastmilk, and Otto bit Christopher while I was using the bathroom. I learned quickly that dresses and jeans could not be a part of my work uniform. By the second week, I had switched to yoga pants and t-shirts. I needed to be comfortable getting on the floor with the kids. Thankfully Jess didn't seem to mind.

The first couple of months flew by. By November, I had deeply bonded with all of the kids. They were good listeners for the most part. They got along well except for the occasional fight over a toy. I cried like a baby when Otto's family moved to Oregon. It broke my heart knowing I would never see him again.

Because of the season, we all made a bunch of fall-themed art projects and stuck them in the windows and on the walls.

"Wow, this place looks great! I love the decorations, and the kids and parents love you, Serena. Honestly," Jess confessed one day when she ventured to the basement.

"Thank you." I blushed as I watched her stumble on her way up the stairs. "Oh my God, are you okay? I put down Morgan's turkey painting to offer assistance.

"I'm fine. I'm fine." Jess waved me off.

"That's not the first time you almost fell on those stairs. Do they need to be fixed or something? I don't want any of us getting hurt." I was mostly concerned for the kids.

"No, I'm just clumsy. Don't worry about it." She left with a hint of irritation in her voice.

The Change

After Thanksgiving break, a boy named Devin came to replace Otto. At six years old, he was the oldest kid at Morning Glory. I didn't understand why his parents wanted a boy his age to attend a home daycare. I watched from the window as he and his parents approached the house on his first day. Devin snatched away from his dad and sprinted up to the gate, ringing the bell five times before his parents caught up to him.

"I'll get the door," Jess said sounding nervous. "Hello there. Come on in," she greeted the family warmly as they walked up the stairs.

Devin was short for his age and chubby. His brown skin was the perfect mix of his parents' complexions. He had beautiful dark eyes and long lashes that framed them.

Unfortunately, my observation was interrupted when Devin suddenly tried to run back down the concrete stairs. His mother grabbed his arm, and he took a swing at her with his left hand.

"No! Let me go!" he shouted throwing his body backward almost hitting his head on the steps.

"Come on big guy." His dad grabbed his left arm and ushered him into the house. Once inside, Devin started screaming at the top of his lungs. The shrieks were so shrill that I was worried someone would call the police on us. I was thankful that the other kids had not arrived yet.

"I don't want to go here! Let me go! Let me go now!" the boy commanded, landing a kick between his dad's legs.

"Devin, you like Ms. Jess remember? She likes you too. You used to have a lot of fun here honey." His mother rubbed his back, and Devin howled directly in her ear.

"And guess what else Devin," Jess added trying to intervene. "We have a new teacher. Her name is Serena. She's happy to meet you." Devin swung his arm and knocked Jess' smoothie out of her hand. Mouth agape, I said nothing.

"Take me home now!" he yelled with his fists balled up at his sides.

"Sorry about that Jess. You know how he can be," Devin's mom stated as if her son's behavior was normal.

"It's fine. Luckily my cup is plastic." Jess picked it up off the floor.

"Devin, guess what. If you're a good boy today, you can watch Mickey Mouse Clubhouse when you get home okay?" Devin's dad's voice strained after the kick to the groin.

"And a movie too," the boy demanded with a frown.

"Any movie you want," his dad agreed too easily.

"I'll be a good boy. Just for today." Devin unclenched his fists.

-

"Hey Jess, are you okay? What was all of that about?" I asked while Devin played in the living room after his parents had gone.

"I'm fine. It's hard for him being back here that's all." She began blending another smoothie.

"Okay, but why is he not in school? Shouldn't he be in first grade?" I yelled over the machine.

"He's six, but his birthday is late. It's in October. He's supposed to be in kindergarten. He has some time to find a school for first grade." Jess turned off the blender.

"So why did he just come to us in November? Where was he before?" I asked not understanding the boy's background.

"Devin… he…he managed to get kicked out of his kindergarten program at St. Benedict," Jess admitted reluctantly.

"How?" I asked scared to hear the response.

"He… was struggling with transitioning to his new school. Apparently, his behavior had only gotten worse since the school year started."

"Jess, what could a six-year-old possibly do that's so bad that he gets kicked out of school?" I braced myself for the other shoe to drop.

"He, uh, peed on another student while they were using the restroom," she mumbled the last sentence so fast that I almost didn't catch it.

"Well, what happens if he does that here?" I folded my arms across my chest genuinely curious about my future at Morning Glory.

"I don't think we'll have that problem. Devin likes being here. I've known him for years. He just didn't want to be at his new school. That's all." Jess sounded unconvinced by her own words.

"He wasn't acting like he wanted to be here. I hope he doesn't pee on any of us." I tried to look her in the eye.

"He won't. I know how to handle him." She avoided eye contact.

"He tried to hit you Jess," I stated plainly as if she wasn't aware.

"Stuff like that happens. Kids have tantrums. He'll adjust soon enough." Her tone was guilty, and I couldn't understand why.

"Good. His parents should be careful. Soon enough he'll be too old to be here."

-

"That boy sounds like he was bad as hell," Maakara said.

"That would be putting it mildly." Serena shivered at the memory.

-

As the days went on, I realized I would not ever get used to working with a kid like Devin who was rambunctious enough to make me rethink my career path. He was dedicated to giving me and the other children a hard time. True to his word, he was a good boy for one day only.

The screaming and temper tantrums drove all of us crazy. Devin made sure we only got peace when he felt like dishing it out. His parents didn't know what to do with him. They were a very polite couple, Black professionals in their mid-40's. They said that they waited until their late 30's to have Devin to ensure he would have the best that life had to offer. They were more than capable of providing for him financially but dropped the ball when it came to disciplining him effectively. They had good intentions, but they chose passivity and coddling because it was best for them, not Devin.

"I don't know how to get him to listen," Devin's mother Karen confided in me one day. "What should I do?"

"He probably needs some type of therapy," I said bluntly before adding, "if you think it's really serious. I also noticed you all reward him even when he hasn't been on his best behavior. If he gets to watch his favorite shows regardless of the way he acts, he has no motivation to be good. Maybe give him some incentive to see what happens."

"I hadn't thought about that! It's easier to just give in to him, but I'll try it. Thanks so much." Karen clearly had never really considered disciplining her son.

-

One day during arts and crafts, I noticed all of the students following instructions well except for one.

"Hey Devin." I reached down and touched his shoulder. "Try to keep the paint on your paper. Let's not get too much on the table."

"No! I don't like you!" he screamed as he threw his paper on the floor and deliberately brushed the table.

"That isn't nice Devin. Now you can't participate in movie time. Maybe if you're a good boy tomorrow, you'll get your privilege back," I offered in the most patient voice I could muster. In reality, I wanted to press his face in the mess he made.

Exhaustion

A few months after Devin's enrollment, it felt like I was caring for 20 kids instead of eight. The original seven were angels, but I couldn't work with the devil anymore.

One morning he hit me when I gave him a time out for screaming in the other kids' ears. The funny thing was little Amari reached out and scratched him right on his cheek when he did it to her. She made me proud, but it didn't make up for Devin's behavior in general. Not to mention the numerous times Devin was determined to keep everyone up during naptime by talking, yelling or wetting his Pull-Up just to spite me.

-

"Hold up, girl. The boy was peeing on himself just to piss you off?" Maakara was in disbelief. "What kind of shit is that?"

"Yeah. His mom wanted me to put him in Pull-Ups during naptime even though he really didn't take naps because he was too old for them. I guess the Pull Ups came in handy on those days." Serena shrugged.

"That is ridiculous. What stopped you from leaving? I wouldn't even have given notice. I would've just left. What was Jess doing about it?"

-

One day when all of the kids were gone, I decided to have a serious conversation with my boss. "Jess, I'm stressed out because of Devin. I haven't found a new job, but I'm going to start looking. I'm telling you because I don't want to quit suddenly. I love the other kids. I don't want to leave you by yourself, but I am overworked and severely underpaid. You haven't been much help. If anything, you've become more distant since Devin started. Since you're okay with things the way they are, I can leave." I let out the breath I had been holding for months.

"Wow, I wasn't expecting this at all." Jess paused to think. "Let me work on it. Don't make a decision just yet. Give me some time."

"See you tomorrow." Before I left out of the front door, I heard her start the blender.

-

After another week with no progress, I couldn't help but to ask Jess about what had been bothering me. "Why were you okay letting Devin come back? His mom told me this isn't the first time he got kicked out of school. He's only six. What's going on?"

"Devin's dad is working on getting him into another private program," Jess offered not fully answering the question.

"And why did you let him come back in the first place?" I asked pressing the issue.

"Once a client always a client. His mom is an old friend. And you all are like family to me." Her weak attempt at camaraderie did nothing to satiate my concerns.

"Maybe if you helped me out a little more it would feel like it," I retorted feeling unusually feisty. "When is he leaving? What did his dad say about the new program?" I demanded to know considering Devin tried to snatch one of my box braids out of my head just that morning.

"Give it another month for his dad to have the school situation settled," Jess suggested as if patience was an actual option.

"Another month?" I asked incredulously.

"Yes. Is that a problem?" she snapped.

"No problem at all." I made a mental note to quit as soon as I found another job.

"Good." She sipped her second smoothie of the day and locked herself in her bedroom.

-

Other than my heated conversation with Jess, that morning progressed almost the same as usual. I only had to give Devin one time out, which was suspicious. His average was four before naptime. Based on how obnoxious he normally was, I knew he had something else up his sleeve. After all of the kids were down for quiet time, he proved me right. Loudly singing off-key was his drug of choice that day.

"Devin please be quiet. The kids are sleeping," I whispered with every intention of looking for jobs in peace.

"But I'm not sleepy!" he whined.

"Okay, but you still need to be quiet," I reminded.

"Don't want to!" He folded his arms and pouted. The singing continued.

"Devin come here." He walked over.

"Do you want to read books until naptime is over?" I asked softly.

"No!" He started to hit me on my knees. I snatched him under one of his arms and pulled him close.

"Don't put your hands on me again. Got it?" I sneered at him, mustering as much hate as I could. "Go sit your butt back down NOW!" I let go of his arm as aggressively as I could without pushing him to the floor.

He rushed over to the cot and sat there with his tail between his legs and fell asleep sitting up. He never hit me again after that.

-

"What's the deal with Devin's new school?" I asked Jess with no preamble.

"He was accepted," she replied furtively.

"Will he be starting this school year or next?" I asked. As much as I hated to admit it, it didn't make sense for him to start in March. He might as well start at the beginning of a new school year.

"I'm not sure," she said slurring a bit and not meeting my eyes.

"He needs to start somewhere soon Jess. He's been here for months, and it's only getting worse. He really gets off on harassing us. Maybe you should keep him upstairs with you," I suggested.

"Is he really that bad?" Jess asked stupidly.

"What do you mean? Of course, he is!" I raised my voice at her for the first time. "Look Jess, I'm trying to be patient because of the other kids, but this is too much!" I almost lost control of my temper.

"Devin is really smart." Jess stalled.

"That boy is smart as hell! Way smarter than he needs to be at his age. He's very strategic. He knows what he's doing, which makes it all the more frustrating," I admitted.

"It'll be fine. Be patient." She took a sip of her smoothie and headed for her room.

"I'll be patient when you pay more money," I mumbled the words at her back. I realized she had been intentionally vague in order to keep me there. She knew I had been doing the work of two employees and getting violated constantly, but she didn't offer any additional help or increased pay. I had to go.

-

By April, I dreaded going to work every day. Working 11 hours took its toll on my body. I could barely pull myself out of bed in the morning. I looked forward to the kids' naptime so I could doze off in the rocking chair. Jess had actually become more distant if that was even possible by that point. I think I would have been slightly less tired if she didn't ask me to do favors for her sometimes. They usually involved her handing me trash from the bedrooms when I was taking out the kids' trash or asking me to wash a few of the dishes she used throughout the day. Her excuse was that she got migraines that prevented her from being too active. I took the trash when I was already on my way out but left her dishes in the sink.

-

"Can I ask you for one more favor?" Jess inquired one day.

"What is it?" I asked scared of what was coming.

"I'm getting nasal surgery. I found out I'm allergic to trees. Can you believe that?" Jess asked more friendly than she had ever been. "I can't even buy live Christmas trees anymore. Anyway, the surgery is outpatient and is supposed to help me breathe better."

"Okay…"

"I have a ride to and from the hospital, but could you just check on me during the day? Make sure I'm still breathing?"

"When is the surgery?"

-

Days later, an associate of Jess' arrived at 9:00 am to chauffeur her to the hospital. "Alright Serena, I'll see you all this afternoon!" Jess hollered down the stairs.

"See you later," I called from the basement. I made sure I heard the front door close before I started the kids on their morning project.

"Hey guys. Since she's going to the hospital, we're going to make get well soon cards for Jess. I'm going to get construction paper and fold it in half then you all can decorate them however you want to. We can use markers, crayons, glitter and stickers. Does that sound like fun?" I asked the class.

"Yes!" screamed a chorus of small voices.

"Let's get started to make sure they're dry by the time she gets back."

Later that afternoon, Jess's associate walked her to the front door. "She's going to need your help getting to her room. She's still a bit loopy from the drugs. Here's her medication. Good luck." She handed me a bag and walked away quickly.

"Thank you…" I hesitated when I realized I never caught her name. "Come on Jess. Let's lay you down so I can get back to the kids." I put my arm around her waist.

"Okay," she responded in a funny voice reminding me of patients on laughing gas.

"We made cards for you. I put them on your dresser."

"Ice water. Throat hurts," Jess loudly whispered as she stumbled to her room.

"Okay. Do you need to use the bathroom before you lay down?"

"No. Just water."

"Fine. Let's get you settled." I flipped back her comforter and sat her on the bed. She clumsily pulled in her legs and threw the blanket over herself.

"Water. Now!" she demanded like a toddler with a raspy voice.

"Whatever you like, my queen." I rolled my eyes and left the room.

By the time I got back from the kitchen, the cards that the kids made were scattered on the floor. "What happened Jess?" I immediately picked them up and sat them down on the dresser next to the cup.

"Water!" Jess yelped and eagerly grabbed for the cup, watering sloshing over the sides.

"I'll be back later," I said heading for the door, but not before Jess sat the cup down too excitedly, spilling its contents onto her get well soon cards. She snuggled down in the bed, oblivious.

-

Later in the evening, I peeked in Jess' room. "Hey, you need anything before I go?"

"Ice water. Dinner too," Jess said in her childish way.

"What do you want to eat?" I asked ready to go.

"Spaghetti."

"Did you make some I can warm up for you?"

"No, can you make some?" Jess requested. I wondered if her meds gave her the audacity.

"Girl, I am not making a pot of spaghetti," I said forgetting I was talking to an employer. "It's time for me to go home. I'll give you some ice water. Call your family to help with anything else you need."

"Fine." She pouted.

"You're welcome Jess," I said pointedly.

"Oh, yeah thanks."

-

"I've noticed you don't seem as happy as you once did. Is everything okay?" Cici's mom asked one morning.

"I'm okay. Just tired," I lied.

"Well, when is a new teacher supposed to join you?" the mother asked indignantly.

"I'm not sure."

She frowned at my response. At that moment, she saw Jess in the kitchen. "Hey Jess!"

"Good morning," Jess said walking toward us.

"When will a new teacher be joining Morning Glory? I noticed Serena seems tired." Cici's mother rubbed my shoulder in a motherly way.

"We have a new teacher coming next month after her background check is processed." The lie flowed off Jess' tongue smoothly.

"That's great to hear. I look forward to it. I'll see you guys later. Take care Serena." Cici's mother made her exit.

"See you. Have a good day." I closed the door behind her feeling thankful for the support. Apparently, Jess didn't echo my sentiments.

"What did she say about me before I walked in?" she pressed.

"Nothing. She asked when I'd be getting an assistant since I seem overwhelmed."

"And what did you say back to her?" Jess asked with her paranoia on full display.

"I told her I don't know. That's the truth. Who is the new person starting with us next month?"

Jess didn't seem satisfied with my answer, but she left me alone. As I rejoined the kids, the blender's hum sounded behind me.

-

Working around toddlers who wiped their noses with their hands and coughed in my face all day finally caught up to me. I was getting sick; I could feel it coming on. My movements were slower than usual. My throat was slightly scratchy; my bones were a little achy. I knew it would be Strep throat by the next day, but I showed up for work anyway. Better me caring for the kids than Jess.

"Good morning Jess," I muttered weakly as I walked in the door.

"Morning," she responded not paying attention to my demeanor.

I washed my hands in the upstairs bathroom before prepping breakfast and setting toys out for the kids. Bending over to put the blocks on the floor almost knocked the wind out of me. I sat down to catch my breath until the kids arrived. Jess silently observed me from the couch.

The rest of the day was much like the morning. When the kids got into fights, I had to rely on them to listen to my commands without me physically intervening. I didn't have the strength to get up from the rocking chair unless absolutely necessary. Jess acted oblivious until it was time for me to go.

"What's going on with you?" Jess asked as I signed out.

"I'm not feeling great. Any time I get sick it's Strep throat. I'm worried that's what this is leading to."

"I hope not. I don't want to have to do your job tomorrow," she said as if Morning Glory wasn't her own business.

"I don't want to do my job tomorrow either. Bye, Jessica." I headed out before she annoyed me any further.

The next morning, I felt like death. My mouth was dry, but it hurt to swallow my own spit. A sip of water burned like acid. My temp spiked to 103.7. The aches prevented me from sleeping soundly. Just as I was about to drift off into unconsciousness again, my phone rang. It was 8:00 am. I was late. Jess needed me. Because of my sore throat, I ignored her call and opted to text instead.

Strep throat. Contagious. Need antibiotics.

The message was left on read.

-

My illness only lasted a couple of days although it felt like a week. After a doctor's visit, the TLC of my mom, and antibiotics, I was back at work on Monday.

"Morning Jess," I said with the residual weakness still in my voice.

"Morning. I'll be gone until the end of the day." Seconds later, she left out of the back door.

A Silver Lining

During naptime, I received a call from an unknown number.

"Hello?" I whispered into the phone.

"Yes, hello can I speak to Serena Davis please?" The caller's tone was unnervingly chipper."

"This is Serena. Who's calling?"

"Hi, this is *MinChoicallingfromTaterTotsintheSouthLoop*. We received your online application and we'd like to request an in-depth phone interview whenever you're available," the caller sped through her introduction leaving me a bit confused.

"I'm sorry who's calling?" I asked again stupidly.

"Sorry. I'm known to talk fast," she responded with a giggle and a deep breath. "This is Min Choi, the director of Tater Tots in the South Loop. We received your application. We'd love to schedule a phone interview with you at whatever time works best."

"I'm actually free right now if that's okay…"

-

Unable to control her excitement, Maakara interrupted again. "Tell me you got the job and left Jess right where she was!"

Holding back a laugh at Maakara's animated voice in the quiet library, Serena replied "Yes, I did get the job, but I still gave notice."

"Shoot girl, you're better than me. How did the bitch take it when you gave her the news? I'm assuming not well."

-

The next morning, I walked in on another one of Jess' migraines. "Maybe you should drink some tea if your head is hurting," I gently suggested.

"Maybe you should mind your own business." Jess sipped her smoothie.

"You're absolutely right Jess. I shouldn't meddle." I smiled at her knowing she couldn't get me down. "Speaking of my own business though, I do need to talk to you. I know you have a headache, but it can't wait."

"What is it?" She groaned rubbing her temples.

"I found a new job," I said as I unzipped my coat. Jess's jaw and smoothie almost dropped to the floor.

"Have you told anybody else before me?" she asked in a paranoid voice.

"Why does that matter?" I asked confusion taking over.

"You should have told me as soon as you found out." Jess' tone bordered on angry.

"You shouldn't assume I didn't tell you immediately. The point is I'm giving you notice now," I stated calmly.

"...When do you plan to leave?" she finally managed to ask.

"Two weeks from today."

"Why are you leaving me? I thought we were a team." Jess sounded hurt. Her eyes were glassy, and I wondered if she was going to cry.

"Well um... because nothing has changed since I spoke with you months ago. It's April now. It hasn't felt like we were a team." My words were shaky, but the point was clear.

"I thought you understood I was working on it. Serena, I've been trying. Trust me. I have been. I thought we were friends. I hope you don't come to regret this decision. Maybe you'll change your mind before then." She took a sip from her cup and retreated to her room.

I felt relieved and slightly guilty, like I'd betrayed her. On the flip side, a weight had been lifted from my shoulders. I could spend the next two weeks with my babies with a clear conscience.

-

I revealed my good news to the parents as they dropped the kids off that morning. Everyone was happy for me, but Cici's mom was the only parent who was not surprised.

"I knew you'd be leaving soon," she said immediately after I confided in her.

"How did you know?"

"I could sense things weren't the same here. Between me and you," she leaned in to whisper. "I'm going to pull Cici out soon too. Anyway, I'm happy for you. Take care." She squeezed my hand then made her way towards the gate, holding it open as another family walked in.

"Good morning! I have some news for you all," I greeted them happily.

"Oh no, what is it?" Elijah's mom instantly braced herself.

"My last day will be the 26th. I'll be moving on to a daycare center."

"Wow, congrats to you Serena. We'll miss you. Elijah adores you," the boy's dad congratulated warmly. "I'm sure my wife feels the same way." He gave her a nudge.

"Oh yes, congrats of course! But we know Elijah will miss you." She gave me puppy dog eyes.

"I will miss him too. I know you all might have a babysitter already, but I do babysit in my spare time. We can still see each other," I offered trying to smooth things over.

"Oh yeah, we'd love that!" the boy's father exclaimed eagerly.

"Cool. I'll put one of my business cards on the clipboard. You all can grab it this evening."

"That's perfect. See you later. Thanks." Elijah's parents walked hand in hand down the steps.

-

After I placed my business card on the sign-in sheet, I took the kids in the backyard for a little fresh air. It was hilarious watching Jada avoid grass. She hated it the same way I hated bugs. Cici and Elijah rolled the ball back and forth between their legs. Christopher and Aiden played with the toy cars, and Morgan was playing in Amari's hair. There was one kid unaccounted for.

"Look, Ms. Serena!" Devin said walking towards me holding a grasshopper between his thumb and index finger.

"How did you even catch that? Put it down!" I shrieked jumping away from him.

"Okay!" He squished the huge insect between his palms. I almost vomited at the sight of it.

"Ugh! Time to head inside guys! Devin wash your hands as soon as we get in!"

I trailed behind the kids as we entered the house. "Take off your shoes! Then put them by the front door. Let's wash our hands. Devin goes first!"

-

As I was making lunch, my phone rang.

"Hello?"

"Hey, Serena."

"What's up, mom?" I asked taking fish sticks out the oven.

"I need you to get two recent paystubs from Jess. Since our co-op is income-based, they need your payment info now that you're over 18 and working full time."

"Okay. I'll see if Jess can print a month's worth."

"Thanks. See you later."

I finished preparing lunch and got the kids settled in their chairs. While they were distracted, I knocked on Jess' door. "Hey, Jess?" No response. "Can I get a month's worth of paystubs? I need them in order to recertify where I live." I heard movement inside just before the door opened slightly.

"Sure. No problem. I'll give them to you later." She gave me a syrupy sweet smile.

"Ummm thanks." I was unable to hide my discomfort, not just from her facial expression but from the smell of liquor on her breath.

-

The next day, the kids made a collaborative art project on butcher paper. Every kid had their own area to draw whatever they wanted. I helped guide the little one's hands over the paper.

"Red!" Cici chirped excitedly over her red crayon.

"Bu," Amari added with a blue crayon in her hand.

"Good job ladies!" I said as I drew a big yellow sun right in the middle of the paper. "Christopher what are you making?"

"A dog!"

"What about you Elijah?" I asked.

"Dinosaur! Ceratops," he exclaimed proudly.

"Triceratops? That's so awesome! Good job guys. I made a sun and a rainbow. We have a dog. Can anyone draw a cat? I think someone should make a house and a car. What about some basketballs? Books?"

After about ten minutes of my suggestions, the paper was almost completely full. "It looks like we're almost done, guys. Let me go get some tape so we can put this on the wall." I grabbed the scotch tape I kept hidden in the bathroom cabinet away from prying hands. By the time I came back, Devin was tearing apart our artwork.

"No Devin!" wailed Elijah's unusually shrill voice. Cici ran up and kicked the menace in the shin.

"Devin, why would you do this? Put it down!" He tore it again before I could reach him. His smug face almost made me strangle him.

"You know what Devin? You can have it. Tear it right up. Guys, we're going to make another one. This time Devin is not allowed to join us." I paused when a thought occurred to me. "You all have been such good listeners today. I might have a treat for you at the end of the day." The kids' faces brightened as I put another piece of butcher paper on the floor.

"I want a treat too!" Devin exclaimed.

"You know you're not getting one. You were mean to your friends. You can't participate in art time or treat time. Have fun ripping up that paper, bad boy," I teased.

"I want a treat! I'm not a bad boy!" Devin pouted.

"Aww, it's too late Devin," I said in a fake sad voice. "Today you'll have Cheez-Its while the other kids have cookies."

Devin started crying. I turned away from him to hide my snicker. I wish I had been the one that kicked him.

-

The office where I lived needed to call my job to verify my income. I was expecting them to give me or my mom a call to confirm that everything checked out. When I didn't hear from them by the following week, I called them myself while Jess was out of the house. "Good morning. This is Serena Davis calling to confirm the recertification was completed. I live in unit 13 with my mother. I handed in my stubs last week."

"Hi, yeah thanks for calling. We did call to confirm that you worked at Morning Glory daycare, but we were told you are not an employee," the lady on the phone replied in a gossipy tone.

Confused I replied, "I'm at work now. When did you guys call?"

"Yesterday morning at 10:00," she replied confidently.

"Are you sure?" I asked, a chilling thought forming.

"Absolutely."

"I work 7:30-6:30. I was here when you called."

"Well, that's what the owner told us," the woman retorted stubbornly.

"I will have a new job after next week, but I've been working here for the last eight months," I assured her.

"We can confirm your pay when you start at your new place of employment. No problem." Her tone was more understanding.

"Thank you." I hung up and stared at my phone dumbfounded then called my mom to vent.

"Mom! I've had it! If one more thing goes wrong, I'm going to curse this bitch out."

"Wait a second. What happened? Who's the bitch?" my mom asked caught off guard.

"Jess lied to the office and said I never worked at Morning Glory. I just got off the phone with them."

"Are you serious?" My mom sounded just as stunned as I felt.

"Yeah. I'm going to quit today before I get fired for putting my hands on her. I've had enough.

"Serena, you have one more week. If you can't make it, then don't go back. I don't want you to get arrested. Say bye to the parents and kids and leave it at that," my mother said firmly.

"I'll talk to Jess as soon as she gets back. She might not let me stay to say bye to the parents, but I'm willing to risk it. I'll keep you posted."

-

When Jess got back at 4:00pm, I had the kids situated in the living room. I didn't want to give her the chance to avoid me. "We need to talk. It's important." I followed her to the door of her room.

"What is it?" she asked with the audacity to sound exhausted.

"Today will be my last day. I know I was supposed to have another week, but I can't do it. I can leave now or wait until 6:30."

"Fine, do whatever you want." She opened her door and closed it quickly, but not before I caught a glimpse of vodka bottles on the floor.

-

"Jess, can you buzz the gate? I'm washing dishes!" I called out when I heard the first parent arrive for the evening. When I didn't hear any movement, I put the dishes on hold and completed the evening pick-ups with no assistance from my boss. In hindsight, it was easier that way. That way my goodbyes were private and personal.

"Hey, we didn't get your business card from the other day," Elijah's dad said when I answered the door.

"Really? I left it on the clipboard for you all." I frowned.

"It's fine. I know you have your hands full here. Just put your number in my phone." He handed it to me.

"Cool. Please keep in touch. I would hate to miss Elijah grow up." I typed in my number and sighed, "Unfortunately today is my last day. I'm leaving sooner than expected, so I'm glad you mentioned it when you did." I handed him the phone back.

"My wife is going to be devastated," he said in a somber tone. "May I ask why?"

"I'm trying to keep things professional here. But I do wonder who would take my card off the clipboard." I gave him a knowing look.

"That bad, huh? Well, we'll definitely be in touch. Good luck with everything." He shook my hand, took Elijah by his wrist and closed the door behind him.

Not one to leave a job unfinished, I checked the basement and main floor to make sure everything was in order. I wiped down the counters and accidentally knocked over a mug. The kitchen instantly filled with the smell of liquor. I soaked it up, washed the glass and left it on the drying rack.

"Make sure you wash those dishes! And take out the trash!" I heard Jess yelling from the living room. It was after 6:30 and my last day; I wasn't doing anything else except heading out the front door.

As I put my jacket and shoes on, Jess struggled to her feet and drunkenly spat at me, "You haven't washed a damn thing! Just because you're quitting doesn't mean you can get lazy." She fished in her pocket for something and fell back onto the couch. "Oh, I heard you talking about your missing little card. Here you go since it's so important to you. It was tacky to leave it on my clipboard anyway." She dropped torn up pieces of my red business card on the floor near her feet.

The weight of her words registered, and then I snapped. "You wash your own damn dishes, Jess! I was trying to end this on a positive note but forget it! I know you lied to the housing people. And you definitely could have helped me more around here. When was the last time you even visited the kids in the basement? You're a jealous, lazy lonely, lying-ass alcoholic who gets off on being able to say you own a daycare, so you don't really have to work. But the gag is, YOU DO HAVE TO WORK! If you're not going to hire two teachers, then get off your ass, put down the vodka, and do what you have to do to keep your business afloat. I'm going to report you. Now that I'm leaving, these kids can't be trusted in your care. I'm going to tell the parents, too. I hope you never get to where you want to be. And you never will, considering what your cheap ass is willing to pay! Goodbye Jessica. Please act like I never existed, and I'll do the same with you." I opened and slammed the door behind me as hard as I could. I jogged down the stairs with tears in my eyes. I wasn't sad. I was angry because I should have given her a piece of my mind long before I did.

-

Maakara stared at Serena for a full 10 seconds before speaking again. "So, you're telling me the bitch was an alcoholic the whole time? How didn't I see that coming?" Maakara paused to reflect. "I'm glad you got to say bye to the kids, but damn I wish you had left sooner. That was ridiculous. Did you ever hear from her again?"

"Yeah, actually the next morning she called me three times. She left two voicemails, one cursing me out, the other apologizing. She sent one belligerent email I never responded to. I told the parents about her. From what I know, they pulled their kids out."

"That would have been enough for me to never work with kids again. That damn Devin needed his little ass beat."

"Girl, it took everything I had not to put my hands on that boy. I despised him. I actually liked working with kids though. I couldn't let one bad situation keep me from my passion, could I? My next job was at a daycare center. More kids and more teachers. It should have been a better experience, but it wasn't."

"Oh my God! Girl, don't tell me it was worse," Maakara clinched at her imaginary pearls.

Serena smirked at her reaction. "I don't know. You tell me."

Tater Tots

South Loop

Glancing through the window of Tater Tots daycare center on my first day of work, I witnessed a heavyset Korean woman grab a toddler by the arm as he made a dash for the front door. Curious about the encounter, I rang the bell to be let in. The woman threw the child over her shoulder and opened the door.

"Good Morning, I'm Min. You must be Serena!" she exclaimed breathlessly.

"I am. Nice to meet you," I replied. "Who is this little guy?" I petted the little boy's mischievous head as he watched me from Min's shoulder.

"This is Evan, one of your new students. He's a little rascal but very sweet." She took a deep breath and set him down with his hand securely tightly in hers.

"Hey Evan. I'm Serena." I held out my hand for a high five, and he slapped it with the force of a two-year-old.

"Big boy!" I cheered.

Min, finally catching her breath, returned to business. "I see your folder. I assume it has your diploma and Tuberculosis test results inside?"

"Yes ma'am. It's all there."

She took the folder out of my hand and shook a piece of her chin length bob out of her face. "Perfect! Why don't we get started with a tour? This is the front office. Duh." She made a goofy face and sat the folder on a desk. "This computer is where you'll sign in for the day. Down the hall to the left is the restroom. Across the hall from there is the infant class, and way down at the end is the toddler class where you'll be working. Upstairs you'll find the preschool classes. Shall we go meet your co-teachers? Great!" She didn't pause for comment.

"FYI, the door doesn't lock so the kiddos run up and down this hall all day," Min informed me then opened the toddler classroom door and let Evan go.

My first encounter with Min and Evan was mild compared to the atmosphere in the toddler room. It was loud and chaotic and smelled like poop. One teacher had a baby on the changing table, and the other was cleaning up what appeared to be vomit. There were dirty dishes stacked in the small sink. Toys were scattered everywhere, and the toddlers, who had been screaming like banshees, stopped in their tracks to peer at the people who had just interrupted them. Their tiny faces were staring up at us with interest when Min said, "Hey guys! I want you to meet your new teacher Ms. Serena. She's super excited to meet you all. Serena these are the toddlers. And here are your co-teachers Patricia Brown and Jasmine Johnson."

My co-teachers nodded short greetings before Min continued her spiel. "On this rug we're standing on, the toddlers have circle time. There's a really simple circle time song you sing to get the kids to congregate. As you know, they can't sit still for too long. This is the perfect time for them to try to escape, so Jasmine and Patricia try to keep someone stationed at the door." She gestured to the cubby area. "Over here we have the cubbies. Each is labeled with a child's name. We try to update the parents on what the students need every day. On top of the cubbies are the daily sheets, which include activities, naptime length, diapering information etc. We also have incident reports in case a kid gets hurt. In Todds, this usually means someone got bitten or scratched. Just fill out the form with the time, location, and the teachers who were present. Am I rambling?" She finally paused to breathe.

"No, I'm keeping up. Please continue." She really did talk unnaturally fast.

"Great! In here," Min moved towards a tall metal cabinet to the left of the cubbies, "are art supplies. The kids love making a mess of things so keep this closed and locked unless you need to use it. Around the room on these short shelves are toys that the students have access to all day. Because the shelves are so low, the room is usually a complete mess unless the kids are napping or doing a project which is typical for toddlers at this age."

"Yeah, all they know is chaos. I think it makes more sense to them than order does." I wondered how I was going to keep the room clean. There was nowhere to hide all of the toys.

"Cool, so you understand the struggle here. We like to hang up art too, but you must use a specific type of tape. Unfortunately, the toddlers like to rip things off the walls, so be mindful of that. Towards the back of the room is the changing table." She walked over to it. "We always sanitize it after each change. In this cabinet above the table are the sanitizers, ointments, powders, etc. The changing table itself is a cabinet so if you open the door near your legs, you'll find all of the wipes. They are all labeled with the kids' names."

Min, realizing we were distracting the teachers and students, sped up. "Sorry for disrupting your class little ones! We're finishing up I promise." She opened a door at the back of the room. "This closet here is for you to hang your belongings… Serena, I'm going to leave you all here to get acquainted. I'll bring you a smock and a Tater Tots collared shirt. Have fun!" She headed towards the door. "Did I forget anything?"

"I do have one question. How many kids are in this class?"

"10 right now. We move five kids to the infant class until we find a new teacher. Usually, there are 15. The ratio is five students to one teacher." She paused before muttering confusedly, "Now what was I about to do?"

"My smock and shirt," I gently reminded her.

"Thank you. Duh!" She chuckled and closed the door behind her.

The Toddler Teachers

Wanting to feel useful, I started picking up toys. "Hey y'all. I'm Serena. Nice to meet you," I said as a toy whizzed over my head.

"Hey. I'm Jasmine. I just turned 20. How old are you?" Jasmine asked bluntly, searching my face for the answer. She was about the same height as me, very pretty, and on the thinner side except for a little beer belly.

"I'll be 19 next month. Do you all like working here?" I asked wanting to get ahead of any drama.

"Well... I'm only here until I can find something that pays more," Jasmine answered quickly. "They don't pay enough for me to move out of my mom's house. I wouldn't be opposed to having one of these single dads take care of me though. You feel me?" Jasmine cracked herself up.

"I guess." I laughed politely.

"Anyway, the kids are cute. You don't have to work weekends. And I like the other teachers. That's about it for me," Jasmine finished weakly.

"Not working weekends is definitely a good thing. How long have you been working here?" I asked hoping it was longer than the eight months I put in at Morning Glory.

"A little over a year now. I was looking for jobs after high school and stumbled across this. So, this is it until I'm ready to move on," Jasmine said clearly not invested.

"I love kids. I've been babysitting in my spare time since I was 12 so I guess this is just an extension of that. I'm excited about teaching. I don't have plans to date any of the dads I work with though." I gave a shy laugh.

"You never know," Jasmine said knowingly.

"What about you, Ms. Patricia? How do you like working here?" I turned away from Jasmine.

"Well let's start with you calling me just Patricia," she asserted with a southern accent. "I know I'm the old lady in here, but you don't have to call me 'Ms.' We're peers. I'm 60, been working with kids for 35 years," she finished proudly.

"Wow! You're a vet! And you don't look a day over 50." I admired openly.

"Well, you know what they say," she said flipping her curly wig.

"Black don't crack." We both laughed. I liked her instantly.

"I can tell you all you need to know." Patricia picked up the conversation. "There's no room for growth here. The pay might increase by 10cents per year, nothing noticeable. Tater Tots doesn't pay enough to live on so most of us have to severely budget. Some of us have roommates, live with family, have two jobs, etc. Carla in the preschool class bartends at night. Kaylen works at clubs on weekends. I have a studio apartment that I make work, but I have my granddaughter to take care of so it's a struggle," Patricia informed honestly.

"That sucks," I replied. "I made $8/hour at my other job, so I'm happy about my little increase. I don't know what you make, but I'm sure it's not enough for your experience."

"You got that right. I do like the kids though... well most of them. This little girl Abigail is bad as hell," she whispered behind her hand. "She's sweet though. We get a couple of them sometimes, but the kids are not the most stressful part about the job. It's the parents, very entitled. Nasty attitudes."

"I'm glad that you all like the kids. I worked with a horrible little boy at the home daycare I came from. I haven't had a problem with parents before though."

"Chile, don't get me started on them. You just brace yourself for what's to come," Patricia said reminding me of my grandmother.

"How do you all like Min?" I asked hopefully. "She seems nice."

"Min is cool, but she always puts the parents' needs ahead of the teachers. She makes it easy to talk to her, but nothing changes. She's nice, but she's not a friend. Remember that," Patricia warned.

The Toddler Class

A few months into my new job, things were going well. The kids were lovable but very rambunctious. I had a few favorites. One was a little girl named Anna Miller. She had short blonde curls like Shirley Temple and was every bit as charming. She was a chubby little girl who showered me with hugs all the time.

My other favorite student was a tiny boy named Jorge Villalobos. His dark hair was styled into a flattering little Mohawk. For some reason, he called me "Pyka." Jorge was a busy body. He climbed on the shelves for fun, and he hit and bit the other kids when they tried to bully him. I admired the little guy for standing up for himself. He was always sweet to me, gave me puppy dog eyes and squeezed my legs when I had to scold him.

My third favorite was a little girl named Cecelia Driver. She didn't talk much, but she liked to be near me. She had long wavy black hair and slightly tanned skin. I assumed her mother was Latina, but nobody ever got to meet her. Cecelia's dad, Donald, was the complete opposite. I was forced to see him every evening. Donald was a tall, bespectacled middle-aged white man who weighed about 300 pounds. He was a high-power attorney who felt like he owned everyone.

Donald thought since he paid $400/week he could gripe about anything. Truthfully, he should have complained if there was an actual issue, but his grievances consisted of him being upset because Cecelia's onesie only had two of three buttons snapped and because her diaper wasn't exactly centered when he got her home at the end of the day. My personal favorite was him claiming that the infant rubber bands I put in his daughter's hair were too difficult to take out. It sucked for Cecelia because I liked doing all the girls' hair. During the last complaint, I mostly nodded as he spoke. Of course, after that he complained to Min that my response to his complaint was not verbal enough.

-

My first few months also revealed more about my co-teachers. I had learned that Jasmine thought acting ditzy was appealing for some reason, or maybe she wasn't acting. Dimwitted or not, she didn't seem to mean any harm. She was very friendly, but I tried to avoid talking to her about certain things if I could. Time at Tater Tots also revealed that Jasmine was seven months pregnant, which explained her sloth-like behavior and what I thought was a beer belly when I started. I liked talking to Jasmine about how her pregnancy was progressing, but after more than a few humdrum discussions about her baby daddy drama, I learned to tune her out. It was easy since she was often distracted by her phone, leaving the daily tasks to me.

Patricia also neglected to do some chores on occasion, but she was easier to tolerate. She wasn't as loquacious as Jasmine, although she did seem understandably bitter about the job. Eventually I found out that there was more to her bitterness than met the eye.

"My daughter is good for nothing," she fussed one morning. "I wish that girl would make her child a priority. She refuses to work and moves in and out of my place with no kind of stability. I don't want to raise my grandbaby. I want to be able to visit her and spoil her like other grandparents do, but she has nowhere else to go," she concluded with a sigh.

"Where is the girl's dad?" I asked feeling sorry for Patricia.

"MIA," she retorted shaking her head.

"Damn, I would be upset too, especially having to share a studio," I said.

"I need more money. I need a bigger apartment. I can't keep doing this!" It took her half an hour to shake off her anger and return to the kids.

-

Patricia feeling unappreciated at work and home started translating over as consistent laziness in the classroom. Most of the time, I was the one who leapt to my feet to grab the toddler who jimmied the door and raced down the hall. My co-teachers never mopped. The room was permanently cluttered. They refused to fill out incident reports for things that happened before I started work for the day, leaving me clueless when parents arrived in the evenings. One time, Jorge hurt himself jumping off of a shelf. He had a bright red bruise on his pale cheek. That happened when I took a five-minute bathroom break. Luckily his mom knew he was an active little guy so she wasn't upset, but it still never should have happened.

Neither of my coworkers ever took out the trash, which left me with one huge heavy bag to take out at the end of the day. Taking out a bag filled with 60 dirty diapers, snacks, meals for 15 toddlers and whatever other trash accumulated over the course of nine hours was absurd. I knew it would only get worse as Jasmine approached her due date. Both of my co-teachers had more experience at Tater Tots than I did. They knew what needed to be done; they just didn't want to do it.

I was not the most creative teacher by any means, but I did try to keep things fun for the kids. I decorated the dramatic play area, so it looked like a grocery store. I also wanted to have the kids color birds, flowers, and butterflies to cover the windows with.

"Jasmine and Patricia, do you have anything you want to do with them? I don't want to take over. I can follow your lead," I offered before I started on the second project.

"What you're doing is fine. The classroom never looked better," Patricia said from her usual spot on the floor.

"I don't care what we do. As long as the kids are safe," Jasmine added distractedly looking at her phone.

"Cool. Another thing, Min mentioned that our room stinks during the day. She asked me how often we take out the trash. Did she say anything to y'all?" I asked suspiciously.

"No, she hasn't mentioned it." Jasmine said quickly.

"What did you tell her?" Patricia asked in a curious tone.

"I told her that I take it out at the end of the evening like always."

"You didn't say anything about us?" Patricia asked mimicking my suspicious tone.

"No, you all can tell her how often you take it out. I only spoke for me."

"Min should stay out of it. We do things how we like to in here," Patricia commented defiantly.

Week of Namrata

"Hey, guys!" Min greeted us animatedly one morning. "We have a new student joining us soon. Ajay from Infant B will be transitioning over next week. I cannot wait for you ladies to show him how awesome it is in the Todd class. He's a sweet kid. He shouldn't give you all any issues. I'll keep you posted." As soon as she left, Patricia turned to me.

"Oh Lord! I've heard nothing but bad things from the other teachers about Ajay's mom."

"What have you heard?" I asked uneasily.

"Apparently Ajay's mom doesn't always speak to his teachers when she picks him up. And she had a screaming match with somebody in the infant class because her son ran out of diapers too quickly." Patricia dramatically bulged her eyes for effect.

"Screaming matches?" I asked in disbelief.

"Yes ma'am."

"Surely that wasn't okay with Min though, right?" I asked expectantly.

"She reassured his mom that everything was fine. Tater Tots is all about their money."

"I was a push over at my last job. I won't let that happen again. I hope the lady acts like she has some sense," I said.

"Be careful with her," Patricia warned like she was scared.

-

Seven days later, Min knocked on our door and ushered in two strangers. "Hey, guys! This is Ajay and his mother Namrata. They will be joining us for an hour."

The mother and son nervously stepped further into the classroom hand in hand. Ajay was the image of his mother with his rich dark hair and warm brown skin. Namrata was short and curvy and looked to be in her mid-30s. Having heard such negative things about her, I assumed she would be just as unattractive as her attitude, but she was stunning. Ajay pulled away from his mom and joined the other kids. She looked slightly disappointed.

"Namrata, Ajay's new teachers are Patricia, Jasmine, and Serena." Min pointed to each of us.

Sensing the tension in the air, I took it upon myself to be as nice to Namrata as Min was to me when I started. "Hey there. I'm Serena. Nice to meet you." I waved and flashed one of my best smiles.

Namrata did not return the smile but managed to mutter in a disapproving tone, "Hello, what do you have planned for Ajay to do while we're here?"

"I was just about to have the kids clean up so we can start circle time," piped up Jasmine. She hadn't taken the initiative or done circle time since I started.

"Can we speed things up? I have errands to run," Namrata commented pompously.

I felt my heartbeat quicken with irritation. Min excused herself while Jasmine took the lead on clean up. I selected which books to read and started the circle time song to gather everyone at the rug. The kids, including Ajay, made their way over. "Um, when was the last time this was cleaned?" Namrata turned up her nose at the rug as if a rat had just run across it. She refused to sit. I ignored her question and began our morning routine. Other than a few questions, she kept quiet before leaving.

Day two of Namrata involved a two-hour visit. Ajay joined us for breakfast. Aside from his mother scrunching up her face at the food and hovering over him to make sure he didn't spill, Ajay thoroughly enjoyed his French toast sticks. Once breakfast was over, I cleared the dishes, wiped the tables, and swept the floors. Patricia washed the kids' hands. Namrata inspected Ajay immediately.

"Did you wash them with cold water? His hands are freezing." She looked at me.

"I don't know. I didn't wash their hands," I replied perplexed. Even more confusing, she didn't follow up with Patricia about it.

We made it through playtime and circle time without a hitch. Then it was time for Namrata to supervise diaper duties.

"Can you use multiple wipes for him?" she asked from over my shoulder.

"Sure, but he didn't poop."

"I know, but I prefer to use multiple wipes to be sure he's totally clean."

"Okay, no problem."

"Make sure to use diaper cream every changing too." She hovered over me.

"Okay," I managed to say again without making eye contact. Her breathing in my ear made me uncomfortable. Luckily the next student's diaper was poopy, so she took a step back.

-

I told myself it was almost over on the morning of day three. Namrata was staying with us from morning through naptime. I was thankful my lunch break cut into her visit. None of us wanted to sit in silence with her for the entire nap period. Without any interruptions, Namrata watched me put all the kids to sleep. Once done, I made myself comfortable in the corner filling out daily sheets and preparing a project for the next day. Namrata decided to take a seat next to me halfway through my tasks.

"What's this for? What did you write on Ajay's sheet? Will he be able to participate in this project you're doing? Tell me about yourself. How old are you? You look young. What kind of experience do you have with kids Ajay's age?" she rattled off.

"I have enough experience to work here. Yes, he'll be able to participate." I handed her Ajay's sheet. My age was not her business.

"Well, I have an MBA and so does Ajay's dad. He works a lot, so I'll be the one picking up Ajay every evening." She glanced at the daily sheet.

"Okay cool. Where does his dad work?" I asked wondering if his personality was any better than Namrata's.

"He works in Arizona… for now. He's been there a year." Her mood shifted suddenly, and she had tears in her eyes.

"Oh, I was just curious about the company he worked for, but I'm glad to hear he's coming home soon. That's great!" I tried to remain positive so she wouldn't burst into tears. "It'll be great to have two parents in the house all the time."

"Ajay's dad is plenty of help. We're going to get married," she offered defensively.

"Congratulations! When's the wedding?"

"We haven't set the date yet. We'll discuss getting engaged when he comes to Chicago."

"Oh, you aren't engaged yet? I'm sorry I assumed..." my voice trailed off.

"I'm going to go." She abruptly left the table.

"Namrata?" I called out before she left. "I'm glad Ajay's in this class. He's a great kid."

"He is. Thank you." She left without another word.

-

The next morning, Min surreptitiously pulled me into the hallway before Namrata and Ajay joined us. "I just wanted to let you know that Namrata was very uncomfortable with your conversation yesterday," my boss notified me in an uncharacteristically somber tone.

"What conversation was that?"

"She said you asked her why she isn't married to Ajay's dad. She said you also implied he's a bad father."

"I'm sorry. I- what?" I stuttered reeling at the words. "I never asked her why she wasn't married. I most definitely didn't say anything about what kind of dad he is."

"Well, that's what she said. I just want to make sure we're being as welcoming and as sensitive as possible."

"I am being welcoming even when she singles me out." I paused trying to shake off my attitude. "Just to be clear, Namrata told me on her own volition that she is marrying Ajay's dad who works a lot. I asked her where he works. I meant the company, but she told me he's in another state. I told her she'll have full-time help, and it's great that he's coming home soon. I asked her when the wedding date was, then she told me they weren't engaged yet. I told her I'm sorry and that I assumed they were when she said they were getting married. Immediately after that I told her what a great kid Ajay is. Why would I ask why they aren't married? I really don't care."

"Regardless, try to shy away from these types of conversations with her," Min said tentatively.

"Yeah, obviously she's very sensitive about them if she's willing to flat out lie. I mean the lady was crying at the mere mention of her baby daddy. She was the one who introduced him into the conversation!" I stated defiantly.

"Serena," Min said authoritatively. "Let's be gentle about this."

"Of course." I scoffed, returning to the classroom.

-

"Wait!" Maakara cut in exasperatedly. "The witch lied about your conversation because she was insecure about not being married? It's not even that serious."

"Exactly," Serena said nodding her head in agreement.

"That's weird." Maakara frowned. "Seems to me like she was mean to the teachers, so they won't ask too many questions. Defense mechanism you know?"

"I thought the same thing."

-

Even though I tried to ignore her, Namrata the nuisance seemed to enjoy giving me a particularly hard time that day. She asked a million questions, raised concerns, and complained about diapering, and cleanliness. She saved all of the questions just for me. And I had the feeling she knocked over a cup of milk just to annoy me. Fortunately for the toddler class, she vanished as soon as Ajay received his lunch tray, hours earlier than we expected her to.

"She has it out for you Serena," Patricia said with a nervous look in her eyes.

"Yeah, she really does," Jasmine added with some of the kids' lunch stuffed in her mouth.

"Oh, I didn't think you all had noticed," I replied sarcastically.

"Of course, we noticed! I'm just not sure what I can do about it," Patricia whined with a helplessness in her voice that irritated me.

"You don't have to do anything. I can handle her. Tomorrow is the last day of the transition anyway. Just one more day."

-

Namrata returned just as Jasmine was scheduled to leave for the evening. "Hello Jasmine," she said packing up Ajay and leaving expeditiously.

"That might have been the first time she spoke to me. You need anything else before I head out?" Jasmine asked rubbing her belly.

"Get that belly out of here, girl." I laughed.

"See you tomorrow." She giggled making her pregnant cheeks look even fuller.

I put a tub of blocks on the floor to keep the kids busy while I changed Cecelia's diaper. Just as I was fastening it, Namrata returned with Ajay's daily sheet in hand.

"Hey Serena, was the meat they served during lunch pork?" She was friendlier than she had been all day.

"I'm not sure," I replied not trusting myself to say more to her.

"Because Ajay doesn't eat pork…"

"I wasn't aware," I managed as dryly as possible.

"That would have been bad if he was allergic," she said probing for a reaction.

"Yeah, it could have been," I said unaffected. "Good thing he isn't allergic, huh?"

"Maybe I should go talk to Min about this," she suggested trying to evoke fear.

"Yeah, maybe you should," I encouraged.

-

Min pulled me into her office before closing for the night. "We need to talk about what happened with Namrata." The serious look on her face was looked out of place. I responded by taking a seat and folding my arms beneath my breasts.

"She's furious about your nonchalance towards the food incident. Ajay doesn't eat pork, so that could have been a problem." Min furrowed her brows.

"At no point did Namrata, you, the other class' teachers, or the cook inform us of his dietary preference." Hot anger rose in my chest. "Sounds like poor communication on management's part if anything. Did Namrata even mention that she was in the room when lunch was served?" I already knew the answer.

"That's not the point. Serena, you need to learn how to talk to these difficult parents. I know it's hard, but you need to work on your attitude," Min urged in an uncharacteristically stringent voice.

"And at what point are you going to pull the parents in here to discuss their attitudes towards your staff?" I tried to keep my tone innocent, but it morphed into something nasty.

"Well, I'm not here to change their personalities," Min said feebly.

"But you're here to change mine?" Silence. "Let me ask you something Min. Is it okay to talk to them the way they talk to me? Is it okay for me to lie about the conversations I've had with parents like Namrata did? Is it okay for teachers to treat parents with the same level of respect they give us? The answer is no. That means you know how rude, petty, and entitled they are, and you all don't do anything about it."

"I just want this transition to go as smoothly as possible." Min rubbed her temples in frustration.

"Me too. But the way you're dealing with this isn't fair. The conversation Namrata told you about did not go the way she said it did. And I'm glad Ajay is okay, although it wouldn't have been my fault if he wasn't." I stood up. "It's after 6:30. Have a good evening."

Min sighed, "Night, Serena."

Walking down the street to the Red Line, I decided to find another job as soon as possible. Teachers were not respected or supported at Tater Tots. I needed to leave before it got ugly.

-

"This Nuisance bitch lied about you again, and that's how your boss dealt with it? She lied twice in her first week there!" Maakara hissed.

"Shhh!" The stranger in the opposite cubicle glared at Maakara.

"Oh, my bad," she said in a hushed voice then looked back at me. "Why even go back to work at that point?"

-

Ajay was already in the toddler room when I arrived the next morning. His mother wasn't, but Min was. She was encouraging Patricia and Jasmine to be extra nice to make up for "the incident".

"Good morning Serena," was all she can manage before scurrying off.

"Girl, she came in here and said yesterday was all your fault," Patricia gossiped as soon as the door closed. "Well she didn't agree, but Namrata blamed you so Min ran with it. She wants Jasmine and me to intervene if you get too close to Ajay in case Namrata comes in and gets upset."

"Really?" I asked unsurprised.

"Yes, girl." Patricia struggled to keep the excitement out of her voice. "I told Min that none of us knew about the pork situation. She knows that. And I mentioned that Namrata was in the room when the food was served. But I guess it's easier for you to be the scapegoat."

"She could have asked Jasmine the same question about the meat, but she deliberately waited until Jasmine clocked out so she could target me. It's cool, though. I won't be working here much longer."

That thought got me through the rest of the morning.

-

Around 5:30, Anna's four-year-old sister Rachel ran into the Toddler class and gave her little sister a tight hug. Their parents, Kirsten and Raymond Miller, walked in hand in hand to pick up Anna as usual, but their faces revealed something was troubling them.

"What is this we're hearing about some parent giving our favorite babysitter and teacher a hard time?" Kirsten asked with a fierce look on her face.

"How did you all know about that?" I asked.

"Rachel's teachers told us. I assume because they know you babysit for us on occasion."

"There's a difficult new mom I'm dealing with this week," I admitted. "I can handle her though."

"You've always been nice to us," Kirsten asserted warmly. "We can vouch for you if you ever need it. The fact that you can spend all day with kids then babysit for us in your spare time? You're a saint." She laughed.

"I appreciate that. Thanks." I kneeled to hug Anna, who was leaning against the classroom door, but it opened causing her to fall straight on her back. Standing at the opened door was Donald Driver looking down at us. He tried to step over Anna to enter the room.

"You just made my daughter fall." Raymond intervened as he blocked Donald's path, then stood his daughter on her feet. Donald tried to walk around him. "Didn't you see that Anna fell because you opened the door? Common sense tells you to say sorry at least." Raymond's volume increased.

"I'm just here to get Cecelia," Donald responded in a shaky voice.

"And you can do that after you tell my child you're sorry." Raymond adjusted so he was in Donald's face again.

"Honey, calm down." Kirsten rubbed her husband's back. "You could have stood her on her feet though. Trying to step over her was rude." She shot daggers at Donald with her eyes then ushered her family into the hall.

-

"Hold the hell up! No, that man did not make the baby fall and step over her like she was trash! Girl, I know you're lying to me!" Maakara looked at Serena stunned.

"I wish I was lying! Her dad felt the same way you did."

"Oooh did he hit him? I hope he hit him." Maakara bounced in her seat eagerly.

-

Donald quickly signed out Cecelia while Min moseyed her way down the hall. "What's going on?" She gave Anna's family her attention first.

"HE opened the door." Raymond pointed into the classroom at Donald. "Anna fell because she was leaned against it. He tried to step over her instead of helping her up and apologizing. Sorry son of a bitch actually tried to step over a child that he made fall." Raymond's voice and temper rose another notch.

"I want his full name. I don't like the way he talked to me," Donald spoke like he intended to press charges.

"I will not give you his name," Min denied politely.

"My name is Raymond Miller. I'd love to know what you think you can do to me after YOU made MY daughter fall, asshole." At these words, he gathered his family and made his way to the front door.

"I'm just trying to take my daughter home, and he comes in here trying to attack me. I didn't know she fell because of me," Donald pleaded his case to Min. "I'm not comfortable with Cecelia being here. I will pull her out of Tater Tots if that man stays." He skirted past me and out of the back door dragging Cecelia along with him.

Jorge's mom, hovering in the hallway, made sure he was gone before giving her two cents. She turned to Min, "I don't know what just happened, but that man is rude. He's always been rude to everybody, even to other parents." She grabbed Jorge and left.

Finally, Min turned to me. "Serena, what the heck happened?" she asked frazzled.

"Anna was leaning against the door. Donald opened the door and Anna fell on her back. Then, he tried to step around her." I paused to see her reaction. "Raymond told him what he did, but Donald wouldn't apologize, so here we are. He's not the victim so I don't know why he acted like he was. I'm so glad there were other witnesses. Maybe you'll be able to understand what the teachers have to go through now."

Min sighed, shook her head, and prepared to leave until she saw who my last kid was. Seconds later, in walked Namrata the Nitwit, who glanced at Min, signed Ajay out, then turned to me. "I don't think you should work with kids anymore. You don't seem to even care about my child. You also really need to learn how to talk to people. I didn't appreciate the way you spoke to me yesterday. I deserve an apology. Just admit you made a mistake and we can move forward amicably."

I looked behind me expecting the person she was addressing to be there. "Are you talking to me?" I asked pointing at my chest.

"Who else would I be talking to?" Namrata's tone patronizing.

"I just needed to be sure before I respond to you and lose my job. Let me make this clear, I'm not sorry about anything I said or did, but you should be. You lied about our conversation, then you watched your son get served lunch and didn't say a word, that is until I was alone in the room when you could put the blame solely on me. Nice try. The meat wasn't pork by the way. I also find it interesting how you're targeting me. The cook and Min knew about his restrictions, but you didn't try to scare them. You're looking for someone to bully, and it won't be me," I finished firmly.

Min was uncharacteristically silent.

"You must not care about this job if you think you can talk to me this way." Namrata looked to Min for support then stepped too close to me, finger-pointed. "I have a right to screen who's around my son. If you can't apologize, then I can't trust you around him."

"You need to get your finger out of my face. Say what you will, but having my personal space invaded by parents is not in my job description. If you're looking for someone to intimidate, you've got the wrong person. Try me." I dared her to get closer. My heart hammered dangerously fast. Min's silence must have given Namrata a boost of confidence.

"What are you going to do?" Namrata got closer. I felt the pad of her wagging index finger graze my forehead. "Nothing I bet!" she mocked.

In a last-ditch effort to exercise restraint, I smirked. "You know what? You're right. I'm just going to go before I do something I wont regret. Min, I'm gone." I turned away to retrieve my things from the closet, but Namrata yanked my polo, pulling me backwards.

Reflex kicked in and before I knew it, I swirled around and my right hand turned into a right hook that connected with Namrata's mouth. My left hook followed up knocking her to the ground. I heard screaming, but I didn't know where it was coming from. "Don't ever put your hands on me again!" Before I could do any more damage, I felt gentle hands on my shoulders snapping me out of it. I looked behind me and saw Min and Ajay staring up at me. The shrieks were coming from him. Namrata was on the floor in a heap with a bloody lip.

"That's enough," Min said calmly.

I grabbed my belongings. The last words out of my mouth were, "Don't worry about me coming back."

An apology is all I heard on my way out the door. I'm not sure which mouth it came from.

-

After a moment of silence, "You almost killed the lady?" Maakara laughed. "Are you serious? You're joking right?"

Something new

As I walked to the red line, I tried to gather myself. Considering Namrata's level of entitlement and victimhood, I expected to hear from the police soon.

"This entitled bitch had the audacity to think she could talk to me any kind of way and invade my personal space?!" I ranted out loud looking crazy to passersby. I started to laugh maniacally when my phone rang. The caller ID displayed *Anna's mom/Kirsten.*

"Hello?" I answered trying to calm my voice.

"Hi, I just want to apologize. I hope we didn't embarrass you or make you uncomfortable earlier," she said sincerely.

"Oh no! Please don't feel bad. Cecelia's dad is an asshole. I'm glad Raymond scared him. He needed some fear in him to be honest."

Apparently, the speakerphone on Kirsten's cell was enabled because Raymond interjected, "It's funny how things happen. We were standing there discussing rude parents, then that bastard walks in and acts like a complete jerk."

"Yeah, it was pretty wild." I smiled in spite of myself. I paused before adding, "Actually I should tell you guys about what happened after you left." My tone turned grave. "My last day at Tater Tots was today. I quit without notice."

"Are you serious?!" Both parents shouted simultaneously.

"Yeah. I didn't feel supported as a teacher. And after what happened with Anna, I had to go." I omitted the full truth.

"Wow. Are you okay?" Kirsten asked in a motherly voice.

"I'm fine." I sighed, "In the meantime, I'll be looking more carefully for a new job."

"I won't take up too much of your time. I apologize for the day you've had. We'll talk later. Have a good evening."

"You too."

-

I was expecting to hear from the authorities the entire weekend following the incident. I checked my phone for missed calls, emails, or texts, but I received nothing. As if reading my mind, my phone rang just as I was about to use the bathroom. The caller ID displayed *Tater Tots*. I rolled my eyes and answered, "Hello?"

"Serena, it's me. Can we talk about what happened Friday?" Min asked hesitantly.

"What do you want?"

"I just wanted you to know that after you left, Namrata tried to convince me that she never intended to harm you. According to her, she grabbed you so you all could finish the conversation," she said objectively.

"Yeah right.

"I told her that regardless of what her intentions were, her behavior was inappropriate to say the least, and that if she decided to call the cops, I would give an accurate account of what transpired. She left soon after that. I'm not sure what her plans are. Serena, I just wanted you to know that although you can no longer work here, I hate what happened. She should never have felt comfortable enough to put her hands on you. I should have spoken to her months ago," Min admitted earnestly.

"True."

"In case you were wondering, I did suggest that she leave the center. I told her to stay home until she's ready to let Ajay be in the care of others who she will treat with respect. It's so unfortunate because Ajay's a sweet little guy," Min concluded.

"Yeah, he is," I said shortly.

"Lastly, I would be open to providing a reference for you… maybe under a different name in case we get into any trouble." She gave a nervous chuckle. "In spite of all the nonsense, you are a great teacher. I would trust my kids with you even though I might be a little scared of you now." She laughed.

"Thanks, Min." I stifled a grin.

"Well good luck with everything," she continued. "Sorry things had to end on such exaggerated circumstances. I'll be in touch if I hear anything."

"Okay. Goodbye," I said feeling a bit lighter.

"Oh, Serena? One last thing," Min added before I disconnected the call.

"What's up?"

"That was a mean right hook!" she exclaimed, back to sounding like her old self.

"Thanks." I giggled before hanging up.

I laid back on my pillows to reflect on the conversation when my phone rang again. I assumed it was Min. "Hello?"

"Good Morning Serena. I hope I didn't wake you." It was Kirsten

"I just got off the phone with Min so I'm wide awake," I said perking up.

"I dropped the kids off at Tater Tots very early this morning. I spoke with Min and told her I'll be pulling my babies out of the school since parents are allowed to be rude to kids."

"Wow! How did she take that?" I asked genuinely shocked.

"She knew there was nothing she could say to defend Cecelia's dad. She just nodded in agreement. She had this disappointed look on her face. I wouldn't be surprised if she resigned soon."

"I hear that. I'm rethinking this career path as well. I've had a lot of drama, and it's only been less than a year." I sighed. "What will you do with the girls now?"

"Funny that you ask. I know you are rethinking your line of work, but would you consider being a nanny for my family? You'd only be responsible for the little girls, not my oldest. They already know you so well."

"...Wow, I've never considered being a nanny before. What would I have to do? Feed them? Teach them? Clean up after them and go on field trips? My answer is yes of course!" Enthusiasm flooded my other emotions.

"Just keep them safe and happy like you already do." I could tell she was smiling through the phone. "What would you need as far as pay?"

"Tater Tots paid me $12/hour, which would be about $1900/month on your end. I think that's fair."

"I can't do $1900. Is there any way we could do $400/week? Untaxed, of course."

Desperate for a steady income and excited at the new opportunity, I agreed to the pay. "Okay. When would I start?"

-

"Damn that's a lot to take in." Maakara processed. "So, you got a new job working as a nanny for the first time. What happened with Nitwit? Did she press charges? And why did you say you were desperate for work? Didn't you live with your mom? Couldn't she help?"

"Good questions. Apparently, Nuisance's baby daddy proposed right after the incident. Min said that he was worried for Nitwit's safety and encouraged them to move to Arizona ASAP. As ashamed as she was about being single, Nitwit leapt at the chance. That's according to Min. All I know is I never got arrested," Serena concluded happily.

"That's crazy! Lucky you!" Maakara said incredulously.

"Please be quiet ladies!" Ms. Jones urged us from the front desk. Maakara looked over Serena's shoulder and mouthed, the word "Sorry" then leaned in for more.

"As far as living with my mom, I was desperate to move out and get my own place. That's why I took the job so quickly. Our rent was way too high once the Co-op factored in my income. And my mom wanted to move in with her boyfriend, so it was time for me to leave the nest."

"Well, what happened with the next family? Being a nanny had to be better right?"

"They were dysfunctional to say the least. I'm so thankful I bought a stun gun after what happened with Namrata."

"No, you did not have to stun somebody!" Maakara's jaw nearly fell into her lap.

The Millers

Mount Greenwood

My employment with the Millers started shortly after my departure from Tater Tots. On my first day Kirsten quickly ran everything down for me, "I think the only thing I forgot to mention is that I want you to serve veggies with every meal. No matter what it is. I'm trying to introduce the girls to better eating habits than the ones I have. I mean look at me." She glanced down at her dumpy body, reminding me instantly of an episode of Roseanne. "You already know where everything is. The keys are labeled and on the dining room table. Oh! I did forget something. In case you hadn't noticed when you were babysitting, certain areas of the house have shoddy cell service. Hopefully it doesn't give you any issues.

That's all for now. We'll see you later. Have a good day, ladies!" She bid us farewell and left in a hurry with her husband.

I took a look around their cluttered three-story ranch style home and realized they had already left me with a dilemma; their 14-year-old daughter Tessa was still home. My contract with the Millers stated that Anna and Rachel were to be in my care full-time. It didn't mention their oldest child at all. I didn't have a personal issue with Tess; she always kept to herself when I would babysit, but there was no way I was going to care for three kids for $1600/month. School didn't start until September 3. I had to talk to my new employers as soon as they returned.

-

The first day flowed surprisingly smoothly. The girls were already comfortable with me, so I didn't have to spend any time getting to know them. We played games, sang songs, and did puzzles. Tessa stayed in her room for the majority of the day. Her sisters seemed confused yet excited about their new schedule.

"You're going to be with us all day Ms. Serena?" Rachel asked staring up at me with wonder in her large eyes.

"If that's okay with you," I answered after breakfast.

"Are you leaving when my mommy gets home?"

"Yep, then I'll just see you tomorrow morning."

"I don't have to go to school?" Rachel asked in a bewildered tone.

"Nope, but I'll be teaching you some preschool stuff here."

"Then we can play?"

"Yes," I laughed. "Then we can play."

Rachel and Anna giggled mischievously.

"Hey! How did everything go?" Kirsten asked later that evening with sweat rolling down her forehead as if she had jogged home. The girls ran over to hug her. "Did you have fun?" She squatted down and peered into their faces.

"We went to the park and danced and exercised. Serena is going to teach me how to write my name. It starts with R!" Rachel informed her excitedly.

"Yeah, it was great," I chimed in. "They were on their best behavior. No tears when you left. Nothing major to report."

"Great to hear that. How was Tessa?"

"About her... she was fine of course, but I didn't spend as much time with her as I did the younger girls. Am I supposed to?"

"Oh, no need to worry about her." Kirsten waved off the question.

"Really?" I asked brightening at the thought.

"Yes, she can feed herself. And she's old enough to be home alone. She's not your responsibility."

"Good to know."

The weight had been lifted.

-

"They didn't think to tell you that the older girl would be in the house with you for a few weeks? That's suspicious. I don't care what the mom told you," Maakara said folding her arms knowingly.

"There were a lot of things they didn't think to mention." Serena cringed at the thought of it.

"Like what?"

-

Since Kirsten convinced me that I wasn't at all responsible for her oldest child, I left Tessa home while the little ones and I ventured to the YMCA where they had free play and activities for preschoolers. As I watched them run around the gym, I took note of the differences between the two girls. Rachel was a sweet little one with a voice like a bird. She was eager to please, very sensitive and loved to play with others. Anna was standoffish and quick tempered. She reminded me more of how I was as a kid. The sisters' appearances differed just as much as their personalities. Anna had a short chubby stature and curly blonde hair while Rachel was taller like her dad and had long dark brown curly hair that rested just beyond her shoulders. Anna usually just wore her hair down around her ears, but Rachel always had two neat ponytails. While the girls did not resemble each other, Anna did have features similar to her mother's, and Rachel's mirrored their dad's. Tessa didn't resemble either parent. Her hair was a lighter shade of brown than Rachel's but equally as curly. I wondered why there was such a big age gap between Tessa and Rachel but only a gap of 15 months between Anna and Rachel. They were learning the preschool basics while Tessa was a full decade older and starting her first year of high school.

There was another little girl at the Y that day. She looked to be about three and wore her hair like Rachel's. As I watched, the girl slowly eased closer to Anna and Rachel then made a dash for the small red ball in Rachel's hand. She pushed Rachel down to the floor and snatched it as Rachel started wailing. As soon as I rushed over, Anna ran away from us.

"Are you okay baby?" I asked kneeling to the floor.

"No," Rachel pouted putting her head on my chest.

"You'll be okay." I hugged her. "We're going to work on you standing up for yourself. If a kid hits you, you hit them back or tell an adult." I looked around the gym for Anna. She was in hot pursuit of the bull. Anna's right foot caught the back of the fleeing girl's shoe forcing her to fall flat on her stomach. The ball rolled out of the girl's hands, and Anna stepped over her to grab it. I couldn't help but to laugh at the savagery of it all.

"My sister ball." Anna announced fiercely, bringing the ball over to us.

"You are so funny, little girl. You had your sister's back huh?" I giggled then hugged her too. The new little girl scurried over to her mother. A part of me hoped her mom would address the issue. Instead, she and her daughter left the gym.

-

After an eventful morning, we came home to Tessa opening the door for us before I could get the key in the lock. "Hey, did the girls eat lunch yet?" she asked me.

"Not yet." I expected her to ask me to feed her.

"Well, I just put a pizza in the oven for them to eat if that's okay," she said shyly.

"That works. Thanks!" I brightened at her presence. "How long until it's ready?"

"Oh, I don't know. But I put it in the oven ten minutes ago."

"How long does it take to cook?"

"Um, 15 minutes I think," she said uncertainly.

"So, it'll be done in five minutes then?" I asked perplexed at her confusion.

"Oh yeah, I guess so." She laughed dopily, vaguely reminding me of Jasmine from Tater Tots.

"Cool, I'll just make veggies to go with it. You pay attention to the pizza for me." I washed the girls' hands and sat them down at their kiddie table. Unfortunately, when I went to heat up the veggies, there was an entire pizza on the floor.

"Tessa, what happened? What's this?" I asked trying to process the scene.

"The pizza fell," she stated plainly.

"How did it fall outside the oven if it was inside?"

"Um, I don't know." She looked as if she was about to cry. I ignored her and warmed a can of ravioli on the stove for the little ones. When I stepped closer to her to clean off the floor near her feet, she flinched.

"What's wrong with you?" I asked irritated.

"Nothing." She left the kitchen silently. I noticed the oven was still on but in my haste to feed the girls on time, I overlooked it. I decided I didn't care what she ate or did during the day as long as she stayed out of my way.

-

About 30 minutes later, Tessa resurfaced during the girls' quiet time. "Can I walk to the deli to get a snack?"

"I don't care." I tried to keep the attitude out of my voice but wasn't quite successful. Her parents could say a million times that I wasn't responsible for her, but I knew I was, at least partially.

"Thank you." She scampered off.

I took a second to relax on the couch while the house was peaceful. Before I knew it, Anna was calling me from upstairs. I checked the time. It had been two whole hours since I sat down. Before I went to get Anna, it hit me that I never turned the oven off. I was sure Tessa didn't either. I turned it off then went upstairs wondering if Tessa came back during my nap. As if reading my mind, she walked through the door and left it wide open.

"Tessa, close the door!" I yelled down.

"Oh, I didn't know," she replied stupidly. Instead of closing it, she sat on the couch. I descended the stairs to do it myself.

"And did you mean to leave the oven on earlier?" I failed to keep the nagging tone out of my voice. Tessa looked at me as if in a daze, then stood to turn it off. "I already did it. You have to pay attention to stuff like that."

"You're right," she replied nonchalantly.

-

The next morning, the Millers' home smelled like gas as I crossed the threshold. Tessa was watching TV in the living room, completely oblivious.

"Hey Tessa, you smell that? Are you cooking something?" I asked sitting my purse on the couch.

"No, I just put something in the microwave," she said a little too defensively as Raymond walked down the stairs.

"It smells like the stove is on. What are you guys doing down here?" He briskly headed towards the kitchen then rejoined us. "The stove was on. You all have to be careful." He grabbed his briefcase and left in a huff. I waited until he locked the door before I turned to Tessa.

"Did you touch the stove?"

"I don't think so." She shrugged.

-

My day with the younger girls progressed without a hitch. After we reviewed our letters, shapes, and colors. We took a walk to the park two blocks away.

"I'm gonna fall!" Anna yelled to me from the jungle gym.

"You're not going to fall, Anna!" Rachel giggled from behind her hands.

"Anna, I'm right here." I sat next to her. "We're not going to fall."

"I'm gonna fall!" She looked down at the porous metal bottom revealing the wood chips beneath us.

"Sit on my lap." Anna quickly took a seat not taking her eyes off the ground. "Rachel, would you show Anna that we aren't going to fall through the holes? Run around and show her." Rachel jumped up and down and ran up along the jungle gym not forgetting to use the slide.

"See Anna? I'm too big to fall through here," Rachel soothed as she joined us.

"Just because you can see the ground, doesn't mean you're going to fall through. We're big girls. Look how big my foot is." I stomped it a few times. "I can't fit through there. Now you stand up and see for yourself." Anna clung to me, burying her face in my leg as I stood her on her feet.

"I'm gonna fall," she stated less fervently.

"Just look down, Anna. We're both safe. Look at your feet."

Anna peeked from behind her pudgy fingers. "I'm not gonna fall?" A smile consumed her face.

"No." I couldn't help grinning back. "Take my hand and jump up and down so you can feel how strong it is. You take my hand too, Rachel. Alright let's jump up and down three times. If we fall through, we'll go home. Deal?"

"Okay!" the girls screamed in unison.

"1-2-3 JUMP!"

By the time I was ready to go, I had to yank Anna off of the slide and carry her home.

-

As lunch finished up, I put the girls on the potty, washed their hands, and put them down for naptime. I quickly realized I had to put them in separate rooms because they insisted on keeping each other awake by chattering. I kept Anna upstairs in her crib but moved Rachel downstairs to the den. After running around all morning, they fell asleep without another word.

In order to make the most out of my lunch, I ate while the girls slept. Half of my turkey sandwich was gone when Tessa walked through the front door. She hadn't crossed my mind the entire time the girls and I had been back. I didn't realize she was gone, but I felt stressed with her back. I didn't bother getting up to greet her, but I was hoping she would remember to lock the door. She entered the kitchen just as I dug into the second half of my sandwich.

"Hey Serena," she greeted in a chipper tone as she walked to the garbage can.

"Hey, Tes-" my voice broke off as the strong smell of weed floated beneath my nostrils.

"Can I watch TV?" she asked.

"Sure, why wouldn't you be able to?" I turned back to my lunch wondering if her parents would find a way to blame me for her behavior. I polished off my sandwich, although it was significantly less appealing with Tessa home, then made my way to the living room to find Rachel on the couch watching TV with her older sister.

"What is going on? Why isn't she in the den?" Vexation instantly washed over me.

"I saw she was awake, so I brought her in here with me," Tessa replied.

"It's naptime. She needs to lay down. No TV," I stated calmly, trying not to snap at her.

"Oh, I didn't know," Tessa lied.

"Rachel, go lay down now," I instructed.

She hiked back to the den with her tail between her legs.

I turned to Tessa. "Listen, if you're going to be here during the day, I need you to be helpful. Otherwise, it feels like I have to handle you too. Don't distract the girls. Let's keep them on their schedule. Cool?"

"Okay," she mumbled obviously offended.

-

For the rest of the day, I debated about telling Kirsten and Raymond about Tessa, but the way Kirsten stormed into the house after work made the decision easy.

"Did you tell Tessa not to play with her sisters during the day?" she asked with hands on her hips.

"Huh?" I replied caught off guard.

"Tessa texted me saying you told her not to interact with the girls during the day." Her breathing was rapid.

"No," I paused getting my thoughts together. "I told her to be helpful when she's around because she distracts her sisters from what we need to do."

"Well, you wouldn't tell me that, so I don't know why you told her that." Kirsten retorted determined to be mad about something.

"You would know to stay out of the way. You know kids don't listen to other adults when their parents are around. Apparently, Tessa didn't know that. I can't do my job if you all are hovering." I kept my voice calm but firm.

"Look, Tessa is going to be here, and I don't want her feeling uncomfortable around you." Kirsten's expression softened slightly.

"If Tessa is going to be here then I need her to be more helpful than harmful. We had a stressful day," I informed.

"What do you mean? What happened?" Kirsten anxiously peered at her daughter. Tessa warily hovered in the kitchen doorway.

"Tessa, since you felt the need to tell your mom about what I said to you, do you also want to tell her about yourself?" I paused for a response but was met with silence. "Kirsten, in the last couple days, she has left the stove on, the oven on, and left the front door unlocked and open when she came back from the store. She also took Rachel out of the den during naptime so they could watch TV together. So, this is why I talked to her," I finished coolly.

"Are you trying to burn down the house? You want someone to come in here and rob us? Tessa, you have to be careful!" Kirsten warned.

"Okay Mommy," she said sounding eager to end the conversation.

"There's another thing I want to follow up on. You're sure I'm not responsible for her during the day?"

"You are not." Kirsten huffed.

"If Tessa leaves the house during the day, then that's no concern of mine?"

"I guess so. What's your point?" Annoyance rose in Kirsten's voice.

"Anything she does while outside of this house is not my issue, right?"

"Right. But I mean I would hope if you were privy to something dangerous, you'd let us know," Kirsten said.

"Okay. Good to know." I chanced a glance in Tessa's direction.

"What am I missing?" Kirsten turned her head at the both of us as if watching a ping pong game.

"Nothing. I just wanted to be sure what my duties are. That's all," I said finally deciding not to reveal Tessa's secret.

Still unconvinced Kirsten said, "Well if that's all, you can leave for the day. Tomorrow will be easier."

"See you all tomorrow." I hurriedly threw my purse on my arm and headed for the door.

Just as my hand grazed the doorknob I heard, "Tessa, what the hell?! Why do you smell like weed?"

-

"Serena! Can you come back in here for a second?!" Kirsten called sniffing Tessa's shirt.

"What's up?" I asked approaching them cautiously.

"Do you know anything about Tessa smoking?" Kirsten asked without preamble.

"I've tried to keep my focus on the girls," I said not completely answering the question.

"She smells like weed. If I smell it now, surely you did earlier." She looked at me shrewdly.

"Maybe this is something you all should discuss in my absence. Seems like a family matter." I wanted to avoid getting Tessa in trouble.

"You're right." She turned towards her daughter. "What were you doing today?"

"I uh…." Fear silenced her.

"Kirsten," I cut in. "I mean this in the most respectful way possible; I think you and Raymond need to talk privately. Maybe she's going through something and wants to talk to you without me here." I hoped to evoke sympathy for Tessa.

Completely ignoring my suggestion, Kirsten asked in a calm but deadly tone, "What the hell have you been doing during lunchtime?" She looked like she wanted to hit her daughter but spared her because of me.

"Nothing I swear!" Tessa's watery eyes were telling a different story.

"Tessa…" Kirsten folded her arms and gave her daughter a stern look.

"M-m-my friends smoke sometimes. I-I don't," Tessa stuttered. "I hang out as long as I can because I'm tired of being stuck in this house with nothing to do. That's it. You have to believe that mom!" She pleaded on the verge of tears.

"We'll talk about this with your dad later." Kirsten glared at her daughter.

"Well, I'm going to head out." I gestured awkwardly for the door. I didn't dare look back.

-

"When you said drama, you weren't joking!" Maakara exclaimed. "That girl did all that and her momma seriously thought you wouldn't feel responsible for her? Wow!"

"After that incident, her view on that changed a bit." Serena recalled bitterly.

-

The next day Kirsten was still in a frenzy about the day before. She was pacing back and forth when I arrived for work. "I can't believe Tessa. She must think I'm an idiot. There's no way she wasn't smoking with her friends. They probably do other drugs too! She's going to end up selling her body just to get the next high!"

"Don't get me wrong. I don't do drugs of any kind, but I think we're passed the days of thinking weed is a gateway drug," I asserted calmly. "Lots of people smoke and never consider trying harder drugs. Maybe Tessa doesn't have an addiction. But if she does, you should find somebody for her to talk to. She might just be acting out. This doesn't have to be the end of the world."

"I doubt we'll be able to get through to her. She needs tough love. I should probably stop giving her money. Oh, I know! I'll take her phone and have you keep an eye on her all day. Raymond will have to pick her up from school too. I bet if I stop buying the foods she likes or take her door off the hinges she'll clean up her act. I'll find a way to set her straight if I have to beat it out of her!" A crazed look contorted Kirsten's face as she ranted to herself. She left the house without another word. I hadn't had time to process her words when Raymond made his appearance for the day.

"Good morning Serena! How are we doing today?" he asked with a smile.

"Honestly I'm worried about Tessa," I stated glumly.

"We had a long talk last night. I'm sure it will be fine from here on out." He patted my shoulder.

"Is there a way you could make sure Kirsten doesn't take Tessa's phone while I'm with her during the day? She said I'd have to keep an eye on her if she takes it. Raymond, I didn't sign up to babysit a teenager," I blurted desperately.

"Don't worry. I'll talk to her and we'll figure out the best punishment once we've calmed down."

"Thank you." I breathed a sigh of relief.

"No, thank you for being so patient with our family drama." He paused before adding, "Can I ask you something?"

"Okay."

"What is your opinion on this idea of the other woman?"

"What?"

"What do you think about 'the other woman'? You know, home wreckers, floozies, etc." He gave a nervous laugh.

"Weird question. Uh… well…" I gathered my thoughts before answering. "I think we should stop blaming the other woman for wrecking the home. The man wrecked his own home by allowing drama into it. Don't get me wrong, the other woman is shady if she knows the man is taken, but we can't hold her equally accountable as the man. He's the one who agreed to be faithful. Also, these days we just call them side chicks, not 'the other woman'." I forced a laugh to hide my discomfort.

"I'm asking because I have a friend who is content being the other woman... or side chick as you would say. She feels that all the good guys are taken so she's fine being the side chick." Raymond looked happy to finally be sharing this with someone.

"Well, it's unfortunate she feels that way. I wouldn't settle for that, but there's plenty of women who do." I shrugged hopelessly.

"Yeah, she told me that the man she always wanted is married, so she gave up on finding true love. I asked her who this man is. She told me that it's me! She's been holding back her feelings all these years." He blushed brightly, clearly flattered.

"It sounds like she's willing to step into that role if you let her. Be careful with her," I advised cautiously.

"Yes, I agree. I will. Let me get out of here. Thanks for chatting with me." He turned toward the door.

-

"What kind of odd ass question is that?!" Maakara hissed as soon as Serena paused in the story.

"Ladies," Ms. Jones said marching over to their desks. "I know the library is nearly empty, but I will have to ask you all

to leave if you keep disturbing patrons. Please keep it down."
She frowned as if the last thing she wanted to do was
discipline someone.

"I'm sorry. We'll try to be more respectful, Ms. Jones."
Serena smiled at her hoping it bought them a little more
leniency. As soon as Ms. Jones walked away, she turned
back to Maakara. "Yes, that was odd, right? And why did my
opinion matter to him anyway? Why was he comfortable
asking me that?"

"This family keeps getting weirder and weirder," Maakara
said stealing a look over Serena's shoulder and
surreptitiously opening a bag of chips. "Continue."

-

We stayed in all day because it rained cats and dogs.
The cloudy sky casted darkness inside the house even with
the lights on. I decided to settle on the couch with a book
while the girls slept.

"Oh hey!" I jumped hearing Tessa trek down the stairs.
"You scared me. How are you feeling today?" I inquired
nervously, still feeling guilty about the day before.

"Fine... I'm sorry about yesterday," the girl replied looking
at her feet.

"No need to be. And I didn't want you to get in trouble. I
just wanted us on the same page." I was relieved she wasn't
mad.

"No, I'm sorry for making things awkward for you. Can I
ask you something?"

"Sure," I said.

"Do you have a boyfriend?"

"Ummm no. Why?" I was caught off guard by the sudden
change of topic. She must have gotten that trait from her
father.

"Just asking." She shifted from one foot to the other.

"Do you have one?"

"No, maybe when I'm older," she muttered in a sad kind of way.

"Why do you say it like that?"

"Boys don't think I'm cute. I don't get as much attention as other girls. I hate my body. I'm too fat." She plopped down on the couch next to me, bursting to confide in someone. Tessa wasn't stick thin. She was about a size 6. I thought her shape and size were fine, but I also knew that what was beautiful in Black culture was not necessarily considered beautiful in White culture. I glanced down at my size 10 frame and compared it to hers.

"You have a great figure. Those boys at school may not notice now, but somebody else will. Self-love is so much more important than what they think though. Don't let them get to you." I nudged her shoulder with mine.

"I'm so sorry I acted out this week." Tears filled her eyes. "Thank you for trying to get my dad to let me keep my phone."

"I can't take too much credit for that. The real reason that I didn't want your phone taken away was because I didn't want to be responsible for you without it. My contract only lists two kids, not three."

"Serena..." Tessa's voice faltered.

"What's up?"

"Uh...I know you've baby sat the girls for awhile now, but I don't think you know this...Kirsten is not my biological mom. My mom is serving a life sentence for felony murder during a bank robbery. She didn't pull the trigger, but she was involved. I haven't seen her since I was two years old. She and my dad were never married. Kirsten has been around since I was three. My dad married her when I was five." The words tumbled out of her mouth then she took a deep centering breath.

Briefly stunned at Tessa's candor, I stuttered, "I-I'm sorry to hear that."

"My grandma told me my mom grew up poor. I guess she wanted a better life. I don't know what happened." She twiddled her thumbs in her lap.

"I can understand your mom wanting more for herself and for you. Sometimes people are victims of their circumstances," I offered to soothe her worries.

"Yeah, I guess so."

A thought occurred to me. "There's a big age gap between you and the younger girls. As a teenager, I know you get tired of hearing about potty training and ABCs. I definitely understand you wanting to get out of the house sometimes."

"The girls do take up a lot of my parents' time… I'm glad we can be friends. I don't know why I didn't try sooner." She scrunched up her face in deep thought. "There's something else I want to tell you." Lightning flashed across her face making the comment all the more dramatic.

"What is it?"

"My mom and dad can be mean sometimes." She avoided eye contact.

"Yeah, parents can forget what it's like to be a kid," I replied misunderstanding her statement.

"No, what I mean is Kirsten can be really hard on me when I screw up. If I don't wash the dishes the right way, she calls me dumb or fat, curses at me, hits me sometimes."

"Does your dad say or do anything?" I asked instantly alarmed.

"He doesn't hit me, but he doesn't defend me either. Well… he does but passively." Her voice quivered. "I do mess up a lot. I know I shouldn't have been smoking. I think I just wanted to get back at my parents… My grades could be better. And I could do my chores better. I'll try harder." Unable to hold in anymore emotion, she finally burst into tears rivaling the weather outside.

After taking a few moments to process the sudden revelation I replied, "Nobody should talk to you like that. Maybe you all could go to family counseling one day. Is there anything else you wanted to share?" I was terrified at what else Tessa might reveal.

"Wel-"

"Shh!" I cut her off. The thunderstorm made it hard to see and hear, but I was pretty sure I had just heard the screen door squeak open. "We aren't expecting anybody, right Tessa?" The front door's lock rattled ominously. I checked the peephole and jumped at the sight of a scruffy looking white man fiddling with the lock.

"Tessa, someone is trying to get in. Do you recognize him?" I whispered to her even though the rain and wind thrashed the windows loudly. She peered through the peephole quickly and shook her head. I pulled out my phone and saw much to my chagrin that I didn't have service. "Go upstairs to Anna's bedroom. Close the door. LOCK IT. Do not make a single sound. Where is your phone?"

"I don't know!" she whimpered preparing to cry again. Lightning flashed plunging us into darkness.

"Shit! Mine isn't working. Do what I said. Secure her door as best as you can. Go!" She scampered away, and I ran to the den and picked up Rachel willing her to stay quiet. I tried to make it back to the stairs, but the front door swung open slowly. I considered running for the back door, but I knew I couldn't make it without being seen. I snatched my purse off the dining room table and hid in the den. Suddenly, I heard two sets of footsteps. One was coming from the back door. I snuck a peek into the hallway and saw a second hooded person. I closed the door as silently as I could.

"Grab the TV! I'll search the rooms," a deep voice commanded. The footsteps faded.

Beads of sweat prickled my forehead as I urgently dug into my purse. I put my ear to the door. Silence. Then I heard the floorboard groan right outside the room. The doorknob rattled. Rachel leapt from my arms and hid in the cluttered closet that only she could fit in. Just as I hid to the right of it, the den's door swung open threateningly. My hand finally grazed what I had been digging for. As the intruder failed to find the light switch, my hand darted out and stunned him right on the neck. Thank goodness he had taken off his hood. He howled and blindly flailed his arms around in the darkness trying to locate the source of his pain. I gave him another shock and he fell to the ground writhing in discomfort having tripped over an end table. I kneeled down and stunned him again right on his balls, something I remember seeing in one of Ice Cube's movies. His shrieks filled the room preventing me from hearing his partner step into the doorway, mouth agape.

-

"What happened next? Don't pause there!" Maakara aggressively whispered while stuffing chips in her mouth.

-

I froze momentarily then flew across the room with the stun gun outstretched. "GET THE FUCK OUT!"

The intruder ran out of the front door. A squad car was sitting in the alley next to the house. I wanted to stop and flag it down, but I was fearful that Rachel would reveal herself to the incapacitated stranger at any second. I hurried back into the den. She was still nowhere in sight, but I sat on the bandit's back and stunned him in the same delicate spot for a full minute until I heard footsteps quickly approaching.

"Drop your weapon!" ordered a man's voice from the doorway. The lightning illuminated him for a split second. He was a tall redheaded cop with his gun drawn. Tears filled my eyes as I put my hands up. "Stand up. Let me see your hands!"

"Don't shoot! These men broke in. I'm a nanny, and there are 3 kids scattered around this house." I took a breath to compose myself. My voice shook with fear. "I need to check on them." I knew cops were supposed to serve and protect, but I couldn't help but be aware of the color of my skin in that situation.

"Sit tight while we secure the perimeter. We saw someone fleeing the building." The cop squatted down and cuffed the guy on the floor, checked his pockets, and found only a wallet and lock picking tools. "I assume this was his partner." He pieced together.

"Yes, they came in the front and back doors. Who called you guys?" I asked confused.

"We received a call from someone in the home. It wasn't you?" he asked with a note of surprise in his voice.

"I have shitty service. Tessa must have found her phone and called."

His Walkie-Talkie crackled, "Suspect secured. Perimeter clear."

"Ma'am you may check on the minors now. I will put this guy in the squad car and be back to get your statement," the policeman said importantly. He yanked the intruder onto his feet, and I noticed the fallen man's fresh limp.

"Ouch!" He hopped on his left foot. "It's sprained or something!" he whined. The cop walked even faster.

I retrieved Rachel from the closet as soon as the men left the room. Her eyes were huge with fear, and she was shaking but overall physically sound. She made her way to me with a soiled crotch. I squeezed her close before leaving the room and hollered from the bottom of the staircase, "Tessa come down! The cops are here. We're safe." Seconds later she wandered down holding Anna who apparently had slept through the whole ordeal. I hugged them both. "Are y'all okay?" I croaked in a hoarse voice. Tessa held up her phone.

"Found it," she smirked.

"Teamwork" was all I can manage before my knees buckled.

-

Even though they heard all the details already, Tessa, Rachel, and I detailed the events again to the Millers. While holding the two youngest girls, Kirsten and Raymond listened again intently.

"So, you heard the doorknob rattling and went to check the peephole?" Kirsten questioned for the third time.

"Yes, I'm so glad we were close enough to hear it. I don't know what we would have done otherwise. The crazy thing is I didn't realize there was another guy at the back door. I'm just so thankful that I got him before he could get us," I replied gratefully.

"You've gone above and beyond for our girls. How can we ever repay you?" Raymond asked leaning forward with his hand on my knee.

"I just did what was needed. But if you insist, I'll think of something." I laughed to keep things light.

"And these weren't guys you've seen before?" Kirsten asked in a suggestive tone.

"I don't think I've ever seen them before. I definitely didn't know them." I tried to keep the defensiveness out of my voice.

"What about you Tessa?" Kirsten started again. "Were these guys you knew from getting high? Drug dealers maybe?"

"What? No! I don't know them, mom!" she asserted clearly affronted.

"Well, did you leave the door open for them?" Kirsten was determined to get the answer she was looking for.

"No, mom!"

"Kirsten, I just told you that the robbers tampered with the lock. The cops confirmed that already," I added firmly with a note of anger.

"You're right. I think I'd feel better knowing it was a crime of opportunity rather than us being a target."

"We will get an alarm system installed ASAP. I want you all to feel safe here." Raymond informed the room at large.

"I would certainly feel better with some security," I admitted.

"Say no more. I can't believe you took this guy down on your own. That's totally badass!" Raymond admired.

"I may not get so lucky next time. Thankfully the guy sprained his ankle when he fell," I replied humbly.

Kirsten, still determined to get her suspicions confirmed, asked one more question. "You aren't covering for Tessa, are you?" She narrowed her eyes.

"Kirsten, can we please focus on the fact that none of them were hurt and that Tessa was able to call the cops?" Raymond was clearly frustrated.

"Fine. Sorry. You're right. Thank you so much for protecting my babies." Kirsten stood up to hug me.

"You're welcome. Can you dismiss the girls for a second? I want to say something they don't need to hear," I said as I released her from the hug.

"Sure," said Raymond. "Girls, go in the playroom for a second." Rachel reluctantly went along with Tessa.

"What's up Serena?" Raymond asked with concern.

"Rachel. I don't think she saw them, but she heard the robbers' voices. When I came back to get her, she had peed her pants. I know sometimes kids start having nightmares and accidents when stuff like this happens, so I want to make sure I pay attention to that from now on."

"Wow, thank you for telling us. Our poor babies," sighed Kirsten with a quivering lip.

"I'm not as concerned about Anna because she only woke up in the aftermath. And even though she's older and helped us a lot today, Tessa might be uneasy too. I'll try to be there for her as well," I told the parents.

"Yeah sure," Kirsten said less emotionally.

"How are you doing though?" Raymond asked me.

"I think I'm okay. I'm glad we got out of this unscathed. Thanks for asking. I'll feel even better once you install an alarm though... a raise would be nice too."

-

"I'm at a loss for words," Maakara said in her normal volume. "That is scary as hell. I probably wouldn't have worked again for at least a year after that. Did they give you the raise at least?" Concern took over her mood.

"I guess you could say that."

-

"Morning!" Raymond chirped happily as soon as I walked through the door the next day.

"Good morning," I replied sliding my purse off my arm.

"The security people are coming in the afternoon. I hope that makes you feel more comfortable," he added in a more serious tone.

"Happy to hear it." I smiled feeling relieved.

"I can always call off work for the whole day if you ladies want some male protection," he said flexing his muscles.

"No!" Tessa answered quickly as she entered the room. "We don't want you hovering over us, dad."

"Okay then I'll just stay until they install the alarm this afternoon." He chuckled. "We have more to tell you, Serena." He looked towards the stairs as Kirsten came down. "We want to give you a bonus, just a little something to show our appreciation for yesterday."

"Oh wow, that's so sweet. Thank you."

"We decided to pay you an additional $50 this week," Kirsten added refusing to let Raymond have all the glory. "Thanks for putting your life on the line for our kids. Thanks for staying with us. And thanks for returning to work so quickly. And here's a Starbucks gift card." She smiled, pleased with herself.

The gesture seemed inadequate, but I tried to hide my disappointment. Starbucks wasn't a place I ever patronized, but maybe I could take the kids for hot chocolate in the winter.

Kirsten's voice cut into my thoughts, "I'm going to head out so I don't miss my train. See you guys!"

"Tessa, can you go up and get the little ones dressed? I need to talk to Serena." Raymond requested immediately after Kirsten left.

"Sure, dad." She made her way towards the stairs. I faced Raymond awkwardly, expecting another weird conversation.

"What's up?" I asked pleasantly.

"Remember that friend I mentioned who has the crush on me?" He lowered his voice furtively.

"Yes."

"Well, she sent me some pictures, of her on vacation..."

"Okay..." I said sensing he had more to tell.

"... in her bikini." He stared at me with wide expectant eyes.

"Why would she do that?"

"She wanted me to see how fit she is now. She's lost about 20 pounds and has been hitting the gym like crazy." I detected admiration and a hint of desire in his voice.

"You sure that's why she sent them?" I asked suspiciously.

"Guess what else!" he whispered loudly. "I forgot to delete the pics. Rachel was playing on my phone and stumbled across them. She showed them to Kirsten!"

"Are you serious?" I asked curiosity getting the best of me.

"Yes, unfortunately. I was going to delete them, but I guess I just never got around to it. We had a horrible argument about it last night after discussing the break in." He shook his head exhaustedly. "Kirsten sincerely believes I'm going to cheat on her. I keep telling her I won't. I'm not going to cheat on my wife!" he said forcefully as if trying to convince himself more than me.

Momentarily taken aback by his reaction I told him, "I don't think you should be friends with this lady. You shouldn't talk to her at all, but if she's that important to you in a platonic kind of way, then the least you could do is demand that she respects your marriage."

"I will talk to her. Thanks for the chat." He turned towards the stairs. "Hey, Serena? Can we keep this between us? I don't want this to get back to Kirsten. I need an objective person to talk to sometimes."

"Uh sure okay."

"Thanks," he said returning to his upbeat mood and skipping up the stairs, passing the kids on his way down.

"Hey girls!" I bent over to hug the little ones. "Tessa, did you sleep okay?"

"Actually, no. I ended up sleeping on the floor of Anna and Rachel's room. I was too nervous to sleep alone. I'm glad the security guys are coming today."

"Yeah me too... I think we'll be fine for the next few hours though. We didn't get to finish our conversation yesterday. Did you still want to talk about it?" I asked careful not to be too specific.

"No, I think I overreacted. She's not so bad." Tessa fiddled with her necklace to avoid eye contact.

"Are you sure?" Without words, I walked the little girls into their playroom so they wouldn't overhear us.

"Well...I already told you she calls me stupid or fat." Tessa's voice remained even.

"She shouldn't be talking to you like that."

"...but I am forgetful sometimes." She looked down at her feet.

"It sounds like you would have benefited from more guidance than criticism." I placed my hands on her shoulders and gave her a shake. "You are not stupid." I walked to the kitchen counter and handed her a napkin for her wet cheeks.

"Thanks," she said stiffly.

"What about physical abuse? I know you said she hits you, but let's talk about it." I hesitated when I realized I was being a little too aggressive. "...Unless you don't want to talk about it. I just want to listen."

"...Well, yesterday she cornered me in the hallway. She was really nasty to me. Kept trying to get me to admit that it was my fault that the robbers got in. She was convinced you were covering for me. I told her this time it wasn't me. She slapped me and said 'Don't you lie to me you little bitch!' I ran to my room and cried." Tessa buried her face in her hands and bawled her eyes out. I hugged her instinctively and looked over her shoulder to make sure Raymond wasn't lurking. I was grateful that the little ones knew how to keep themselves entertained.

"Your mom took her anger out on you, but she was mad about something else. That wasn't your fault. Do you want to keep talking?" I pulled away from her to look at her face.

"One time," she sniffed before sharing more. "She wanted me to wear my hair in pigtails like a little kid, so I fixed it when I got to school, but I forgot to put it back the way it was. She went bat shit crazy and cut my hair to make it uneven. I had to tell my friends I wanted a haircut."

"What did your dad do?" I asked without emotion.

"He told her he wished she hadn't cut it. He told me I should not have changed my hairstyle." She looked at me with betrayal in her eyes. She took advantage of my silence and continued, "I think the worst thing she ever did was when I was six. Dad wasn't home. I hadn't cleaned my room. When she found out, she made me touch the radiator in the bathroom with my bare hands. She told me 'either you do it or I hold it there myself', but I couldn't do it. She held my hands there for what felt like forever. I had blisters afterward and couldn't use my hands properly for a while. She told my dad it was an accident. He believed her, and I was way too scared to say anything."

"Healthy relationships are not abusive," I replied choked up. "You need to know that. And I am so sorry that happened to you." I wiped a tear from my own eye.

"I hate it, but I love them. Please don't tell them I told you. Don't tell anybody." She pleaded with her eyes.

"Of course not," I said immediately, unsure about my intentions.

"Serena? Please?" Tessa read my thoughts.

"Huh? Oh yeah of course, but the least I can do is look out for you while I'm here."

"Thank you… Hey, I know my dad told you about the pictures on his phone." She abruptly changed the subject again.

"Oh, you knew about that?" I looked down guiltily.

"Yeah. I don't get why he would he do that though." Her eyebrows scrunched up in confusion.

"I don't know either. Does your dad have friends?" I knew I was being unprofessional, but I had to know.

"Yeah, a couple of guys he plays poker with sometimes."

"I wonder why he doesn't talk to them about it."

"Probably because the lady in the picture used to date one of my dad's friends," Tessa informed me darkly.

"Whoever she is, your dad needs to be careful. I told him that."

"Her name is Lindsay. I'm not sure how they got so close, but I don't like it," Tessa said worriedly.

"What does she look like?" I wanted to confirm my suspicion.

"Thin, bleach blonde, big boobs. Every guy's fantasy," Tessa said dreamily.

"Maybe every white guy's fantasy," I mumbled to myself.

"What did you say?"

"Huh? Oh, I was just thinking about something."

"What is it?" Tessa asked curiously.

"Well, I don't presume to understand all white beauty standards, but I do know you just described the holy trinity: thin, blonde, and big boobs. Your mom is on the chubbier side with dark brown hair. Maybe she's insecure and takes it out on you. This probably isn't the first time your mom has had trust issues with your dad. You're probably a constant reminder of your mom's insecurities."

"But I was born before they got together!" Tess shrieked incredulously.

"I know, but I think in her mind you're the only person she can take her anger out on. And you're the evidence that your dad was ever with another woman, even if it was before her time. She's not going to take it out on her little ones. They're innocent in her eyes. She's not going to leave your dad, so she chose to pick on you. And she's able to do it because for some reason your dad doesn't defend you. I can't quite understand it myself."

"That's ridiculous." Tess folded her arms in protest.

"It is! But maybe this can help you understand Kirsten better. She has her own issues that aren't your fault. Don't be so hard on yourself." I placed a comforting hand on her shoulder.

"Yeah okay," Tessa said not totally convinced.

"Did you want to talk about anything else?" I asked. I might have a little more AP psychology knowledge stored in my brain somewhere."

"No. I'm okay. Thanks. I really do wish we had become friends sooner. I like talking to you."

"Unfortunately, so does your dad." I muttered to myself so she couldn't hear me.

-

"Damn, I hope they got therapy. I can't believe that lady was putting her hands on that girl, and the dad allowed it! Just sad. You're a better person than I am because I would have reported her ass," Maakara said angrily.

"I strongly considered it. It was hard. Trust me."

One less kid

"Have a good first day, Tessa." I hugged her a couple weeks later as she prepared to leave for her first day of school.

"Thanks, Serena. See you later." She grinned at me ready to go tackle freshman year.

"Hey Serena, will you and the girls be here when I get back from dropping Tessa off?" Raymond inquired as he ventured down the stairs.

"We will be."

"Okay, I need to talk to you about something. I'll see you in a bit."

Tessa gave me an inquiring look. I shrugged my shoulders at her behind Raymond's back. Once the two had left, I found the preschoolers. "Alright, little ladies. Let's have breakfast then review our flashcards. Cool?"

"Hooray!" Rachel yelled.

-

"What is this?" I asked holding up a card 45 minutes later.

"Blue triangle!" Anna quickly yelped with excitement. She liked answering before her sister.

"Good job Anna! Rachel, can you tell me what this is?" I held up another card.

"The letter R! R is for Rachel R-R-Rachel!" My chest swelled with pride. She was such a fast learner.

The alarm chirped signaling Raymond's return.

"Excellent job Rachel. What about this letter?" I held up the letter A.

"A!" Anna shouted.

"Great job Anna!"

"Really good job big girl!" Raymond cheered from the doorway. "Hey, Serena can we talk for a second?" He looked concerned.

"Sure." I scrambled off of the floor and stepped into the hallway.

"Have you told Kirsten about any of our conversations?" His eyes bored into mine.

"No, why?" I asked a bit unsettled.

"The other day she told me I talk too much for my own good. I was wondering why."

"I'm not sure why she'd say that, but I haven't talked to her about you," I assured him.

"Hm. Well just so you know, I vent to you because my family doesn't care for Kirsten. I don't want them treating her any worse than they already do. They are very traditional. They think she's too independent, too strong, too outspoken. And I think I made matters worse by venting to them earlier in the marriage."

"What were you telling them?" I asked curiously. "...If you don't mind sharing, I mean."

"Kirsten can be too critical of me in a lot of different ways. Let's use cooking for example. If I want to make a big breakfast, I'll go to the store and get what I need. If I forget to buy butter and there's none in the house, I prefer to run back to the store to get some. Kirsten prefers me to just stay home and substitute it. She fusses at me if I have to leave the house again. Seems small but it can be annoying after a while."

"Well…" I cut myself off opting not to delve any deeper into the conversation.

"What is it?" Raymond asked eagerly.

"Nothing. I already feel like I know too much of you all's business." I struggled to fight my desire to butt in.

"Serena, please tell me. It could be something helpful." He looked desperate.

"Can I be frank since you insist on having these conversations?"

"By all means." He waved his hand in acceptance.

"Maybe she doesn't want you leaving the house because she's worried that you're interacting with other women. I only say that because of what you told me about your friend who has a crush on you," I concluded tentatively.

"I just can't believe she doesn't trust me. But that's definitely something to consider," he muttered more to himself than to me. "And she's overly critical about me as a father. When she doesn't like the way that I raise my voice or discipline the younger girls, she'll tell me not to yell at her kids, as if they aren't my kids too!" he cried in disbelief.

"Interesting."

"And sometimes when she's really mad at me she'll say things like 'You're not the prize in this relationship. I can find better.' She also doesn't think I'm ambitious enough. She wants me to push harder to make more money." I stared at him until he continued. "You're right about one thing though... She's convinced I'm going to cheat on her, even though I'm not going to." Again, he left me with the impression that he was mostly trying to convince himself.

"Sounds like you all need to sit down and have a real conversation. Maybe get counseling too," I offered.

"Yeah, I know. It's so tough sometimes. I appreciate you listening to me." He gave me a brief hug.

My phone rang from my hand. "It's Kirsten," I told Raymond, and he walked out of the room. "Hello?"

"Hey, just calling to let you know tomorrow you'll be driving me and the girls to their doctor's appointment downtown. This is so you can get familiar with where it is in case you have to take them yourself. After the appointment, you can just drop me off at work."

"What time are we going?" I asked looking forward to a change of scenery.

"Appointment is at 10:00 so we'll head out at 9:15. Cool?"

"Fine with me."

As I reviewed more flashcards with the girls, I wondered if Kirsten would rip a page out of Raymond's book and spill some tea about her marriage on the way to the doctor.

Doc's visit

As soon as I finished washing dishes after breakfast, I made sure the girls looked presentable. Kirsten checked them over after me, looking for something to complain about. Not finding anything, she directed us to the car. After listening to the girls sing along to Pharrell's "Happy" for three full minutes, the song concluded, and the radio host began discussing a gospel singer whose husband had been unfaithful with countless women.

"I don't know how she took him back after that. I would be scared he'd bring an STD home," I said then turned to look questioningly at Kirsten as I merged on the expressway.

"I hear you. I told Raymond the only thing I will not put up with in this marriage is infidelity. I just have no patience for it at all," she stated resolutely.

"And you shouldn't have to. I understand some women deal with things differently than others, but I don't think I'd stay if my husband cheated multiple times."

"No woman should have to go through that kind of pain." Kirsten remarked darkly.

-

The fancy doctor's office was plush enough to be a hotel lobby. I wondered how good the Millers' insurance was to afford going there and if the doctors were any better than the medical card approved doctors I went to. I couldn't wait to see if they were punctual.

"Follow me please." The nurse instructed us at 10:03. We followed him to room number two. "I'm just going to check your temperatures and get your height and weight okay?" He busied himself getting the ear thermometer and gloves. "Okay, who's going first?"

"Me!" Rachel eagerly skipped over to the nurse.

"I'm just going to check your temperature." He checked it and recorded the reading. "Now step onto the scale. Let's see how tall you've gotten since your last visit." He recorded her height and weight then repeated the process with a more reserved Anna. "The doctor will be with you shortly." He let himself out.

After a few minutes, Dr. Jackson walked in. She looked to be about 40 and had the most beautiful shade of brown skin I had ever seen. "Hey, there little ladies! How are we feeling today?" The girls smiled back in return.

"How are you doing, Kirsten? And who is this?" The doctor looked at me.

"I'm their nanny, Serena. Nice to meet you."

"Same to you. So!" She clapped her hands together. "Let's see what's on the agenda for today." She checked the clipboard. "Just a checkup. Okay. I'm going to step out of the room. Undress the girls down to their underwear, and I'll be back."

"She seems great," I commented undressing Anna.

"Yeah, everyone is nice here," Kirsten said undressing Rachel. A moment later, a knock at the door signaled the doctor's return. "Ready!" Kirsten called out.

"I'm looking over your body to check for any rashes or bruising. Your skin looks healthy," she informed the girls examining them carefully. "Now, I'm going to check your lungs and reflexes.

After a thorough examination Dr. Jackson proclaimed, "Everything looks perfect. How are their appetites?"

"Excellent," I offered immediately. "They eat well at breakfast and lunch."

"I'm happy to hear that. How long have you been a professional nanny?"

"About a month."

"How do you like it?" Dr. Jackson asked from over her clipboard.

"I like it. These girls make it fun." I winked at Anna and Rachel.

"Have you ever considered healthcare?" Dr. Jackson asked with interest.

"Like being a pediatrician like you, you mean?"

"Sure. Or a child psychiatrist. Lots of options."

"If school was free maybe. I don't want to take on the debt," I admitted.

"I see. We could really use more women in medicine, Black women specifically. Black people tend to be a little more suspicious of doctors considering our negative history with experimentation. It would be nice to see more faces like mine." She smiled at me.

"Thanks for saying that. Considering the substandard treatment Black expectant mothers are receiving, maybe I will consider it."

"Maybe you should." She gave a pointed look over her glasses.

-

By 11:00, we were back at the car. The girls were in good spirits with stickers on their foreheads and lollipops in hand. Kirsten loaded them in then told me how to get to her job.

"Hey, do you think you could start washing all the dishes in the sink?" she asked me suddenly from the passenger seat. "Not just the ones you and the girls use."

"I can only wash the dishes I use. I thought washing dishes was Tessa's job."

"Well, what about cleaning the house? Straightening up when the girls are sleeping. Sweeping, mopping. I noticed sometimes you don't straighten the pillows after the girls play on the couch."

"Does that come with a pay increase? Even still, I respectfully decline. I'm not a cleaning lady, but I will be sure to clean up after the girls better."

Kirsten appeared to try to think of a reason why I should perform the other tasks. Unsuccessful, she dropped the subject. We rode in silence to her job.

-

"I do not like this lady." Maakara shook her head. "She thought you were stupid. Glad you told her no. She should have been more worried about her marriage and family than some damn throw pillows. And I'm waiting on you to tell me the husband cheated on her. He's so damn lonely it's pathetic." Maakara adjusted in her chair and waited for Serena to continue.

"Speaking of that…"

-

When we pulled up to the Miller home, Raymond's car was outside. He wasn't supposed to be there that day but was relaxed on the couch pigging out and watching TV. You would think the girls hadn't seen him in ages with the way they rushed over to him.

"Hey girls! How was the doctor?" Their dad asked brushing crumbs off his hands.

"We had fun daddy!" Rachel said hugging him and looking to steal some food. I excused myself to go warm up lunch. As I heated the Beefaroni on the stove, Raymond put his plate in the sink and waited for me to notice him.

"So, I had a meeting today." He began with a smirk. "As I was setting up my presentation, a woman walked in early. I told her good morning and we briefly engaged in small talk. She stared at me kind of… lustfully, if I do say so myself, and told me I looked like trouble. Of course, I asked her what she meant by that, but before she could answer, a few other people trickled into the room. At the end of my presentation, I asked her again what she meant by her comment. She told me, 'You'll just have to find out' and winked at me. Can you believe that?" His face turned the same shade of crimson as his tie.

"Really? Wow," I said dryly. I doubted how truthful the story was.

"It was a major ego boost. Kirsten isn't always the most affectionate person." He looked away from me embarrassed.

"Well, you should talk to her about that. I understand wanting to feel attractive, but as a married man, other women's perceptions shouldn't matter that much to you. Again, I think maybe you all need counseling. Just throwing that out there." I put my hands up defensively.

"You're right; I will. I must admit I do have a bit more pep in my step though!" Raymond beamed and headed for the front door.

His conversation had left my mind by lunchtime. I could barely place the food on the table before the girls were scarfing it down. "Did you guys like going to the doctor today?"

"Yes! It was fun!" Rachel immediately answered with a mouth full of food.

"More fun than you have with me?" I asked in a mock sad tone.

"We like you too." The girls giggled.

"Am I your best friend?" I laughed teasing the girls.

"Of course!" yelled Rachel spitting food everywhere.

After two helpings, the girls washed up at the sink in the downstairs bathroom. Then I brought Rachel upstairs with me to tuck in Anna before heading back down to tuck her in on the couch in the den. Since the break-in, I hadn't left her in the room by herself yet. She didn't say she needed it, but I made sure she knew I was always nearby.

"You ready for naptime baby?" I tucked her in gently.

"Yes," she replied sleepily.

"I'm going to sit on the floor by the door until you fall asleep. Okay?"

"Thank you, Ms. Serena." She yawned.

Mistrust

Two months post break-in, things were flowing smoothly between the Miller family and me. Tessa hadn't mentioned any more abuse. The girls knew all of their shapes, colors, and letters. Rachel could spell and write her name, and Raymond hadn't shared any more inappropriate stories. The pay could have been more, but work was easy and enjoyable otherwise.

One unseasonably warm October morning, I decided to take the girls on a long ride to Brookfield Zoo. Hundreds of kids gamboled around in their adorable 90's Halloween costumes. The girls were dressed as Phil and Lil from "Rugrats", and I followed the festive theme by dressing as Ashley from "Fresh Prince". I was sure to take tons of pictures and send them to Kirsten. As fascinated as I was with the costumes, Anna and Rachel seemed to be equally as interested in finding the kangaroos.

"Look girls! You see them?" I pointed in the animals' direction.

"What's wrong with her stomach?" Rachel gaped repulsively.

"She probably has a baby in her pouch. You see the small kangaroo hopping around next to the momma? Maybe the baby has a younger sibling in there." At that moment, a tiny kangaroo head popped out of the pouch.

"Oooh, I see it!" Rachel pointed hopping from foot to foot. Anna mutely peered at the scene.

At the girls' insistence, we ventured to every single other exhibit the zoo had to offer. We ate a homemade lunch of turkey sandwiches, and the girls let me usher them to the car without a fuss. "Did you girls have fun?" I asked glancing in the backseat before exiting the parking lot.

"Yes." A sleepy Rachel yawned. Anna's eyes were glued shut. They both drifted off before the engine started. After a long quiet drive, we arrived home well after their usual nap time. I carefully put them on the couch and snuggled next to them before exhaustion got the best of me too.

-

I was home watching my shows when I received a text from Kirsten at 8:06 pm.

-Who is Kamroo? The girls said you took them to her house today to see her baby.

The text made no sense, so I ignored it.

-

As soon as I entered the Miller home the next morning, Raymond had his phone to his ear asking me if I got Kirsten's text the night before.

"No," I lied.

"Honey, she says she didn't get the text," he spoke into the phone ostentatiously, making sure I knew the line of questioning was Kirsten's doing. "Serena, Kir wants to know what this Kamroo business is about." He enabled the speakerphone.

"What are you talking about?" I asked tersely.

"Kirsten says that Rachel told her that you all went to somebody named Kamroo's house, and she had a baby? Is that true?"

"Yeah, I don't want her taking them to strange people's houses or anywhere I don't approve of!" Kirsten griped angrily, apparently unaware of the speakerphone.

"I don't know what you're talking about. We went to the zoo yesterday," I answered unaffected.

"Ask Rachel again. Call her in there," Kirsten ordered her husband.

"Rachel?! Come here!" he summoned. Rachel stumbled into the room. "Did you say something about Serena taking you to Kamroo's house yesterday?"

Rachel looked at me mischievously then said, "We went to the kangaroo house; she had two babies. One was in her belly."

"Kir, you heard that? Yeah, she said Kangaroo house, nothing about Kamroo." Raymond turned off the speakerphone.

"You all know I took them to the zoo yesterday. I even sent pictures," I said stoically, but inwardly I was affronted.

"Yeah Kir. You probably should have thought about that before sending the text. See you later. Bye." Raymond rushed off the phone. "Sorry about that Serena. She should have investigated that before confronting you." Not meeting my eye, he left swiftly. I was sure he wanted to know where I took the girls just as badly as his wife did. He also could have verified Rachel's comment just as easily as Kirsten could have, but he chose not to. I wondered why they didn't trust me.

-

Later that evening, Kirsten came home in a radiant mood. "Hey!" she greeted me with a smile.

"Hey," I said not returning it.

"Funny about that 'Kamroo' thing huh?" She laughed, a complete 180 from her attitude that morning.

"I need you to respect my time when I'm off the clock. I'm not going to respond to you after hours, especially over something untrue." My tone was more aggressive than I intended it to be.

"Okay, I won't text unless there's an emergency." Kirsten seemed surprised by my firmness.

"And it seems like you all don't trust me," I continued. "The way this was handled made me uncomfortable. You were on the phone with Raymond waiting for me to get here this morning so you could ambush me."

"Well, if I think you took the girls somewhere inappropriate, I have a right to know. You didn't text back, so yes I wanted to talk to you," Kirsten replied with a hint of anger.

"Again, I don't have to respond in my personal time unless it's urgent, but you're right. You do have a right to know everything I do with the girls. I just don't appreciate the way you went about it. It backfired, and it will continue to because I'm not doing anything inappropriate with them. If you don't trust me, then why am I here?"

"I guess Raymond and I could have confirmed this with Rachel before assuming the worst. I do feel silly now." She gave a nervous laugh and scratched the back of her neck.

I felt slightly mollified as I headed out the front door.

-

One January morning was particularly freezing. "Great day to leave my scarf at home," I muttered sarcastically to myself as I stomped into the Millers' home.

"I need to get Tessa to school early today. No time to talk now but can we talk later?" Raymond addressed me in a rush, throwing on his coat.

"Sure… okay." I looked at Tessa. "How are you?"

"I'm fine. I'll see you later," she replied moodily. The two of them stepped into the freezing air, and I wondered what was in store for me. I fixed the girls oatmeal for breakfast and let them watch Sesame Street while they ate.

"C is for cat!" Anna screeched excitedly.

"I love Elmo," Rachel informed us with a mouthful of food.

Watching them shout out the new things that they had learned was so rewarding. It felt good knowing I was doing something right. Just as I stood up to clear the girls' dishes, Raymond marched back into the door bringing the wind with him. The girls were completely glued to the TV, oblivious to his return. I grabbed the dirty dishes and retreated to the kitchen. Raymond followed me.

"You know what I noticed?" he started as soon as the girls were out of range.

"What's that?" I faced the sink half interested in the conversation.

"Ever since I've been married, I don't get as much attention from the ladies as I used to.

"Is that so?" I doubted he ever got that much attention.

"Yeah," he continued. "I got more action like 10 years ago. Now women don't ever approach me."

"That lady at your meeting a few months ago came on to you." I turned to face him.

"Yes, but that was the first time in years!" He chuckled.

"Why does it matter to you?" I asked coolly.

"I just want to understand it," he said desperately.

"Well, you look like a nice guy. Maybe women see your wedding ring and actually respect it." I tried not to reveal my true thought: he wasn't very attractive… at least not to me.

"Yeah maybe. But a friend of mine from high school was always successful with the ladies. He's married now, but he still gets a lot of attention."

"What do you consider a lot of attention?" I asked curiously.

"My buddy gets hit on weekly. That seems like a lot to me. Sometimes I'll innocently flirt with the cashier at McDonald's or a girl at the gas station just to see if I still got it. You know?"

"As long as you and Kirsten still think you got it that's all that matters," I reminded him with a note of finality.

"True… I'm going to go relax. I have a meeting later."

"Okay." I turned back to the dishes feeling Raymond was one step closer to cheating.

Paranoia

"Good morning! It's super windy out there today." I shivered as I entered the Millers' home and took off my coat and shoes. "How are you feeling?" I looked at Kirsten expectantly.

"You haven't been taking showers here have you?" she asked from the couch looking troubled.

"What?" I asked thrown off guard.

"Rachel mentioned that you took a shower yesterday," Kirsten replied seemingly determined to have a conversation that pained her.

"Why would I take a shower here?" I asked bemused.

"You're saying you didn't take one?" Her paranoia revealed itself.

"No, I didn't," I answered not understanding what the problem would be if I did.

"I was going to tell you that we can't have you taking showers during the day," Kirsten warned.

"Great because I didn't take one," I responded flatly.

"This isn't the first time that she's said this you know." She searched my face for a lie.

"Well, I don't know why she would say that. Maybe she just wants me to shower here? Maybe she wants me to spend the night or something? Sometimes kids lie about stuff they want. Rachel also told me her dad is buying her a pony. I assumed it wasn't true, and she said it because she wanted one," I responded sensibly.

"I see." Kirsten sounded unconvinced. "She has been talking about a pony, but we haven't agreed to get her one. Anyway, I'm going to work."

I could see her mind trying to process what I'd said as she prepared to leave. I wasn't sure why a simple shower would cause her to behave this way, but it left me with an ominous feeling in the pit of my stomach.

-

"Girl! Her behavior only got worse after that. Didn't it? I just know it did." Maakara stuffed a few more chips in her mouth. "This family is crazy as hell!"

"You make story telling so fun." Serena giggled.

-

Deciding to put any thoughts of Kirsten out of my mind and focus on the girls, I packed them up before going on our favorite field trip: the YMCA. On the way, I stopped at the gas station. I was trudging back to the car wanting to escape the frigid air when I heard someone calling my name.

"Serena? Serena? Oh God, I hope I remembered your name correctly." I turned to find a professional-looking Black lady who looked vaguely familiar. "Hey, you may not remember me but I'm Anna and Rachel's doctor, Dr. Jackson. We met at one of their visits." She walked towards me.

"Ohhh that's right!" Recognition washed over me as I filled up my tank. "How are you?" Every time I opened my mouth, I could see my breath dancing in the cold air.

"I'm great. Hey, there little ones!" She waved at the girls through the window then focused her attention on me. "I'm happy I ran into you. It's way too cold for us to talk right now so I'll just give you my information. You text me later okay? I have a business opportunity for you." She reached in her purse and handed me a card.

"Thanks."

"I'll let you get back to the girls." She almost slipped on the ice as she ventured back to her car. I finished filling my tank and hopped inside my car, relishing the warmth. I looked down at the card before pulling off. The doctor's full name was Michelle Jackson. Instead of waiting until I got off work to see what the business opportunity was, I texted her.

Hey there Dr. Jackson. It's Serena. Just texting so you'll have my number.

I hit the send button then pulled off.

-

Before the day was done, Dr. Jackson called me.

"What's up Doc?"

"Totally here for the Bugs Bunny reference, but please call me Michelle. I wanted to connect with you so we could discuss a babysitting opportunity."

"What did you have in mind?"

"My husband and I need a date night sitter," she informed me.

"I'd be open to that but what made you reach out?" I asked curiously.

"I trust Kirsten's judgment. I've known her for years. She doesn't play when it comes to her kids. And honestly, it feels much more comfortable than going through a service."

"That makes sense."

"How soon could you start? What do you charge for two kids? Do you work on weeknights? Sorry, I'm rushing this. I'm glad I've found someone." The doctor gave an excited giggle.

"We can start ASAP. I charge $15/hour for two kids. I do babysit during the week, but it would have to be after work. I can send you my resume too. Whatever you need."

"Perfect. I'll be in touch."

-

The next three weeks progressed with no drama. I started babysitting for Michelle and her husband Ryan to make some extra cash. They happily paid me $15/hour for their two kids. It was such a stark difference from working with the Millers who were stingier with their money. As far as the Miller family was concerned, Tessa seemed to be doing fine, and Raymond hadn't started any more irrelevant conversations. I assumed one day in particular was going to end on a similar good note, but as I walked into the Millers' house, Kirsten had yet another question about yet another lie.

"Hey, you didn't have the girls in some other nanny's car, did you?" she asked me quickly intending to catch me off guard.

"Why would they be in any other car except mine?" I asked.

"Rachel said when you all went out for hot chocolate that you rode in another nanny's car."

"I drove us to Starbucks and parked in the lot. We met my friend Elizabeth and her kids there. We didn't need to be in another car."

"I can't have you guys in someone else's car," Kirsten responded wearily.

"And luckily for you, we weren't so…." I rolled my eyes in frustration.

"Maybe we should get one of those location apps so I can track the whole family," Kirsten muttered more to herself than to me. She appeared unhinged.

"Maybe when you get back, we can talk to Rachel to find out why she's telling these lies," I offered softly, careful not to upset Kirsten's delicate state.

"No, it's fine. We're good. No worries." She brushed me off and left for work.

-

"Let's review your letters and numbers," I suggested to Anna once we finished reading *Green Eggs and Ham*. "Rachel, you can either join us or practice writing your name." I held up a flashcard. "Anna, how many hearts are on this card?"

She pointed to the card and counted. "Nine!"

"Good Anna! You're ready for preschool girl! Okay, let's do some letters." I held up the stack of flashcards.

" A is for Apple a-a-apple…B is for Ball b-b-ball… C is for cat c-c-cat." And on she went until we reached the letter Z.

"A is for AWESOME! Anna! You're amazing! Let's see how Rachel is doing with writing… How's it going?"

"I wrote my name again and again until the page was full. R-a-c-h-e-l." Rachel beamed.

"Good baby! We're going to have to start writing your last name too. M-i-l-l-e-r. It's the same length as your first name. You can start writing both names together. I have to challenge y'all. You girls are too smart."

"Thank you, Ms. Serena." Rachel blushed and hugged me. "...Are you going to move in with us?"

"No, why? You want me to?" I gave her neck a little tickle.

"My daddy likes you. He's always talking to you." Her face was suddenly serious, too mature for a four-year-old.

"Oh no, don't worry about that Rachel. Your mom, dad, and I are all friends. We all talk to each other. Your daddy loves your mommy so much!" I hugged her tight.

"Serena... are the bad guys ever going to come back here when I'm sleeping?" Her face contorted with anxiousness.

"No of course not! Your parents installed the alarm system to keep you safe. If any bad people try to get in here, the alarm will go off and the police will come to protect you. Remember?"

"Oh okay." Rachel hugged me back with relief. She might have felt better, but I felt worse. Why would she think her dad liked me? What had she heard?

-

April breezed in and brought relief from the cold. It was only 50 degrees outside, but it felt balmy compared to the usual 25. The melting snow and change in temperature lifted my spirits. Reporting to work, I saw I was not the only one the weather had affected. Raymond strutted around the house whistling. I could sense another one of our little chats coming on.

"Good morning Serena. How are you today?"

"I'm alright. You're in a good mood I see."

"I'm great! Work is good. My kids are healthy and so am I!" he sang.

"Kirsten good too?" I asked noticing he neglected to mention her.

"She's okay, I guess." His tone was suddenly darker. "You know…my sister Rebecca is getting married soon. She isn't sure if her partner is the one for her. She loves Amber, but she's not certain that she's her soulmate. I told her being in love with someone is the only reason to get married. Unfortunately, I got married under different circumstances, so I would know."

"What are you trying to say, Raymond?" I asked annoyed at the implication. "Never mind, I don't want to know."

"I respect my wife so much. She's extremely hardworking and committed. She's an excellent partner," he pleaded.

"That's good to hear," I uttered quickly before he could share too much. "I need to go check on the girls. I don't want to talk about this stuff anymore." I scurried away.

"Yeah of course. I should head to my meeting. See you later," he called dejectedly to my back.

Chaos

"Hello?" I answered my cell phone one morning as I walked through the Millers' front door.

"Good morning. How are you?" Kirsten greeted in a friendly voice on the other end of the line.

"I'm alright," I responded concisely suspicious of the reason for the call.

"So, what are you wearing today? Nothing crazy right?" she asked in her uncharacteristically friendly tone.

"Ummm what? No." I answered bemused, my heartbeat quickening.

"Oh, no need to be offended. Just asking. They said something about you having cleavage out," she replied in an off-hand kind of way.

"What? I'm wearing the same t-shirt and yoga pants I wear every day," I stated already offended.

"Oh okay. That's all I wanted to know. I'll see you later." She hung up.

Before I could process how to react, Raymond entered the living room with Tessa. "Good morning," I said brusquely.

"Good morning." Raymond mimicked my tone and heading towards the kitchen.

"How are you?" I asked Tessa, but she avoided eye contact and made to follow Raymond. "What's wrong?" She flinched as I grabbed her arm.

"I don't want to talk to you." She twisted away.

"Wait, Tessa. Please tell me," I implored.

She furtively glanced towards the kitchen, "My parents argued last night. Probably about you."

"Wait, what happened?" I whispered hurriedly.

"My mom was pissed about something last night, then she tripped over a pile of laundry I left in the hallway. She pinched my arm really hard after that. It's still a little sore."

"Can I see?" I reached out with concern and inspected her arm. "She bruised you. Maybe she didn't mean to, but she did. What did your dad do about it?"

"He told her to leave me alone, but he didn't come out of the bedroom," Tessa informed me disappointedly.

"I don't understand him!" I said in a fierce whisper. Tessa shushed me. "Why doesn't he speak up?!"

"I don't know. Maybe it's my fault but he's my dad…" she trailed off sadly.

"The abuse could be worse, but that doesn't make this okay." I gave her a look filled with pity.

"Please don't say anything." Her eyes watered instantly.

"I'm going to report this," I stated firmly.

"No, please!" she pleaded.

"I-" I cut myself off because Raymond was heading toward us. "I'll see you later Tessa. Have a good day." I smiled and patted her shoulder in an effort to seem normal.

"We'll see you later Serena," Raymond inserted, closing the door behind them.

-

During breakfast, I turned on the TV to keep the girls occupied while I tackled my intrusive thoughts. *Should I call DCFS to protect Tessa? What if her new home is worse than this one? What if I don't report her and something worse happens? I need to talk to Kirsten. I'll quit if the conversation doesn't go well. And I can't let her think insulting my wardrobe is okay. Maybe I should just make today my last day. Kirsten doesn't trust me anyway! But if I leave, what will happen to Tessa?*

That question haunted me for the rest of the day. I decided to type a letter of resignation. I planned to send it to Raymond and Kirsten just in case only one parent relieved me at the end of the day. I needed them both to hear my words straight from me.

-

"Hey!" Kirsten called as she walked through the door at 6:00 sharp with Raymond in tow. She floundered in the doorway when she saw my facial expression. "Oh no, what's wrong?"

"That comment you made about my attire earlier? I know you said don't be offended by it, but I'm highly offended," I informed her.

"Why are you offended?" she played dumb.

"Because I don't dress crazy!" I cried in frustration. "Where did that question even come from?"

"They said something about you having cleavage out," she repeated in a mock innocent voice.

"What are you talking about? Who is 'they'?"

"Raymond. Well, actually it was Rachel."

"Rachel? What did she say exactly?" I looked briefly at the little girl.

"Rachel said that your 'boobies' were showing in your shirt. I assumed that meant you had cleavage showing. She also said you wore some type of shirt showing your belly last week. I didn't see you myself which is why I asked." Kirsten shrugged.

"A crop top? Are you serious? In this weather?" I asked, her tone annoying me.

"Raymond, you saw Serena last week. Did she wear anything inappropriate?" Kirsten turned to her husband, determined not to take my word for anything.

"I don't recall that. I don't really pay attention to what she wears. I couldn't care less." Raymond stepped further into the house.

"Just back me up for once, Raymond. Jesus Christ! You were right there when Rachel said it. You should have corrected her!" Kirsten fussed.

"I didn't think it was that big of a deal honestly. I also didn't know you were going to address it."

"You should have known me better than that," Kirsten retorted.

"Listen, I wear the same thing every week," I interjected trying to keep the focus on me. "That includes yoga pants and t-shirts. I have never tried to accentuate or expose my body at work." I looked at Rachel feeling betrayed. "I'm not sure why Rachel said these things, but they aren't true. Even if they were, your use of the word crazy is my first issue. It's offensive. Second, at no point have we ever discussed what my attire for work should be. And considering my uniform has been the same for months, I don't understand why you would believe this. You believe everything Rachel tells you. I guess you should; she is your daughter, but obviously there's an issue of trust here. If you don't trust me, then it doesn't make sense for me to keep working for you." My voice quivered. I was furious but hurt too.

"This time I thought it was true not just because Rachel told me but also because Raymond could have spoken up in your defense, but he chose not to for whatever stupid reason." She glared at him disdainfully.

"True, but you could have confirmed it with him before addressing me. You wanted to believe the worst about me. Why that is, I don't know, but this is not the first time we've had this issue," I said.

"Well as long as you're not dressing inappropriately, I don't have a problem." Kirsten waved her hand dismissively.

"Again, there is nothing about attire in the contract. You didn't determine what was work appropriate then and you definitely won't dictate it now all because of a lie. If I had come in here in a skimpy outfit, I could let this go, but your lack of trust is pissing me off to be completely honest. That coupled with the fact that you have not once apologized for using the word crazy or for how you talk to me in general makes me want to leave this evening and never come back." My temper forced my chest to heave.

"I apologize." Kirsten looked as if I was overreacting. "We weren't trying to offend you. I never thought it was this serious," she continued flatly as if unwilling to express the emotion it took to convince me of her words.

"Since we're already discussing sensitive topics, I will quit and be forced to report you if Tessa gets another bruise." I stood to my feet preparing for a fight.

"Uh... I what?" Kirsten looked scathingly at Tessa.

"I care about these kids more than you know. I haven't said anything before now because Tessa is scared, but I can't do this anymore. DO NOT take your anger out on her. Don't hit her or disrespect her. It's bad for her self-esteem and you know that," I concluded firmly.

"You're right. I'm so sorry Tessa," Raymond cut in. "We've been taking our problems out on you, and it's not fair. Kirsten, obviously we have to do better especially if Serena has noticed our bullshit." He walked over and hugged his oldest daughter.

"You're telling me you've known this about me and never said anything? Tessa, how could you tell our family business?" Kirsten had the audacity to sound victimized.

"I-" Tessa started to speak, thought better of it and remained quiet.

"Kirsten, what was she supposed to do? Keep her emotions in forever?" Raymond retorted. "She didn't want to talk to us. Obviously, she was comfortable enough to talk to Serena. Serena, thank you for giving my daughter a safe space to vent. I didn't realize we were doing her a disservice."

"Serena, you should have told me what Tessa was accusing me of," Kirsten said stubbornly.

"So she could get in trouble for it?" I asked hotly.

"It's none of your business."

"Why did you do it?"

"I… don't want to talk about this. This conversation is over." Kirsten sounded uncomfortable for the first time.

"Maybe a family counselor would be a good idea. I just want the kids to be okay," I admitted with a calm desperation in my voice.

"We will look into that. Thank you, Serena," Raymond said determined to put an end to the unpleasant conversation.

"Look, I wanted to talk to you all, and I've overstepped. Today can be my last day. This arrangement clearly wont work."

"No! No! We want you here! We trust you with the girls. Hopefully, we can get beyond this. Please stay. We'd love to have you right, Kir?" Raymond looked expectantly in her direction.

"You figure it out. I'm done here," she replied indifferently.

"How about I put in my two weeks' notice today to give you all time to find someone else? I think that's best," I offered fairly.

"You don't have to do that!" Raymond insisted with alarm in his voice.

"What we pay you is easier on our pockets than Tater Tots was. Whatever you want to do is fine with me," Kirsten said slightly reconsidering her position.

"I should stay because it's easy on your pockets? Not because you trust me to keep the girls safe? Not because they're happy? Not because I'm here every day on time but because I'm a cheap date? Yeah, let's consider this my two weeks' notice." I rolled my eyes.

"Please reconsider. Just think about it and get back to us tomorrow morning. We don't want to lose you," Raymond pleaded.

I gathered my belongings in silence. The atmosphere was thick enough to cut with a knife.

-

"No, that heifer did NOT ask you if you were dressed crazy. I would have been offended too! And she wasn't even sorry." Maakara shook her head reflecting Serena's sentiments.

"Exactly. She thought she could say anything to me, and it would be okay. She thought wrong."

"So how did it go on your last day?"

-

"Hey, Serena. Can I talk to you before my dad comes downstairs?" Tessa asked me the morning after the blow up.

"What's up?"

"I was hoping you wouldn't say anything to my mom and dad about what I told you-"

"I know I-" I interrupted.

"I'm glad you did though! I think my mom needed to be embarrassed. I'll miss you. Stay in touch when you leave okay?" Tessa smiled and gave me a strong hug.

"Of course." I hugged her back, as Raymond descended the stairs.

"Morning Serena. I'd love to talk about your decision, but I'm running behind. When do the girls go down for their naps?" he asked in a hurry.

"Around 1:00."

"Okay, we'll talk then."

-

Ahead of us was another free day at the YMCA. Riding trikes, hula hooping, and chasing each other around the gym were sure to have them worn out by lunchtime. Before the girls and I could get to the fun stuff, we needed a bathroom break. As I took Anna off the potty, Rachel asked "Are you mad at me Ms. Serena?"

"Why would I be mad at you?" I refused to meet her eyes.

"Because I told my mom a lie about your clothes."

"Why did you do that?"

"I thought that you would get in trouble," she admitted tentatively.

"Why would you want me to get in trouble?"

"Trouble for talking to my daddy."

"Why shouldn't I talk to your dad?" I asked squatting down to her level.

"I thought my daddy liked you. If you get in trouble, then mommy would make you go away." The little girl was on the verge of tears. I hugged her until she pulled away. "I love you, Ms. Serena. I'm sorry."

"I love you too, but it's not okay to tell lies. Now I understand why you lied about the showers and riding in the other nanny's car." Rachel nodded in response. "Let's go have some fun okay?"

"Okay," she agreed and hugged me again. Anna remained quiet but hugged me too.

-

Waiting on the water to warm, I put the dirty dishes from lunch in the sink. The alarm chirped notifying me of Raymond's return. I held my breath and waited for him to come to me.

"Hey Serena," he greeted after a couple of minutes.

"Hey." I turned around to face him.

"I hate the way Kirsten spoke to you yesterday. She really shouldn't have used the word crazy. That was inappropriate. We talked about her word choice last night." He gave me what would-be a sincere look if I trusted him.

"Yeah, I wish I had your support in this too since you were standing there when Rachel told the lie." I gave him a pointed look.

"Yes, in hindsight I should have. I didn't think it was a big deal, but I was wrong. Will you consider staying on with us beyond the two weeks?"

"No."

"No? Why not?" Raymond pouted.

"I don't feel like you all trust me. You believe everything Rachel tells you, which is good for her but bad for me. I don't want to feel responsible for what happens with Tessa. And I'm no longer interested in those personal conversations we have either," I reiterated plainly.

"We don't have to have those conversations anymore!" he cried desperately. "I've talked to Kirsten. And you're going to love this," he added with a small laugh. "Rachel thinks something is going to happen between us. She thinks we like each other. Isn't that crazy?" he asked with a smirk.

"Yeah, it is crazy. That just makes this situation worse," I said disgusted.

"How so?" He questioned moving closer with a worried look on his face.

"Because I'm not here for you!" I yelled losing my temper. "I'm here to get these little girls ready for preschool. That's it!

"Why are you so offended? She's not the first person to think it. When our friends and family heard we were getting a nanny, there were some suggestive jokes made."

"See, this is flattering for you. If anything was to happen between us, people would write you off with the whole 'a man will be a man' bullshit. Sleeping with a younger woman does wonders for the male ego, which is obviously what you need. But I would be deemed a home wrecker. I would never under any circumstance have an affair with a married man and especially not with one of my married clients! And it upsets me that you don't get that. To hell with these dishes." I took my phone off the counter and turned to leave the kitchen. Raymond seized my wrist.

"Please don't leave," he muttered desperately yanking me towards him.

"Let me go!" I tried to pull away, but he forced his lips onto mine. I raked my nails across the side of his face.

"Ouch!" He yelled and let my arm go. I raced towards the front of the house. "Serena wait!"

I picked up my jacket and purse and ran out of the front door leaving it wide open. I didn't look back or catch my breath until I was home safely.

-

"He did what?!" Maakara shouted spilling her remaining chips on the floor.

-

Once in the parking lot of my complex, I gathered myself and checked my phone. Raymond had already sent five messages.

Hey, where did you go?

Why did you leave?

Who's going to watch the girls?

Are you coming back?

What was all of that about?

There were no missed calls. He couldn't be deluded enough to think I left for no reason. Or was he really smart? On second thought, I knew what he was doing, setting it up to look like I left suddenly for no apparent reason. Asking innocent questions so he can show Kirsten our conversation. I planned to give her my version if she tried to contact me. It didn't matter if she didn't believe me. She needed to hear it. Before I could get out of the car, my phone rang.

"Hello?" I answered hesitantly.

"Raymond said you attacked him when he tried to convince you to stay with us. And you ran from the house without saying goodbye? What is going on?!" Kirsten screeched.

Momentarily stunned, I finally managed to say, "Your perverted husband sexually assaulted me in your home while your girls slept in the next room! Did he tell you that?" Silence. "Did he say I scratched his face because he forced his lips on mine? Do not call me with this bullshit! Talk to your damn husband!" I hung up the phone. Angry tears filled my eyes as I walked into my house.

"Mom..." My voice cracked.

"What's the matter?" She sat up immediately on alert.

"I quit today. Raymond grabbed my arm and kissed me. I scratched him and ran." I shivered at the thought of his lips touching mine.

"God dammit! You're going to need a gun."

-

Hours after my mom consoled me and banned me from ever talking to the Millers again, I received yet another phone call.

"OH MY GOD TELL ME IT'S NOT TRUE!" a familiar voice wailed.

"Hey," I said calmly. "Sorry, it had to end like that."

"You left the house without giving us a chance to say goodbye. What happened?" Tessa asked.

"What did your parents tell you?" I did not want to relive it.

"That you left with no notice and scratched up dad."

"I'm going to be honest with you since I'm sure your parents won't be. I was having a conversation with Raymond during the girls' nap time. I tried to walk away from him, and he grabbed me and kissed me," I summarized.

"He did what!?"

"Yeah. I scratched his face and ran."

"Oh my god! You have to be kidding." Tessa said incredulously.

"No, I'm not. It was really upsetting to be honest," I admitted heavily.

"What is wrong with my family?!" she howled into my ear.

"I don't know. I'm still processing this myself. Listen, you have my number. Please stay in touch. I have to go." I was not strong enough to tackle her emotions and mine.

"I hope you're okay. I believe you the same way you believed me. Talk to you later. I'm sorry. Bye."

I hung up the phone and confronted the thought that I'd been trying to deny. What if he tried to do more than just kiss me? I needed to brush my teeth for the third time. I could still taste him.

The next morning, I woke up feeling refreshed and relaxed until I remembered what happened the day before. Anxiety intense enough to make me weak flooded my body.

Before I fell asleep the night before, my mom suggested I take my time finding a new job. I decided to listen.

-

"I'm rarely speechless, but here I am without speech," Maakara said finally picking her chips up off the floor. "I wish you were making this up."

"Wish I was too."

"So, you were finished being a nanny by then right?"

"Not exactly."

The Atkinses

Hyde Park

Three months after fleeing the Millers' home, I hadn't heard from Raymond or Kirsten, but Tessa stayed in touch weekly. She told me that neither of her parents had filed for divorce, but things were tense with their constant bickering. The girls finally stopped asking why I hadn't come back. Apparently, they were in preschool bored with reviewing the basics. Most importantly, Kirsten hadn't taken any more anger out on Tessa.

It had been peaceful on my end. I hadn't worked in months, but I was itching to get some money in my pocket and quite honestly, I missed working with kids. I had just started applying to babysitting jobs on Nannytown.com when I connected with a mom named Emily Atkins. She was only looking for someone to watch her son twice a week. She was offering $12.50/hour for seven hours. From the picture on the profile, I could see her one-year-old son Ethan had a bright smile. Emily wasn't smiling but looked very well put together for the family photo. After corresponding for a full day, she wanted to meet the following afternoon at the Dunkin Donuts in Hyde Park. I was looking forward to starting fresh with a new, much smaller family. I felt more at ease since Emily hadn't mentioned being married and there was no dad in the family picture.

I dressed in my usual work uniform: yoga pants and a t-shirt. I wanted Emily to know upfront exactly how I dressed everyday so there were no issues. After I lucked up on a space in the small parking lot, I found two employees behind the counter at Dunkin, one customer at the register, and a white lady with dark hair holding a little Black baby at a table. She waved me over. I smiled and walked towards them.

"Hi, are you Serena?" she asked enthusiastically.

"I am. Emily?"

"Yep. And this is Ethan." She stood the little guy up on her lap.

"Nice to meet you."

"My husband Jabari is running late from work. He should be here soon. Please have a seat."

"Oh, you didn't mention you were married," I said trying to keep the nervousness out of my voice as I sat down across from them. I did not want to work in close quarters with a dad again.

"I should really update our profile pic so there's no confusion," she admitted weakly. "We've been married for three years." She gazed at her son who took an immediate interest in me.

"Hey, little guy. Nice shirt." I reached out and touched his hand. He was wearing a brown onesie with a lion on the chest. He smiled at me with a slobbery grin.

"Oooh he likes you. I guess we're off to a good start then," Emily said optimistically.

"Yeah, I guess so." I smiled back at Ethan.

"Just so you know, I'm a stay-at-home mom. Full disclosure, I get overwhelmed being home sometimes so we decided it would be best for me to have some time to myself during the week," Emily admitted.

"That's understandable. And good for you. I wish all moms could do that."

"But enough about me." Emily waved off the uncomfortable topic. "Tell me about yourself. I saw online that you're CPR certified, and you have some experience babysitting?"

"Yes, as I said yesterday, I've actually cared for my younger cousins, as well as some of my mom's friend's kids in the past. More recently, I've been babysitting for families I worked with from the home daycare and center."

"So, you really enjoy working with kids?" Emily asked with a note of surprise in her voice.

"Absolutely. I always knew I would work with kids in some way. I'm thankful you all are even considering me for this."

"Of course. Is $12.50/hour okay with you?" Emily peered at me shrewdly.

"Yep."

"Fantastic…oh here comes my husband," she said glancing over my shoulder.

I looked behind me, and my heart skipped a beat. Seemingly in slow motion, the most handsome man I had ever seen strode through the door. I was pretty sure I heard Whitney Houston's "I will always love you" playing in the background as he made his way towards us. Emily's husband was at least 6'3 with very dark skin and beautiful white teeth that contrasted with his short dark beard. His body was equally as alluring as his face. He was noticeably muscular but not bulky or thin. His white button-up and black slacks were tailored to perfection, complimenting his strong frame. Streaks of sunlight danced across his face through the windows as he finished his journey to us.

"This is my husband Jabari. Jabari, this is Serena," Emily piped up immediately.

"H-hello," I stuttered closing my mouth, which had been hanging open. I blushed under Jabari's piercing gaze and extended my hand.

"Hey, nice to meet you." He took my hand and shook it.

I wasn't sure if it was the sound of his deep voice or his hand that affected me but when we touched, a jolt of electric energy shot from him to me. I wondered if he felt it too. "Do you all have any questions for me?" I asked trying to gain some composure as the handsome man took a seat next to his family.

"We saw you had a few references listed online. Is it okay if we contact them?" Jabari's voice flowed through my ears like warm honey.

"Absolutely. I listed the families I worked with at the home daycare. I still babysit for them in my spare time." I tried to keep my eyes focused mostly on Emily.

"Excellent. Are you CPR certified?" Jabari asked making eye contact.

"Yes. J, she answered that already." Emily answered with a hint of irritation.

"Are you comfortable putting little ones down for naps? How do you usually get them to sleep?" Jabari ignored his wife.

"Most times I ask parents what they prefer. My preference is to lay the child down and leave the room. I'm comfortable with the self-sooth method, but sometimes I like to lean over the crib and rub their backs until they fall asleep or play soothing music. I prefer to get the baby accustomed to sleeping without me holding them. I think it makes it easier for all of the adults involved."

"Sounds good. I think we can work with that. What do you plan to do with Ethan when he isn't napping?" Jabari asked looking at me intently.

"I like to dance, play music, and exercise. If you are okay with us leaving the house then we can go to the park or take a walk. Reading books kind of goes without saying," I offered with a friendly smile.

"Of course. Well, I'm done grilling you." Jabari chuckled. "Emily, do you have anything else to ask?" He turned to his wife.

"No, I like her. Let's call those references today. She already had a background check done through the website."

"Can I ask if there's anything I need to know about Ethan? I know your profile said there are no allergies," I mentioned putting the icing on the cake.

"Good question. He's an easy-going little guy. He does struggle with naptime a little, but I'm sure you can work your magic, right?" Emily asked almost desperately.

"I'm sure I can," I assured her.

"I do have one last question," Jabari said seriously.

"What's that?" I fully faced him, bracing myself for the impact of his beauty.

"Can you babysit from 7:00 to midnight Friday?" He grinned.

"I can do that." I grinned back.

"Since Nannytown.com already ran your background check, we'll be in touch after we speak with your references," Emily added.

"I can't wait to hear from you." I stood to my feet. "It was nice meeting you all, especially you Ethan." I leaned over to touch his hand again.

"Thanks for the meeting. You'll be hearing from us soon." Emily said sounding grateful.

"See you soon," chimed in Jabari.

"Have a good one." I turned and walked away smiling to myself. I thought the interview went extremely well, but I wasn't sure the smile was because of the job.

-

"Girl! I've never seen a man that fine!" Maakara admitted impressed. "I wish I could see him in person."

"It was hard being around him. That's how fine he was. He gave me butterflies. I felt like I was always blushing around him. My heart didn't beat normally. It was so odd." Serena shook her head at the memory.

"Could he tell you had a thing for him?" Maakara asked conspiratorially.

"I did my best to be professional. I'm not sure how successful I was to be honest with you."

"But how did you think it was too soon to be working around a man again? Especially in that environment."

"That is another reason why I was uncomfortable for sure. I spoke with the mother about that."

-

Later that evening after the interview, I was sitting on the couch watching TV when I got a call from an unknown number.

"Hello?"

"Hey, Serena. It's Emily. I didn't want to use your number until I knew we were sure about you."

"That's understandable. Nannytown tells us to hold off on sharing personal info until we're sure it's not a scam."

"Don't we know it. We've encountered some already. I'm glad you're not one though! We called your references. We'd love to extend the part-time offer to you if you're still interested," Emily paused for a response.

"I'd love to! Do you still need a sitter for Friday?"

"We do. Does that work for you?" Emily asked hopefully.

"Absolutely. Yes, but I have a question."

"What's up?"

"Will I be mostly seeing you in the mornings and evenings? Or will your husband be there? I'm just asking because talking to moms about their child's day seems to be better than talking to dads. Moms listen better." I tried to laugh off my anxiety.

"That is true. Since I'm more flexible, it should be me who relieves you at the end of the day."

"Cool. Text me the address for Friday." I hung up the phone happy to have a little cash flow and some security.

<u>Friday</u>

South Shore

The Atkinses only lived about seven minutes from my house. I arrived at their building five minutes early and squeezed into a space right outside the front door. It must have been my lucky day because South Shore was not known for good parking. The Atkins' place was dark brick and looked like it had multiple other units inside. The exterior was old, not much to look at, but I suspected the apartments were impressive. I rang the bell, got buzzed in without hearing a voice on the intercom, and headed up to the third floor. The hallway was just as dark and old as the outside. The stairs foretold my arrival as they creaked like toads.

On the top floor, I almost stumbled from shock. Jabari was waiting at the door shirtless. I fought hard to keep my mouth from hanging open this time. His chest looked just as beautiful bare as it did with a shirt on it. I found a spot on the wall behind him and focused on it.

"Hey, Serena come on in!" He opened the door wide and took a step back.

"Hey, thanks." I stepped over the threshold. The front door lead directly into the living room. It was spacious but very cozy, covered in shades of brown and burgundy. The floors and paneling were wooden. The bookcase extended from one end of the right wall to the other. It was completely full. The dark brown couches with colorful blankets paired well with the tan and red multicolored rugs, adding warmth to the room.

"Here's Ethan," Jabari grunted scooping the little guy off the floor. "You'll be responsible for putting him to bed tonight." Ethan instinctively reached out for me, and I took him from his dad's arms.

"I'm glad he likes you. Let me give you a tour... This is the living room. To the left is the dining room."

There was no door separating the dining room from the living room. We walked straight into the tiny kitchen from the dining room, which only housed a table. The kitchen was completely white. The tile was dated and clashed with the browns from the other rooms. Before Jabari could continue, Emily entered in her robe.

"Hey, Serena. I'm so glad he likes you!" she exclaimed.

"Huh?... Oh, um yes of course!" I hugged Ethan closer to me realizing she meant the child, not Jabari.

"We keep everything pretty simple. He already ate dinner, but I suggest giving him a cup of milk before bed. There are snacks in this cabinet for you and Ethan." Emily gestured to the cabinet above the sink then turned to leave the kitchen through the second doorway. "Follow me... down this hall are the bathroom and three bedrooms. One bedroom is just a guestroom. Feel free to relax there. Ethan's room is down the hall to the right and ours is across the hall from his."

Emily opened the door on the right leading to a pale green nursery. There was a white metal crib on the far wall, two white dressers, a closet full of clothes, and a diaper genie. "Ethan's diapers are stacked on top of the dresser along with his ointments. His books are on the floor next to his bed. We already put on his pajamas."

"You following all of this Serena?" Jabari cut in. "Or is this too much?"

"I got it," I said quickly making eye contact then focusing back on Emily before Jabari's beauty could distract me.

"Turn on his sound machine before leaving the room. It's important because this door creaks and so do the floors. I think that's all for now since he'll be sleeping most of the time. Any questions?" Emily asked in a rush.

"So, I should change him, give him milk and turn on the sound machine?" I asked summing things up.

"Yep!" both parents answered in unison.

"Well, then I only have one more question."

"What's that?" asked Jabari.

"Can I get the Wi-Fi password?" They clearly didn't have cable. I hadn't even seen a TV.

"Sure, I'll get that for you," Jabari offered helpfully. "Em, you finish getting dressed. I'll be there in a minute." Emily walked away without another word.

"Follow me," Jabari instructed.

I could smell his deodorant and cologne as I followed him back down the hall. I found his scent intoxicating. Maybe it would help if he put a shirt on. His back was perfectly sculpted. I was already drunk at the sight and smell of him in the 10 seconds it took to walk to the living room. Suddenly, my face collided with his back when he stopped. "Hmph! Sorry, I wasn't paying attention." I wiped off my forehead.

"I see!" He smirked and kneeled on the floor, which was lucky for me because I didn't want him to see my look of embarrassment.

"Here's the router. Type the password in and you should be fine. I'll be back in a few." Jabari finally walked away, taking Ethan with him. I connected to the Wi-Fi and browsed the books on the shelves. I wasn't familiar with most of the titles, but the genres included mystery, politics, racism, and religion. I hoped I could borrow some in the future.

A few minutes later, the Atkinses returned completely dressed and ready to go. I almost didn't notice Emily because Jabari was so stunning. "You guys look good!" I said standing up to meet them at the door. I looked at Emily first, then snuck a look at her husband.

"Thanks." Emily checked her hair. She was wearing a little black dress that accentuated her abnormally large boobs. It highlighted how small her frame was. Her hair hung flatly by her shoulders. Black gladiator sandals covered her feet. By contrast, her husband's attractiveness was completely understated in a periwinkle polo shirt and jeans that fit just right. He finished off the outfit with crisp white Nikes.

"We're just headed to a game night at a friend's house. We may come back earlier than midnight," Jabari told me.

"Okay, have fun."

"Any other questions for us before we leave?" He asked as he hugged Ethan.

"Nope. I think we're good," I said reluctantly making eye contact.

"Okay well, we're going to set the alarm before we go. The code is 1994 if you need it," Jabari informed.

"See you guys later."

"Bye Ethan," Jabari said kissing his son on the cheek.

Emily was out of the door.

-

Once Ethan and I were alone, I hurriedly texted my friends about my new employer. I couldn't keep my emotions contained.

Oh my God! The dad I'm babysitting for is FINE AF

-OMG, what does he look like?! Is he single?

-Send a pic if you can.

He's tall and dark skinned. Sexy AF. He's married, but my hormones don't know that!

-Damn, he must be fine then. I don't think you ever said any of the dads you worked with were cute before.

-Send us a pic! I gotta see him.

Maybe I shouldn't keep working for them.

-Lol nah, I like this. It's exciting.

-It's so cliché, but at the same time, it's fun hearing you talk like this.

Y'all are bad influences

-I fully admit this.

-It's really crazy because the last dad you worked with was such a creep! You said he was ugly and insecure and you'd never cross that line, but now you turn around and you're instantly attracted to this new dad. Like wtf? Just be careful.

I think I'll be fine as long as he doesn't try me...

-

With the little time left to spend with him before bed, I sat Ethan on my lap and read "Good night Moon" as he dozed in my arms. I stood him on his feet and walked him to the kitchen for his milk. As sleepy as he was, he gulped it all down. I quickly changed his diaper and put him in the crib with a tiny plush toy. I turned on the sound machine and turned off his light before heading towards the door.

"Good night Ethan. Sleep tight." I closed the door gently behind me.

I kept busy for a little while by perusing the bookcase. The family pictures on top caught my attention. There were wedding photos with Jabari and Emily looking young and in love. It was interesting to see the contrast between Jabari's family and Emily's. I wondered if they ever had to deal with racism from their in-laws. After hours of browsing and watching shows on my phone, mom and dad returned.

"How did it go?" Jabari asked taking off his shoes.

"Great! Ethan is a good kid. He went right to sleep at bed time. He didn't even cry when you left. He drank all his milk after we read a story. I changed his diaper before bed and didn't forget the sound machine. That's pretty much it."

Jabari turned to Emily, "We're glad to hear that. I'll pay you. Em, can you go check on Ethan?"

Why did he insist on us having private moments together?

"Good night Serena. Thanks again. I'll see you next week," Emily said and walked away.

"You're welcome. See you."

"I appreciate you taking care of Ethan so well. Maybe we can make this a long-term arrangement?" Jabari reached in his wallet and handed me $65 in cash.

"I hope so!" I uttered a little too enthusiastically. "... Or um that would be nice." I awkwardly pocketed the money.

Jabari chuckled at my embarrassment then said, "We won't keep you any longer. Should I walk you to your car?"

"No, I actually parked right at the front door. Thanks though." I put my shoes on expeditiously.

"Okay, I'll just watch out of the window then," Jabari said politely.

"Thanks. I'll see you all next week." I opened their door without looking back at him.

"Drive safely. Will you text me when you make it home?"

"I will. Bye." I blushed as I headed down the stairs.

"Goodnight." I heard him say as he closed the door.

I couldn't resist looking up into the living room window to see if he was watching once I stepped onto the concrete. He waved at me. As my butt hit my car seat, I wondered how it was possible for me to be attracted to this man so soon after what happened with Raymond. I was thankful I wouldn't have to see too much of him.

Tuesday

I reported to the Atkins's condo at noon. Emily was already completely dressed. Ethan was sitting on the floor observing while his mom gave me the rundown.

"Ethan can have lunch now. Put him down for his nap when he finishes. The keys are on the counter. They're labeled. His stroller is in the hall. Do you need me to explain anything else to you before I go?"

"Yes, but it's unrelated to Ethan."

"What's up?" she asked clearly ready to leave.

"Do you plan to go back to work any time soon? I think I forgot to ask that before."

"Maybe when Ethan can talk, I'll go back part-time. It's not important to me right now. As I said, sometimes I just need a break from being a mom 24/7. I don't want to work, and I need a break from my kid. Does that make sense?" She gave a nervous laugh.

"It does. What's on your agenda for today?"

"Lunch with a girlfriend then the spa. I should be back by 7:00." She picked up her purse.

"That sounds fun! Enjoy. See you later."

"Bye." She closed the door behind her without acknowledging Ethan.

"Alright. What do we have for lunch today?" I asked walking towards the kitchen with Ethan trailing behind. "Looks like chicken nuggets, steamed broccoli, and rice. Good combo. Let me heat this up then you can dig in." Ethan looked up at me expectantly. He wasn't much of a talker yet. As the food warmed, an email alert caught my attention. It was from Nannytown.com.

-Hello Serena. I'm Aleyda Apaza. I saw your availability listed online, and I was wondering if you were still looking for work. I have six-week-old twin boys named Oliver and Oscar. We call them Oli and Ozzie. My husband Mauricio and I are looking for someone to start full-time Monday. It's 40 hours a week, eight hours/day. 8:00-4:00. Sorry for the short notice! I've been nervous about making this transition. We're willing to pay $16/hour…

At that point, I stopped reading because if my math was correct, that was $640/week untaxed. I was only getting $175 for my two days with Ethan. The job sounded too good to be true.

-We've already called your references. We are associates with one of them so we have faith you'd be a good fit. If you're interested please give me a call at your earliest convenience.

She left her number at the end of the email. I quickly fed Ethan so I could call Aleyda while he was sleeping. I felt nervous as the line rang.

"Hello?" a woman with a Hispanic accent answered.

"Hi, can I speak to Aleyda Apaza please?"

"This is Aleyda. Who's calling?"

"This is Serena Davis. You emailed me on Nannytown.com."

"Oh YES! Thank you for getting back to me so promptly! How are you?" the woman asked in her unique accent.

"I'm great. Thanks for asking."

"I won't take up too much of your time. Mauricio and I would like to offer you a job. It sounds strange to finally be able to say that," Aleyda admitted.

"Can you tell me more about your family?" I asked nervously.

"Just a little background on us. Mauricio and I are Bolivian. I'm 38 and a personal injury lawyer. Mauricio is finishing up his Master's degree. He's 32. We struggled to get pregnant so we ended up investing a lot of money into in-vitro fertilization. We're so thankful for our two little blessings, but because of what we had to go through to get them, we're a little scared to leave them. On Monday, I'm going back to work after a ten-week maternity leave. I'm not quite ready to work yet, but we need my income so we're opening our home to a caregiver. Daycares seem too hectic. Since we're first-time parents, we need someone to be just as patient with us as they are with our babies. Does any of this sound appealing?" the woman asked hesitantly.

"Yes, of course. Which one of my references do you know? I'd love to thank them."

"You babysit for Dr. Michelle Jackson. She made you sound like a godsend."

"Wow that was so sweet of her. I'll be sure to thank her later," I replied gratefully. "Aleyda, you seem like a nice lady. I'd like to meet your family before I start. Is that okay?"

"Absolutely. The sooner the better."

"How's tomorrow at 10 am?"

"Excellent. I'll text you the address."

-

After the phone call with Aleyda, I realized I would have to tell Emily as soon as she got home that I had an interview the next day and might be quitting soon. I hated that it was such short notice, but I wanted to warn her as quickly as possible. I didn't want to seem flakey, but I'd be making hundreds of dollars more than what I was currently making. As far as Emily was concerned, she'd be fine. She wasn't working, so she wouldn't have to call off to stay home with Ethan if I accepted the new job. Most importantly, I wouldn't have to see Jabari every week. Leaving seemed like the smartest option.

By the time Ethan and I got back from our walk, it was 4:30. In our remaining time, I straightened up while Ethan played alone. I heard a key in the door around 5:00. Emily was home early. I was mentally prepared to tell her everything when Jabari walked in. "Oh, you surprised me. I wasn't expecting you," I admitted as my heart pounded. His outfit of choice was a blue, violet, and white plaid short-sleeved shirt that hugged his biceps.

"Sorry. I got off early. How'd it go today?" he said sitting his briefcase on the couch.

"Great! We read books and played then we went for a walk after Ethan's nap. He ate all his food and slept for about two hours. I guess he's comfortable with me because he didn't cry not once."

"That's good to hear," Jabari said tiredly.

"I have some potentially bad news to tell you though." I looked at him anxiously.

"Oh no, not more bad news. What is it?" he asked sounding defeated.

"It's about me. A family reached out while you were at work. They want me to start full-time Monday. I wasn't still looking, but I do want to interview for the job. If I take it, I wont be able to work for you all during the week anymore. I wanted to give as much notice as possible. But I can still babysit on weekends if you need me!" I offered desperately to soften the blow.

"Okay, that's fine." Jabari sighed. "I'll tell Emily."

"When you commented about more bad news, what did you mean? What bad news did you get before?" I asked worried.

"Oh, nothing. It's just hard to find someone to work with our schedule."

"And I'm sorry it's such short notice. I wasn't expecting anyone to reach out. I should have updated my availability."

Jabari's dark eyes probed mine for what felt like days. He made it hard for me to breathe then said, "It's totally fine. Don't worry about it." He picked up Ethan off the floor.

"I'm meeting the family tomorrow. I can call or text you guys to let you know what I decide."

"Yeah, that'd be great."

"Can I ask you something?" A thought suddenly occurred to me.

"Sure."

"It's totally irrelevant to the job but… how old are you guys?"

"How old do you think we are?" Jabari challenged playfully.

"I figure you're about 30. The same for Emily."

"I'll take that. I'm 32. She's 30. Usually, people think I'm younger than I am," he replied sheepishly.

"Yeah, you do look young, but you're so mature and seem to be doing so well for yourself that I figured you had to be at least 30."

"Thanks." He flashed a smile that made me blush.

"What do you do?"

"I have a Ph.D. in Psychology. I share a practice with a former classmate of mine."

"How do you like your work?" I was genuinely intrigued.

"I love it. It was hard putting myself through school, but I refused to have to pay loans for decades," he said resolutely.

"I feel you. I won't bore you with the way I feel about school."

"Humor me." He smiled, and I melted.

"Well… I don't like the idea of taking on that much debt either. I didn't go to school. It wasn't because I didn't have the grades to get in but because getting a degree doesn't guarantee anything. They aren't worth as much as they used to be. The debt isn't worth it either. But I do respect people who stick it out," I finished gently.

"I agree. Maybe one day you'll go to school for free," Jabari said hopefully.

"How? Are you going to pay for it for me?" I always asked that question when people suggested I go to school, but saying it to him sounded flirty for some reason.

"We'll have to see about that. But what I was trying to say was that maybe college will be free by then." He laughed.

"Oh, my bad...I-I noticed you have a lot of books. Can I borrow one?" I asked needing to change the subject.

"Sure." He instinctively grabbed a book about racism in America post-Obama's election. "Keep it. I think you'll like it."

"I can keep it?" I was shocked. "I never give books away."

"Yeah, I read it twice. Maybe we can discuss it when you finish," he said positively.

"Absolutely. Did Emily read it already?"

"She never finished it. Discussing these things make her uncomfortable." For the first time, a dark look shadowed Jabari's face.

"She has a Black husband and son. She might want to get in tune," I said disappointed.

"Yeah, she doesn't get that. She lives in her own little world," Jabari retorted bitterly.

"Sorry to hear that." I regretted asking the question.

"It's fine. Hopefully, you'll never have to deal with that in your relationships."

"I don't see how I'd be in a relationship with someone who doesn't want to discuss race or racism," I said repulsed at the idea.

"Yeah. I wouldn't have predicted this for myself neither, but here I am." He shrugged helplessly.

"You seem happy, though. So obviously Emily's doing something right." I offered wanting to think the best of her.

"Yeah, I guess… you're attractive and smart. I'm sure you get a lot of attention from guys. Let's talk about your relationships instead." He leaned against a wall, not so subtly changing the subject.

"What's it to you if I get a lot of attention?" I asked coyly.

"You're right. It's not my business. I just didn't want to talk about Emily." He smirked.

"I understand." I wanted the conversation to last forever, but I couldn't think of anything else to say.

"You're really leaving us huh?" Jabari asked changing the subject again.

"Yeah, maybe. This new job is 40 hours and pays more per hour. I'd be crazy not to look into it. My mom wants to move in with her boyfriend, and I do not want to be bothered with that. I need the money for my own place. Like I said, I can still babysit sometimes though. Just let me know."

"I'll be in touch for sure." The suggestiveness in his voice paralyzed me momentarily.

"Okay, so I'm going to head out. Please talk to Emily for me," I requested awkwardly, finally managing to pull my eyes away.

"I will." Jabari straightened up, and his tone became professional again. "If you know anyone looking for a few extra hours of work, let us know." He hugged me with Ethan in his arms. He smelled delicious; I wanted to nuzzle his neck, but I pulled away.

"See you, Ethan! You're such a cool little guy." I looked at his dad. "Thanks for trusting me with your son. It was great spending time with him."

"The pleasure was all mine." His tone remained friendly.

"Bye." I jogged down the stairs before he could see me blush.

A grin spread across my face as I walked to my car. I know I shouldn't have been, but I was happy my attraction to Jabari was mutual. It made me feel good unlike the way Raymond made me feel. I tried to put Jabari out of my mind, but the smile remained plastered on my face until I started the car. Before pulling off, I got a text.

-Ethan started crying as soon as you left. We're going to have to get you back over here for sure.

Aww poor baby! Just say when.

Heat flushed my cheeks. Was I flirting? I didn't know. And it didn't matter how I felt in that moment. I wouldn't be seeing Jabari regularly anymore. I was safe. Reputation intact, I drove home wondering what it would be like had we met under different circumstances.

-

"Whew!" Maakara fanned herself and cracked open a forbidden Pepsi. "Girl, I'm glad you went for the other job because Jabari sounds irresistible. I don't think you would have been able to keep working with him and be professional at the same time."

"Yeah, it was tough being around him. Luckily, I accepted the new job. The family was really nice. It was such a change from what I had dealt with before. But dealing with them brought on a whole different set of problems."

Maakara nearly choked on her drink from swallowing so hard. "What other kinds of problems could there be? I feel like you already had them all!"

The Apazas

Hyde Park

The Apaza's lived on the 23rd floor of a luxury apartment building with a winding driveway. Finding parking near their place was a struggle, however the short commute made it worth it. Once I was permitted beyond the front desk and up the elevator, a thin pretty lady with dark hair greeted me at the apartment door.

"Good morning, Serena! So nice to meet you. I'm Aleyda," she welcomed in accented English.

"Nice to meet you too."

"Please, come in!" The tiny woman, who was a nearly half a foot shorter than me, stepped aside. Just on the other side of the apartment door, there was a short hallway with mirrored closets for walls. The thick carpeted floor urged me to remove my shoes.

"Let's go see the boys, then we'll do a tour." Aleyda gestured for me to follow her.

The apartment was shaped like the letter T. On the right end on the hall was the living room. The sizeable window consumed the entire eastern wall and faced Lake Michigan. An average looking man with dark curly hair was sitting on the couch with two infants. Even though he was sitting down, he looked almost as small as his wife.

"This is Mauricio, my wonderful husband." Aleyda smiled.

"Hello, Serena. I would shake your hand, but mine are kind of full." He laughed. His accent was equally as thick as Aleyda's.

"Nice to meet you. I love you all's accents."

"Thank you. It definitely makes us stand out."

"Amor, I'm going to give her a tour and we'll be back." Aleyda walked into the next room. "Here is the kitchen. Just enough space for appliances. The master bedroom is next door. Nothing special in there either. At the other end of the hall is the twins' room with a bathroom we use exclusively for them. Let's go take a look." She walked to the other end of the apartment into a simple white room with all the fixings for twin boys.

"Everything you need is here. Diapers, wipes, and creams are on the changing table. Clothes are in these drawers beneath the changing table and in the closet. They have plenty of toys and books as you can see. The twins are mostly content just relaxing on the floor, so you don't have to do much to entertain. Let's go join them." Aleyda sat on the couch next to her husband and took a baby from his arms. I settled on the floor next to them with my legs crossed.

"This is Ozzie," Mauricio said pointing to the little baby in blue on his lap. "This is Oli." He pointed to the little guy in red sitting on Aleyda. "Ozzie always wears blue or yellow. Oli wears red and green. Never forget their colors. As you can see, they are identical. We'd hate to mix them up."

"That makes sense. Have you all considered getting them bracelets/anklets? Maybe with their names engraved?"

"Actually, we hadn't, but maybe we should. What do you think, amor?" Mauricio looked at his wife.

"That's not a bad idea. We just need to find materials that won't irritate their skin."

"I have a bracelet that's made out of cloth. Something like that would be perfect for the boys. The store I got mine from probably doesn't have sizes that small, but maybe you can have something customized," I suggested.

"Good idea! Thanks," said Mauricio gratefully.

"No problem."

"So, Serena. Tell us about yourself." Aleyda gazed at her baby boy.

"Uh well, I'm 20. I've worked with dozens of kids, and I've been babysitting in my spare time since I was 12. I worked at a daycare center in a classroom with 15 toddlers, so I know I can handle working with multiples. There were eight kids of different ages at the home daycare. That really helped me become more organized. At this point, I would say I'm looking to find a long-term job as a nanny. I've struggled to find a good fit. Hopefully this is it." I gave them my winning smile.

"All of that sounds great. Sounds like we made the right decision in choosing you. But there's something I think we need to be honest about." Aleyda looked nervously at her husband. "Once Mauricio finishes his Masters, he might have to accept a position in another state. You may only be working with us until May unfortunately."

"Oh… well… that's okay," I replied a little let down. "I'll be happy for the experience of working with twins. Tell me about these little guys."

Aleyda's face instantly lit up. "Ozzie is three minutes older than Oliver. That's the only difference honestly. They both have the same appetites and schedules. They look exactly alike. They're easy-going. They don't cry unless they're really hungry. This is why it's so important to be able to tell them apart. They haven't developed their own personalities yet." The new mother looked worried.

"We'll get to know each other so well that we won't even need the bracelets. Just watch," I assured her. "By the way, I think they look exactly like you."

"See amor? I told you they look like me," she taunted her husband playfully.

"But they have little curls like you, Mauricio," I added for good measure.

"I'll take that. They really do look so much like Aleyda already though," he confessed.

"Serena, if you decide to accept the job, we would like you to start Monday at 8:00 am. Mauricio will be here with you to monitor your first week and answer any questions."

"Okay good to know. Thanks."

"How often would you want to receive payment? We like the idea of every Friday. That's how often I get paid," Aleyda informed.

"That works for me!"

"Do you bank with Chase? We can QuickPay you."

"That's perfect." I was glad things would be efficient.

"Great. Anything you want to ask us?"

"Actually yes. It's unrelated to the kids, but are you all originally from the US? I'm only asking because of the awesome accents."

"Oh, thank you!" Aleyda blushed. "Like I said, we are Bolivian. Both of our families are from Sacaba. Maybe one day we'll move back home, but we plan to stay in America for a while."

"Maybe you all could speak some Spanish around me so I can learn more of the language. I know a little bit."

"We speak to the kids exclusively in Spanish so that'll be very easy!" Aleyda beamed.

"Great. They'll hear Spanish from you and English from me."

"We're off to a good start then. Since we just wanted to meet you face to face today, I think we can let you go. Now that you know where our house is, it'll be easier when you start Monday... that is if you accept," Aleyda said innocently.

"I most definitely accept."

"Great!" Mauricio chimed in happily.

"I will see you all in a few days then." I stood to leave.

"I'll walk you to the door, Serena." Mauricio handed Ozzie to Aleyda and stood to his feet. I was right; he was short only a couple inches taller than Aleyda who looked to be about 5'1. I wondered how tall the twins would be.

"Thanks again, Aleyda."

"No problem. ¡Hasta luego!" she called from the couch.

"We look forward to starting this new adventure," Mauricio said as he watched me put my shoes on.

"Me too."

"Drive safely. Que tengas un buen día." He opened the door for me.

"You too," I said happily. Once outside the door, I felt grateful. I would be earning more money than ever before and working with a seemingly drama free family. Almost equally as important, I was glad I didn't find Mauricio attractive at all. He seemed to be in love with his wife. And most importantly, due to his small size, I thought I could fight him off if he tried anything inappropriate.

First-time parents

As I approached the Apaza's building for my first day of work, I felt slightly anxious. Considering the drama that I'd experienced so far, I wondered what was in store for me. Would Aleyda end up paranoid like Kirsten? Would Mauricio be an asshole like Cecelia's dad? What if I didn't like the twins? What if I ended the job on a bad note like the others?

The one thing I felt prepared for was the possibility of a physical altercation. Just in case I had underestimated Mauricio's abilities and things turned sour, I had my stun gun and a newly purchased pocket knife discreetly stored in my backpack. Dozens of negative thoughts rushed through my mind as I knocked on the apartment door and was greeted by a tearful Aleyda.

"Good morning Serena." She sobbed.

"Hey Aleyda, what's wrong?"

"I don't want to leave my babies." Tears flooded her face. She let me step inside.

"If it makes you feel any better, the kids are more than safe with me." I placed a gentle hand on her shoulder.

"I know I know. It's not you. It's me. I'm not ready. I wish I didn't have to go back."

"Hopefully when Mauricio finds a permanent job, you can stay home with the kids for a while." I comforted her.

"Yes. I hope so." She wiped her face and suppressed another sob.

"When my mom had me, she ended up leaving work for six months because she missed me so much. It's normal, but to make you feel better, I'll send you pictures throughout the day. That's one thing that has changed since I was little, lucky for you."

"You're right. Please do that. It would really help." She looked desperate. Her husband approached us, holding both infants.

"Have a good day. Buena suerte, esposa. I love you." Mauricio sniffed away his own tears. The family hugged and kissed. It was one of the most intimate scenes I had ever witnessed at work. I left the hallway to give them a moment and busied myself by straightening up the living room while they talked. I was putting some toys away when Aleyda called me back.

"Mauricio and I want you to download an app. It's a baby app with the boys' info. You can upload their meals, naptimes, and activities during the day. In addition to seeing the pictures, I can monitor what they do from work."

"No problem."

"Mauricio will give you the information. I'm going to go. I don't want to miss my train." She choked back a sob.

"Have a good day Aleyda. I'll send you a picture once I get them dressed," I reminded her.

"Okay. Don't forget!"

"See you later, mi amor." Her husband leaned in for a quick kiss. Aleyda finally left, leaving me alone with her family.

"Okay Serena, I think the boys need changing. Can I watch you do it? I just want to see you do a few things before I leave for a while," Mauricio said immediately perking up.

"Where should I change them?"

"Let's go to their room." He walked down the long hall into the bedroom and finally let me hold one of the infants. "This is Oli," he said nervously.

"Hey, Oli. I'm just going to change your diaper, okay? It doesn't smell like poop so I will make it quick," I told the infant. Everything on the changing table was right where I needed it as I laid him down. I took off the boy's pajamas then threw the diaper in the genie.

"Mauricio, he's a little red. I'm going to put some ointment on him. I'll mention it in the baby app."

"Aleyda will be happy to know you noticed that. I was going to tell you to use cream, but I didn't have to. I like that," he commented like changing diapers was rocket science.

"Of course. Where do you want me to sit Oli down?" I asked as I finished diapering the first baby.

"On the floor for tummy time is fine."

I gingerly laid Oli on his floor mat. Mauricio put Ozzie on the changing table and waited for me to take his place. I attempted to repeat the same process with Ozzie, but his diaper was completely soiled and some of the poop soaked through his pajamas. I unzipped his clothes and removed them. With one hand, I took off his diaper and dropped it in the diaper genie. With the other hand, I held his tiny legs in the air and wiped off as much poop from his back as I could with one wipe. Because Ozzie only drank breast milk, the poop was super viscous and green; it didn't have a strong smell and wiped off easily. Then I used another wipe just to be sure he was completely clean. I didn't want my new boss thinking I used too many wipes, but I also wanted him to see how thorough I was. My week with Namrata had me a bit self-conscious. Since Ozzie didn't have a rash, I decided to just put a clean diaper on but Mauricio intervened.

"We like to put cream on during every changing, rash or not."

"Alrighty." I thought it was a waste of cream but did it anyway.

"Okay, now that you're finished, put Ozzie on the floor next to his brother. I want to show you what we do with dirty clothes."

"Okay." I carried the naked boy over to his equally naked twin then picked up his clothes.

Mauricio walked across the hall to the twins' bathroom. There was a container in the sink filled with sudsy water. "Here we usually soak the dirty clothes so they don't stain.

Just wet it, spray it with this hypoallergenic stain remover and rub the stain before soaking it."

"Got it." I nodded and did as he said. "Like this?"

"Exactly," he affirmed

"I think I should pick out their clothes for today."

"Excellent." He followed me back to the bedroom.

"If I recall correctly, the clothes are in the closet and these drawers here." I pointed towards the drawers under the changing table.

"Good memory."

I kneeled on the floor and picked out a yellow t-shirt with a bumblebee on it. Black cotton shorts to match for Ozzie. I selected something with Christmas colors for Oli. I sat on the floor with the twins while Mauricio hovered over us. "Oh no! I put them down and didn't keep track of who was who!" I exclaimed.

"I was waiting for you to notice that." Mauricio laughed. "I actually marked Oli's foot with a marker before you got here. Just wanted you to see how easy it is to get confused."

"You scared me for a sec!" I laughed nervously.

"I knew that would happen. I wanted you to learn. Now you know."

I turned away from him and slid little Oliver to me, then put his clothes on quickly but gently. I knew Mauricio was watching, waiting on a mistake, but I didn't make one. I repeated the process with Ozzie. Aside from a little cooing, the twins didn't make much noise. They didn't seem uncomfortable with my touch.

Mauricio interrupted my thoughts. "They prefer laying on their backs and aren't as fond of tummy time, but if you could get them to do it that would be great. We would like for you to read to them during the day as well. They're pretty easy to deal with. I hope you feel the same way." Mauricio smiled insecurely, letting his nerves shine through for a split second.

"They seem like sweet boys." I tried to put him at ease.

"I'm glad you think so. Let's just play for a while then we'll try to feed them." He clapped his hands together.

"Sure. Let me just download the app and send Aleyda pics."

"Oh yeah. Glad you remembered. It's called 'Baby Drop'. It's free. Just type in my name or Aleyda's. It'll connect you to us then we'll allow you to see our page for the boys. We have to add you as a family member or caregiver in order for you to see it."

"I've never heard of this app before. It's innovative though," I said as I installed it.

"Let's see how well it works. We haven't had someone else use it with us yet."

"I'm signing in now."

"The process should be simple."

"Yep! I'm in. You have to accept my request." I couldn't wait to use the app.

"Let me grab my phone." Before Mauricio could have possibly made it to the living room to get it, my request was accepted.

"Did you accept it that fast?" I called down the hallway to him.

"What? No." He returned with his phone in his hand. Realization dawned on him. "Aleyda must have done it. She probably has her phone in her hand waiting on pictures." He looked down at his cell. "She's calling me now. Hola, mi amor. Cómo estás?... They are right here on the floor in their room. Serena is about to update the app for you... She just changed them. She was about to take a picture, but she wanted to update the app first."

I could tell he was speaking English out of consideration for me. I appreciated it. I uploaded information as he spoke. There wasn't much to input yet. It was hard to focus on the kids with so much instruction going on. I took a picture and sent it while Aleyda was still on the phone. Mauricio put her on speaker.

"Ohhh, Mauricio! Mira los bebés! Qué hermosos! Gracias, Serena. Les quiero," she whined.

"I know, mi amor. Serena is doing great so far. She remembered the app, and I almost forgot it." He winked at me. "I think the boys will be fine. This is hard for me too." He disabled the speakerphone. "Yes, they should eat. I'm going to show Serena what to do. No, I'm not going to stay on the phone to do it. Fine, I'll Face Time you when we feed them. Bye." He hung up. "Sorry about that. It's 9:00. In a half-hour, we're going to feed them. I'm going to leave you alone until then. Have fun." He smiled and left the room.

I turned on some music, and when "Hakuna Matata" came on, I sang to the twins and played with their skinny little legs and arms while they laid on their backs. It seemed like Oli smiled a little easier than Ozzie. Although Ozzie was a tiny baby, he appeared slightly heavier than his brother too. I stored this information for future reference. Once the playlist ended, I decided to lay next to the infants and read The Very Hungry Caterpillar. They stared off into space, wriggling around on the floor.

"Hey Serena, can you grab one of the twins and follow me to the kitchen? I'll carry the other," Mauricio requested as he entered the room.

"Sure. It doesn't even seem like it's been 30 minutes already." I realized I'd forgotten to ask the parents about outings. "Mauricio, how will I be able to take the kids on field trips? Where's the stroller?" I scooped Oli into my arms.

"Don't worry about that. We don't want you leaving the house with them just yet."

"Oh… okay." I tried to keep the disappointment out of my voice. I'd go stir crazy if I had to stay in the small apartment every day until May.

"Okay so now I'm going to show you how to warm the breastmilk." He looked down at the twins. "You know what? Let's put these little guys on their boppy pillows in the living room. I need both hands so I can call Aleyda."

We sat the kids down just before Mauricio got a text. "It's Aleyda. She's asking if we're about to feed them." He sighed and rolled his eyes. Instead of replying, he called her on FaceTime. "Yes, mi amor. We are in the kitchen now."

"The babies are not in the kitchen with you? I wanted to see them," she whined, ruining her lovely accent.

"No, mi amor. They are in the living room waiting to eat."

"Can I just see them quickly?"

"Fine." He walked to the living room and held his phone over the twins. "See? They are in their own little worlds. They will get cranky if we don't feed them soon. Back to the kitchen."

"Oh yes. Hurry." Aleyda said wanting to slow us down and speed us up at the same time.

"Okay, Serena. We have a lot of frozen breastmilk in the freezer, but sometimes you'll find some in the fridge too. For now, I'm going to just show you how to use the bottle warmer for refrigerated milk." Mauricio took 2 plastic packets of milk out of the fridge, walked over to the sink and retrieved two clean bottles from the dish rack. "All you have to do is fill a small cup with water, pour it inside the warmer, and put this lifting basket inside so it can hold the bottle. Press B if the milk is room temp. Press E if the milk is chilled. In this case, we'd press E. This warmer is made to heat a few ounces at a time," Mauricio instructed.

"E for chilled milk. Got it."

"Have you used this warmer before?" he asked.

"Actually no. At the home daycare, I used this electric tea kettle type thing. It warmed the water in like three minutes. We just sat the bottles in a bowl of warm water. It was much faster than a regular kettle."

"Well, this is what we have. Will this work for you?" Aleyda asked anxiously over the phone.

"Of course! Seems simple enough."

"Great, because we haven't actually used it yet. I've been with the boys every day up until this point, so they haven't had to use a bottle. I want to see how they do." She made it clear that she wanted to witness it, not hear about it.

"She's very nervous about this transition. To be honest, I am too," Mauricio said needing assurance.

"I've never had a problem with feeding a child, but from my understanding, if someone is hungry enough, they will eat."

"We want you to feed them every two hours. At least two ounces each feeding." Aleyda stated from what appeared to be her work desk.

"Okay. No problem."

"Great! Now let's see you warm the bottles," she encouraged.

"Okay." I filled the warmer with water and poured the milk from the packets into the bottles. The basket was already in the warmer so I just sat the bottle inside and pressed E.

"Excellent," Mauricio cheered.

"Good." Aleyda sounded like she had been expecting mayhem. She checked her watch. "Dios Mio! I have to go! Can you please record the feedings?"

"Por supuesto, mi amor," Mauricio replied in a tired voice. He hung up the phone as I heard one of the babies starting to fuss. The bottle was done warming, so I took it out and prepared the second one. I tested the milk's temperature on my hand. It was perfect. I propped Ozzie up on my arm and put the bottle's nipple to his lips. He hungrily accepted it as Mauricio recorded him.

"Success!" Mauricio shouted gratefully. I couldn't tell if he was excited that his son had a good appetite or that Aleyda wouldn't have to harass him about it. As Ozzie gobbled down his milk, the warmer alerted me that the second bottle was ready. Mauricio quickly grabbed it. He tried to feed his other son on his own without recording. Oli opened his mouth then turned his face away from the plastic nipple. As I watched the new dad struggle with the feeding, Ozzie finished his bottle.

"Mauricio, can I try to feed Oli while you burp Ozzie?"

"Let me try one more time," he remarked as stress lines formed across his face.

I burped Ozzie quicker than expected and laid him back on his pillow. Mauricio, defeated because Oli had started to cry, set the bottle down. He put Oli in my arms, and I tried to feed him the same way his dad had. Mauricio recorded the interaction. I received the same results. Oli turned his head away from me and wailed. I kept at it for five minutes before I decided he did not want the plastic nipple.

"He wants the boob, Mauricio. He's probably not hungry enough to take the bottle right now. Maybe we can put them down for naps and when they wake up, we can feed them both. Oli should be even hungrier in the next couple of hours. I can tell they're already sleepy. He won't suffer if he waits a little while."

"He won't be too hungry?" the dad asked me anxiously.

"That's the point. We want him to be good and hungry so he'll eat this time."

"Let me try one more time." Another five minutes went by that yielded the same outcome. "Okay let's let them rest and see how it goes later." Mauricio checked his watch. "Actually, I have somewhere to be in one hour so I may not get to see this. But you'll keep me posted, won't you? And I'll send these videos to Aleyda."

"Of course. Should I just let them sleep in their Boppy pillows?"

"Yes. It looks like Ozzie doesn't need any help. Let's see what Oli does."

Oli was more restless than his brother, so Mauricio put him in the vibrating swing instead. In two minutes, Oli was knocked out too. "I'm going to head out early since the boys are asleep. I'll just shower and be on my way." Fifteen minutes later, Mauricio was out of the door, and I was alone for the first time with the two sleeping babies. I updated the app before Aleyda could call me with questions. For the next two hours. I read books and straightened up in the nursery room while they slept. I wasn't sure if Aleyda had a meeting that kept her away for all that time, but she started excessively texting all of a sudden.

-Oh my gosh, Mauricio sent me the videos!

-I'm so proud of Ozzie!

-But I'm worried about Oli!

-What should we do?

-Was the milk warm enough?

-Should I come home?

-Are you feeding them again now?

I'm going to feed them both when they wake up. It will be fine. I'll send pictures.

Right after I sent the text, the babies started stirring in their sleep. I immediately removed the frozen bottles from the freezer and ran one of them under hot water in the sink while I waited for the other to finish warming. One of the boys started to fuss. I wished the milk would heat faster. It'd be just my luck that Mauricio walked in while the kids were screaming. As if they could sense my anxiety, both boys started howling. Since Oli was the picky eater, I gave him the bottle that had been in the warmer. I hoped Ozzie would be okay with room temperature milk since he wasn't so particular.

I took the bottles to the living room and sat in between the boys' pillows then tilted the milk towards their mouths. Ozzie stopped crying and gulped greedily. Oli's cries were quieted a bit as he fought the nipple. He took one aggravated suck and continued to cry. He knew it wasn't his mom, but he had to get used to it. I decided to focus on feeding Ozzie first. It would be great if they were old enough to hold their bottles on their own. Even though he was only six weeks old, Ozzie finished his bottle in record time as his brother wailed with hunger. I burped Ozzie and sat him under his play gym with the swinging toys. Then I picked up Oli as gently as I could.

"Oli baby. Please eat your food. You have mommy worrying about you. This milk is nice and hot, straight from mom." I talked to him in as soothing a voice as I could muster. He continued to scream his head off. I rocked him back and forth and started singing to him. The song came out to the same tune as "Frere Jacques." "Little Oliver, little Oliver. Eat your food. Eat your food. It's time to eat. It's time to eat. You will love it. You will love it." Oli calmed down but was not interested in the bottle. He started to close his eyes again.

"Will you drink it while you're half-sleep? Come on baby. At least drink one ounce for me," I whispered desperately.

He suckled a little bit. Success! He managed to drink half an ounce before he stopped responding to the bottle completely. He had exhausted himself. I had just put the bottle down when Mauricio opened the front door. He rushed in with a look of concern. His curly hair stuck to his face with sweat. I wondered if he ran all the way back.

"How's it going? Did he eat?"

"He managed to get down half an ounce." I took a picture of the babies and tried to update the app.

"That's all? I guess that's better than nothing," he said disappointed.

"Yeah, it's something." Before I could send the picture, Aleyda texted me.

"Is that my wife?" Mauricio asked.

"Yep." I giggled.

"She was calling while I was out. Let me just give her a call to update her." He took a seat on the couch and looked down at his boys.

I looked into other ways to feed infants. One alternative that stood out was using a syringe by squirting a little bit of milk onto the tongue. The other option was using a spoon to scoop the milk in. I kept the ideas to myself. I thought the best option was to make sure Oli was hungry enough to use his bottle first.

Mauricio's conversation with his wife cut into my thoughts. "Serena just updated the app, amor. Yes, he just took half an ounce. Ozzie drank a full bottle…This is the first day. We have to see how he adjusts. You fed him a lot before you left. He'll eat more when you get here… Yes, I'm worried too, but it doesn't help if we're both freaking out… Yes, you are freaking out. He's just tired now. We will try again in two hours. I'm sure it will be better by the end of the week. We just have to get through this rough patch." He paused. There were tears in his eyes. "Don't cry, amor. I'm sure he isn't the first baby to reject his bottle. By the end of the week, it will be better."

Stubbornness

Unfortunately, Mauricio underestimated just how strong-willed his tiny son was. By the end of the week, Oli had made sure to only consume a total of two ounces in the eight hours I was with him. He filled up on fresh breastmilk the 16 hours I was gone. Aleyda was more than happy to provide it. As a first-time mom, she liked feeling needed. It was great that Oli ate so much with her, but I was getting worried that he would not even try to get full during the day. I knew he would eat more if Mauricio wasn't hovering over me, begging me to feed him every two hours and if Aleyda wasn't expecting pictures and videos every 30 minutes.

Instead of testing it out, I shared my alternative suggestions until I could be alone with the boys. "I saw a video of a mother spoon-feeding milk to her infant daughter. I also saw a video with an infant being fed with a syringe. The parent was squirting just a little bit of milk on the tongue so the infant could taste it. Maybe we could try something like that with Oli. What do you think, Aleyda?" I asked cautiously.

"Oh my gosh yes! Why didn't you tell me this sooner? Mauricio go find a baby spoon for Oli. He needs it today! Serena let me go get you the syringe that came with the children's medicine. Just use that until we get a new one." She wandered away with a hopeful determination in her step.

"Bossy little thing, isn't she?" Mauricio asked with a smirk.

"Really? I hadn't noticed." I laughed because even the description of high strung wouldn't quite grasp the intensity that was Aleyda.

"I'm worried too, but she stresses me at times. She's a great mom though," Mauricio added. "She means well."

"She does," I whispered as Aleyda returned with a small syringe in her hand.

"Let me know how it goes. Feed Ozzie first. Don't put too much milk on Oli's tongue. I don't want him to choke," Aleyda warned.

"Thank you. I won't," I said as positively as I could, but the truth was I was already exhausted with so many instructions.

"Serena, I'm going to head out with Aleyda to grab the stuff for Oli. Good luck today. Send pictures!" Mauricio threw on a pair of shoes.

"Yes, please do send LOTS of pictures. See you all." Aleyda kissed the twins looking as sad that day as she did days before.

"I'll feed them around 10:00."

"Great. Bye." Aleyda gave a final wave. I quickly closed the door behind them. I could breathe with them gone. I couldn't do that with Aleyda in the room. She made sure that everybody worried just as much as she did. I had to be patient because she actually meant well and didn't seem to be a bad person like Kirsten or Namrata.

I played with the boys without feeling stressed or being supervised. I turned on some Disney tunes and sang my favorite song, *Part of Your World*, while they stared up at me. I loved that they couldn't judge my horrible singing voice yet. I picked up Oli for a dance then did the same with Ozzie. Next, I read to them. Before I knew it, it was 9:00. Like clockwork, I got a text from Aleyda asking if I had changed their clothes and for pictures. I rolled my eyes in response. I hadn't been able to leave the house with the kids yet so I wasn't sure why it mattered what they wore or how early I dressed them. Regardless, Aleyda was their mother. I tried to understand that she struggled to conceive so she was even more nervous than any other first-time parent would be. I carried Ozzie to their bedroom then did the same with Oli. For some reason, I wasn't quite ready to carry them both at once. I picked out a plain olive green t-shirt and blue jean shorts for Oli and a plain navy blue shirt and blue jean shorts for Ozzie. I quickly changed them and took a picture for their mom.

As soon as the picture was taken, I heard a bubbling sound come from Ozzie. He had pooped up his back again. He'd done that every day that week. I was getting used to dealing with it. I snapped the picture then rushed to remove his shorts before they got soiled. His little blue t-shirt was a lost cause. I removed it then wiped off his back. When it was clean, I laid him back on the carpet while I scurried across the hall to put his tiny tee in the sudsy water in the bathroom. I found a striped yellow shirt to switch out with his dirty blue one then changed his diaper. In all this time, the little guys didn't make a sound. Aside from the messy pooping and poor eating habits, they were easy babies. I couldn't wait to see their personalities develop. Before doing anything else, I updated the app with everything we had done so far. I decided to practice holding both infants at once. While I adjusted to what it felt like to hold two babies the exact same age at the exact same time, I got a text alert.

-*Where is the picture*?

I realized I never sent the picture I took because of Ozzie's accident. I quickly sent it without text hoping to quash Aleyda's incessant questioning.

-*I just checked the app. Did Ozzie poop up his back again?*

Do you want me to include when Ozzie soils his clothes?

-*Please.*

Okay

-*So, did he?*

As always.

-What songs did you sing?

Part of Your World. I don't remember the rest.

-That's nice! What are you all doing now?

They're waiting for me to stop texting so we can play.

-Oh! Don't forget to send pictures!

-

It was 10:00 on the dot when I took the first bottle out of the warmer. My phone chimed with another text.

-Are you going to feed the boys?

I wanted to tell her I hadn't planned on feeding them at all that day, but I put my irritation aside. I didn't reply at all. She was distracting me from my task. I'd send her another picture when I was feeding them if I could manage it. I put Oli's bottle in the warmer and fed Ozzie first. He greedily guzzled down his meal as usual. His appetite was so good that I wondered if he'd need baby food earlier than six months. Ten minutes later, he surprisingly had finished four whole ounces. I breathed a big sigh of frustration as I considered waiting longer to feed Oli. I knew he'd do better with the bottle if we fed him every four hours instead of two, but I tried the syringe for the time being. Maybe once the Apaza's were more comfortable with me they'd give me more room to experiment.

I grabbed the syringe and lukewarm bottle then cradled Oli in my left arm. First, I tried to put the nipple to his lips to see what he did. He took the nipple in his mouth for one suckle then started to fuss. I was at it for about two minutes before I moved on to the syringe. I twisted the top off the bottle and filled the syringe. Between Oli's cries, I squirted his tongue with a little milk. He stopped crying and opened his dark brown eyes as he registered the tasty liquid. He smacked his lips appearing to want more. I squirted his tongue, and he swallowed it faster than before. I kept squirting little by little. In 15 minutes, the milk was gone. Four ounces down the hatch! Success! I burped him and laid him next to Ozzie.

"You did it, Oli! You did it! And you both ate more than I expected you to!" I cheered. The boys looked at me with clueless smiles. I updated the app and sent Aleyda a picture of the empty bottles, then stepped into the kitchen to wash them. Once cleaned, I found multiple messages from the nervous mother.

-Yes! Did he eat it all?

-Did you burp him?

-How did he like the syringe?

-Did he cry?

-Did you get a video?

He ate it all. He seemed to like it. I can't take a video if I'm holding him and feeding him.

-How's he doing now?

He's great. We are going to read and then go down for a nap.

-Send pics of them sleeping.

-

"Girl, she was out of control asking for so many damn pictures all day. She clearly wasn't ready to leave those kids yet. Sucked for her and you," Maakara told Serena as she polished off her Pepsi.

"Yeah, the first week really showed me how anxious she was. I don't think it was intentional though, which is why I was so patient. I really wanted to do my job well and be compassionate, but it was hard as hell sometimes!" Serena admitted.

"Please tell me it got better though," Maakara said rifling through her book bag for more snacks.

"When you say 'better', what exactly do you mean?"

-

I decided to read a book on potty training before I set the little guys up for a nap. I loved how their big dark eyes followed the sound of my voice. I knew their vision wasn't quite clear yet, but they still managed to look at me with happiness. The little swings that the twins took naps in were heaven-sent. They were different than any swings I had seen so far. They weren't the old school tall white swings that went back and forth. These short swings swung side to side like hammocks and vibrated at different levels. When using them, I didn't have to help the twins fall asleep at all. Before the boys could even start fussing, they were fastened in with the vibration on the lowest setting. I was taking pictures of them when Mauricio ran in the door.

"Hey! How's it going?"

"Shhh!" I shushed with my finger to my lips and ushered him away from the living room. He snuck a peek at the boys as we walked away.

"So how did their feeding go? I have the new syringe and a few spoons! So how was the feeding?" Mauricio repeated.

"Aleyda didn't tell you already?" I asked suspicious.

"Uh well... yeah. She did." He grinned embarrassed and looked away. I could tell he wanted to talk about his babies almost as much as Aleyda.

"I figured." I laughed. "It went smoothly. We played. We read some books. I sang to them."

"And mealtime?" He rushed me to answer what he was most curious about.

"I fed Ozzie first. He gulped down his whole bottle as usual. I tried to give Oli the bottle. He wouldn't take it, but the feeding with the syringe went extremely well! I kept refilling it until the milk was gone. I didn't want to completely fill his mouth; I just covered his tongue with milk. It seemed to surprise him at first, but once he got the taste of it, he was ready for more. He drank four ounces. I burped him, read to him again, and put him down for a nap. Both of their eyes had just closed when you walked in."

"WOW, so I guess the syringe is the best thing for Oli for now."

"I see nothing wrong with it. But I will still try to get him to take the bottle," I said getting ahead of him."

"Of course. Should we try the spoon?" Mauricio asked.

"Totally up to you if you want to use it. Just let me know." I shrugged.

"So, everything really went smoothly so far huh?"

"Always the note of surprise with you." I smirked.

"Oh sorry. I just feel like I've been holding my breath since Aleyda went back to work. It feels good to know my babies are safe."

"I understand," I said gently.

"But you've made this transition so easy for us. I appreciate it. Thank you for being patient with Aleyda... and me."

"No problem. You guys are nice people. I've struggled to find that in this line of work," I confessed.

"I guess I'll sneak a peek at the boys then head back out for an hour or so. I'll let you take it from here." He lightly touched my shoulder then left the room. I knew I couldn't stay with them long term, but I wished I could until the twins were ready for pre-school. It felt good that Mauricio was trusting me more already. That was one obstacle overcome. Aleyda was next.

-

The next few hours passed by peacefully. There were no more poop accidents and no more issues with feedings. Aleyda came home at 4:00 as if she hadn't seen her children in weeks. Her frenzied presence clashed with the calm atmosphere.

"Hey, how did it go today?!" she practically screeched jarring the boys out of their sleep.

"Fine. They were just dozing off," I said struggling to keep a frown from creeping across my face.

"They're awake? Great." She settled on the floor between her kids' swings gazing at them with a crazed look on her face or maybe it was just love. I couldn't tell. "Tell me everything that happened that wasn't on the app."

She took Oli out of his swing and cradled him in her right arm. She lifted her shirt preparing to breastfeed, then looked up at Mauricio standing in the doorway. "Hola, amor! How'd it go today?"

"Serena did a good job keeping the boys happy. Next week I'm going to stay out of the house more. I think she can handle this." He winked at me.

"Yes, but how did the other feedings go?" She looked at us desperately.

"We just played and read books all day. We did tummy time, sang songs. And the feedings went smoothly too. The syringe was a good idea."

"Oli didn't fight it at all?" she asked obviously disappointed.

"No, he didn't. Isn't that a good thing?"

"Oh yes of course!" she said quickly hiding her face. "But did you still offer him the bottle too?" She asked almost desperate to find a problem.

"I did. Every time."

"We still have to try to get him to adjust to the bottle. He probably shouldn't use a syringe forever."

"Yes. I know, which is why I offered him the bottle multiple times today," I said closing my eyes to keep from rolling them.

"Serena did everything we wanted her to do. She knows what she's doing," Mauricio assured.

"Thanks, Mauricio."

"I guess you can go, Serena. We won't keep you. I'll ask Mauricio to fill me in on anything you left out," she said dismissively, so she could hurry back to her family without being reminded that they could be okay without her.

"See you guys," I said getting to my feet. "I'll see you Monday."

"Thanks, Serena! I'll Quick pay you in a second." Mauricio took a seat next to Aleyda. I let myself out and took a deep breath in the hallway. It would be better next week. It just had to be.

Monotony

Monday morning was off to an easy start. Aleyda was her same neurotic self. Ozzie had already had his daily poop-up-the back accident, and the boys were in their assigned outfits. I had just sent Aleyda a picture of them and was updating the app when Mauricio popped his head in to say bye. It was my first day alone with the boys for most of my shift. I wished I could take them out on a walk while it was still warm. I needed to talk to Aleyda about having outings. It would be hard staying in every day for the rest of the summer.

"Hey, Serena? I almost forgot." Mauricio poked his head around the corner. "Please try to send Aleyda pictures of the twins as soon as possible. She really worries. I know it's hard on you sometimes, but she needs it. I just want to make this easier on all of us."

"Should I send you pictures too?" I asked knowing Aleyda was not the only one who worried.

"If you want to, sure. No pressure. But I think this will go smoothly if you send her pictures all day."

"I've sent her pictures every day since I've started, every few hours."

"You don't understand." He laughed wryly. "If you want to stop Aleyda from being so anxious, you're going to have to send her a picture every hour at least. I wish I was done with school so we wouldn't be in this situation. Anyway, I just think texting her before she can text you is the way around her stressing you out. Does that make sense?"

"It does. I will try to remember that. Thanks." I paused before adding, "I know Aleyda wants me to keep suggesting the bottle with Oli. That's no problem. But I really do think the only way he'll take it is if I wait longer than two hours. I just wanted to mention that again."

"You want to try to see if he'll take the bottle when he waits twice as long?"

"Only if it's okay with you," I said hopefully.

"Okay. Let's see what happens. We'll keep this between us. Just tell Aleyda whatever you told her last week. No sense in worrying her. If it goes well, eventually we'll tell her the truth. But tell me first. Cool?"

"Cool," I said feeling relieved.

"See you later. Good luck today." He rushed out of the door.

The morning continued with no problems from the kids. I tried to send Aleyda pictures every hour in order to avoid her constant texting. At 10:00, I texted her a picture of the plastic refrigerated bottles before she could ask if I was going to feed them. Her response annoyed the hell out of me.

-Are you about to feed them now?

I guess she realized how stupid her question was.

-Let me know how it goes!

We had already agreed that I would update the app and send pictures after feedings. I didn't understand why she thought I needed constant reminders. I shook off my irritation and turned to the bottle warmer to get Ozzie's bottle. I was so thankful that the babies were easy-going. I wasn't sure how long I could work there if they were as needy as their mom. I was glad I was waiting longer to feed Oli. When he started to get fussy, I'd introduce the bottle. I was determined to not only have him drinking from his bottle by six months but holding it too.

Just as I was heading back from the kitchen, Ozzie started fussing. The little guy was very serious about his feedings. I didn't blame him. I got cranky when my blood sugar was low, too. Propped up on their Boppy pillows, the boys looked so sweet. Even though Ozzie had his mouth open in a small cry, he was still a handsome little guy. They reminded me of baby Tarzan from the Disney movie. They had big dark eyes, thin lips, button noses, and dark hair.

The feeding went just as smoothly as all the others had. It didn't seem to matter what the temperature of the milk was, Ozzie gulped it down. I liked the kid's energy. I uploaded the app with Ozzie's feeding. Without feeding him, I decided to upload two ounces of milk by syringe for Oli. I knew it wasn't entirely truthful, but I'd tell Mauricio how our little experiment played out.

The great thing was Oli didn't appear to be hungry yet, so I put the boys in their bouncers and read a few books to them. I almost forgot to send a picture before Aleyda texted me. I was sure she was hungrily reviewing the app wondering what we were doing. I sent a pic before the infants started to doze off. I thought I might take a quick nap while they dozed off too. I was on the floor next to them when my phone chirped.

-Oli ate with the syringe?

Yes. Did I forget to add that to the app?

-No, I just wanted to be sure.

-What are they doing now?

I sent you a pic. Did it not come through?

-Yes, I got it.

I read the message then curl up on the floor next to the dozing boys and drifted off until I heard low cries from Oli. His timing was perfect. I scrambled up from the floor and grabbed the bottles out of the fridge to warm one at a time. While they heated, I grabbed a couple of diapers and wipes to change them.

"Hey, little one. Ohhh it's okay baby! I have your milk coming right up. Let me change your diaper first okay?" Oli screamed in response. I laid him on the floor and changed his wet diaper. Luckily, he only peed. I tossed the old diaper in the kitchen trash. The first bottle was ready, so I put the second one in. While Oli screamed, I changed Ozzie. It was my lucky day. There was poop, but it didn't go up his back. After a quick change, both bottles were ready. For the first time, I picked up Oli first since he was actually hungry. I gave him the warmest bottle and watched to see if he accepted it. In mid wail, Oli stopped and suckled the nipple.

He had a dissatisfied look on his face, but his hunger almost got the best of him; he continued to drink for all of 30 whole seconds. He was ravenous but stubborn. I took off the top then syringe fed him. It took what felt like forever, but Oli drank four whole ounces. Once he finished, I burped him then focused on his brother. By that time, the milk wasn't as warm but Ozzie didn't care. I was so proud of them that I didn't even get frustrated when I heard my phone chirp. I took a pic and sent it before Aleyda could ask for one.

After rinsing the bottles in the sink, I played some music and put the boys under their activity gyms. There were so many different toys hanging from them. The lights and music kept them entertained for half an hour. As I watched their eyes light up, I picked up my phone for another check-in with Aleyda.

-How did Oli do this time? Did you try the bottle?

Of course. Was I not detailed enough in the app?

-Yes. I just had the boys on my mind. Can I get another picture?

I took a deep breath and sent a picture of the babies playing. The monotony of my days was going to drive me crazy. I was already bored and it had been less than two weeks. I planned to talk to Mauricio about taking short field trips. I thought going outside would help the days go by faster.

At 3:55 Mauricio came home.

"Hey! How did it go today?" He made a beeline for the twins.

"It was great! Guess what!" I said excitedly.

"What is it?"

"Oli actually drank a little from his bottle! It wasn't much but it was slightly more than before. He drank four ounces by syringe. Maybe next week he'll drink a full ounce from the nipple.

"De verdad?! Dios Mio! What happened?"

"I waited four full hours before feeding him. He was ready to eat but his stubbornness wouldn't let him drink the whole bottle, so he only drank a little. Luckily he let me try with the syringe again, and the rest is history."

"Eso! That's my big guy! I'm so glad to hear it! Did you tell Aleyda?" He was suddenly serious.

"No, but she does know that I tried to give him the bottle every time."

"Good. Let's just keep that up this week. We'll see how that goes, and then we'll tell her what we did. I'll take all the blame for it. Or maybe we won't tell her at all," Mauricio considered.

"Got it. Just so you know I've been making sure what I say in the app matches up with how much milk is left over so there's no confusion on her end."

"You're right! I didn't think of that. Do what you have to do. I trust you." He winked.

"Cool. Aside from that, all we did was sing songs, read books, and played with the toys, nothing different."

"No issues?"

"Nope. The boys are some of the best kids I've ever worked with," I said earnestly.

"I love to hear that." Mauricio blushed.

"I do have something else to add though," I said hesitantly.

"What is that?"

"Is there any way you and Aleyda could consider us taking daily field trips? Our days will be pretty much exactly the same otherwise. I think it's important for them to get some fresh air while it's warm outside too."

"I'm not sure Aleyda is ready for that. She has to get adjusted to having a nanny and being away from the kids. You know we had such a hard time conceiving. We just want to be cautious," Mauricio said carefully.

"Absolutely. And I do understand that. What do you think though? Would you be okay with us leaving the house just for a quick walk?" I pressed knowing if I never mentioned it, we'd be indoors until May.

"I'll get back to you about that. Okay?"

"Of course. One last question. Can I use the stroller and walk around the building at least? It's such a large place. If you leave keys, we can walk around for maybe 20 minutes and come back. We could do that a few times a day without ever going outside," I mentioned hopefully.

"That sounds more than fair to me. I'll talk to Aleyda."

"Excellent! Please tell her how great things went today. Maybe that will make her comfortable enough to allow us to leave the apartment."

"Will do."

"Thanks. I'm going to head out."

"Okay. We'll see you tomorrow. Thanks for everything." Mauricio hugged me.

-

As I rode the elevator up to their apartment the next morning, I was hopeful that the Apaza's would let us leave the building in the next few weeks.

"Buenos Días," I greeted Mauricio.

"Buenos Días, Serena."

"How are you?"

"I'm alright. How are you?" he asked as we walked into the living room where Aleyda was breastfeeding both boys.

"Good thanks."

"Good morning Serena," Aleyda said with an unusual grin on her face.

"Morning."

"We thought about your field trip proposal. We're not comfortable with our boys leaving the house without us yet. So, we just want you to stay in for now and we'll let you know when the time is right."

"Okay," I said emotionless.

"But," Mauricio cut in, "it's okay if you want to walk around the building with them. We'll leave a key so you can get back inside," he added and gave Aleyda a meaningful look.

"Yes, that'll be fine," she said less enthusiastically than a minute before. Clearly, she had hoped that he would keep that bit of information to himself.

"Great! I think it would be good for the three of us to move around, not be so cramped you know? Add a little variety to the twins' day."

"I guess so," Aleyda replied in a jealous tone.

"I think it's a good idea. Let us know how it goes. The stroller is set up in the hallway whenever you need it. The keys on are the table," Mauricio said supportively.

"Of course. But please don't go outdoors," Aleyda interjected. I suspected she didn't want me doing more with her kids than she could.

"Yes, I've already said I wouldn't so I won't. I'm just glad to expose them to something beyond these walls."

"Aleyda let's head out," Mauricio suggested impatiently.

"Please don't forget to send pictures!" Aleyda mentioned as she laid the babies on the floor. I responded by taking a seat next to them.

"Let's go, mi amor." Mauricio ushered his wife towards the door.

-

I decided to keep the morning routine mostly the same: change clothes and Ozzie's poopy diaper, send Aleyda a picture. After doing my duties, I checked out the stroller. It was unique; I had never seen one that held two infant car seats at once. They were detachable so you could load them into the car easily. I put the twins inside, grabbed the keys, and backed out of the front door with the stroller following me. We took the elevator to the first floor and walked the perimeter of the entire building. We greeted the doormen and the employees at the front desk. The twins caught the attention of a few of their neighbors. I took note of the location of the indoor gym. Right around the corner was the natatorium. It was very spacious with a bunch of chairs and tables surrounding the pool. The ceiling and three of the walls were made of glass. I imagined that it looked magical in there when it rained or snowed. There was a small Jacuzzi on the far wall. The coolest part about the whole natatorium was the small restaurant called Maravillas. I had no idea it was there. I pushed the stroller over and took a look at the menu. They had a good variety of foods: chicken quesadillas, fries, Philly cheesesteaks, burgers, pasta, salads, etc. My mouth had started watering by the time a middle-aged Mexican man walked over to us.

"Can I help you?"

"Oh no, I was just looking, but what do you recommend?" I asked with interest.

"Everything is good here, but I do recommend the quesadillas and fries. We also have new breakfast options that aren't on the menu yet."

"Oooh, that sounds so tempting!"

"What's stopping you from buying?" the man asked curiously.

"We were just looking around the building, exploring. I didn't even know this was here. I didn't bring my wallet, but I'll be back another day for sure."

"I'll tell you what. How about I give you an order of our new hash browns today? If you like them, then you come back another time with your wallet," the man offered.

"Bet! I love hash browns," I said as my stomach growled. "I work in the building so you'll see me around."

"You don't live here?"

"No, I'm a nanny to these two little guys here." He leaned over the counter to catch a glimpse of the twins.

"Ohhh, that's cool. Sit tight. Your browns will be out in a sec."

"Thanks so much!" I walked the boys over to a nearby table and checked on them. Their eyes were wide open. I expected them to have dozed off. It was already 9:45. We needed to head upstairs for their feeding soon. I sent a pic of them while we waited. Five minutes later, I had my piping hot hash browns and the kids in tow. If the elevator was running fast enough, I would have been able to feed Ozzie right on time.

Once inside the apartment, I left the kids in the stroller in order to get the first bottle heated, then I took them out of their seats and laid them on the floor with soft toys and checked their diapers. Only Ozzie needed to be changed. The feeding went the same as usual with Oli showing no desire to eat.

Once done, I checked my phone.

-You went for a walk? How did they like it?

-Are you going to feed them?

-How's it going?

The boys were quiet the whole time. I thought they were sleeping when we were walking around.

I updated the app instead of responding to the last two questions. The twins started to fall asleep without me helping them. Their schedules had been so predictable. I put them in their swings then dug in to my nearly forgotten hash browns. The cook from the restaurant mixed in peppers and onions. I took a bite and instantly fell in love. It wasn't often I ate hash browns cooked that way. I didn't realize how much I had missed them. I made a mental note to keep my wallet on me on our future walks. I would definitely be a repeat customer.

-

November eased Fall into the Chicago area four months later. The little guys were almost six months old. They were holding their heads up on their own, and their personalities were becoming more apparent. They smiled at the sound of my voice and rolled all over the carpeted floors. Their hair was longer and curlier, which complimented their round faces. The skinny little legs they had when I started had vanished. In their place were chunky thighs with rolls. Oli finally adjusted to the bottle and regular feedings after a month of maneuvering. Mauricio never told Aleyda our little secret. In contrast to Oli, Aleyda's behavior had not changed much, so I still sent her pictures as often as possible. Luckily, I had much more interesting footage to send since the boys were more active.

The twins weren't the only ones who had gained about 10 pounds. After eating lunch at Maravillas almost every day, I could see it reflected in my midsection. The restaurant served the best French fries I had ever tasted. I couldn't stop eating them. No matter the meal combo, I had to get fries on the side. I wasn't sure what kind of drugs they put in them, but I was addicted. Eating there gave me something to look forward to outside of the apartment every day.

Aleyda still was not comfortable with us leaving the building. She started using the weather as an excuse for us to stay in. She claimed she was fearful the kids would catch colds. Fortunately, as predictable as our days were, I did my best to spice them up. Sometimes I dressed in the twins' signature colors so we would match in the selfies we took. Multiple times a day, we walked around the building taking pictures by the pool or by the couches in the lobby. Unlike their parents, I could get them to smile in pictures. If I called their names in an annoyingly high voice, they would grin in my direction. The staff around the building had gotten used to stumbling upon our playful antics in the hallways.

-

A couple of weeks before the twins' half birthday, Mauricio informed me that our schedule would be temporarily changing to accommodate someone new: his mother. "Ozzie and Oli are her only grandchildren. She's super excited to be visiting all the way from Sacaba. I can't wait for her to meet you and the boys. She'll be here by the time you arrive Friday, and she's staying for three weeks. I haven't seen her myself for a few years," he said giddily.

"That sounds like fun. We need some excitement."

"Por supuesto! Mi mama es wonderful! The nicest 62-year- old you'll ever meet. She's such a good mother. She did a great job of raising my brothers and me," Mauricio spoke more passionately than I'd ever heard him.

"I can't wait to meet her!"

"You're going to love her." Mauricio smiled big enough to show every tooth in his mouth.

-

"So, I take that to mean that you 100% did not end up loving her?" Maakara surmised.

"I'll just say that Lupita was an interesting character to say the least," Serena laughed.

The Grandmother

Friday morning brought with it a few immediate changes. The house seemed louder and busier than usual when Aleyda let me in. "His mother is here. I'm leaving," she muttered in a strained voice. Without words, I took off my boots and went to the living room.

"Ah! Serena! This is my beautiful mother, Lupita. Mom, this is Serena, our amazing nanny." I turned to face a petite Bolivian lady with shoulder-length curly hair like Mauricio's.

"Hey there. Nice to meet you," I greeted as she used a cane to stand to her feet with Oli in one of her arms. She was less than 5'0 ft. tall.

"Igualmente," she replied with a slight smile.

"My mother speaks great English. She works at the embassy. She prefers Spanish though, so she would be great to practice with." Mauricio turned toward his mom. "Mama, Serena is practicing her Spanish so talk slowly or speak English." Lupita nodded at him then resumed her seat on the couch.

"Serena, I will be busy today so I won't be here to help you all get acquainted. Can you just walk my mom through your regular schedule? She's excited to see how the boys' day goes."

"I'd be happy to." I smiled at Lupita, but she didn't return it.

"Okay great." Mauricio turned to his mother. "Adios mama. Nos vemos." He kissed her on the cheek.

"Hasta luego, hijo." She leaned over and picked up Ozzie.

"See you later, Serena. Have a good day," Mauricio mumbled as he kissed his sons.

"Have a good one," I told him as he walked away. "Lupita, how was your flight? What time did you get in?"

"I landed at midnight. Got here at 2:00 am. The flight went smoothly," the grandmother said in a clipped way.

"Oh wow! You must be tired! I'll try to keep the boys out of your way until you get some rest."

"That won't be necessary. I'll sleep when you leave." Lupita turned her nose up at me.

"Okay, well I'll take one of them with me to change his clothes then we'll switch." I ignored her cold shoulder.

"Show me where the clothes are. I'll do it myself."

"No, I'll do it. It's my job." I frowned. "You're more than welcome to watch first then assist after you're more familiar with our schedule." I kept my tone soft.

"Just let me care for them while my son is gone," Lupita insisted.

"It would be inappropriate to take advice from anybody other than my employers. Sorry."

"I guess you're right about that. But I know what I'm doing. I want to spend time with my grandchildren. I don't need you here. I'm not sure I trust my son's judgment anyway," Lupita said reminding me of Namrata.

"Do you have a problem with me?" I asked.

"Honestly, it's not personal. I want to spend time with my family without a stranger lingering around," she answered disdainfully.

"I can understand that, but you need to understand that I don't work for you. We don't have to bump heads about the kids. You can play with them, but I will be keeping them on their schedule in the meantime," I informed her politely. I took Ozzie from Lupita's arms as she mumbled something in Spanish. "I'm sorry. What was that?" I asked not intending to come off as confrontational but also wanting her to know that I wasn't there to play games.

"I said I didn't come from my country just to have someone supervising my time with my grandchildren. I already have to share my son. Now mis nietos tambien!"

"What do mean by share your son?" I asked confused.

"She wasn't the best choice for my son. You probably aren't the best choice for my son's kids either. My son can do so much better."

"What? Who isn't the best choice for your son?" I asked wondering if the lady had lost it.

"Aleyda," she spat like the name was poison.

"Oh…" I paused awkwardly. "Well if it helps, I think Mauricio is very smart and nice. He's an excellent dad, too. He and Aleyda seem good with each other from what I can tell. And they made an excellent choice in choosing me as their nanny if I do say so myself. You don't have to like me, but I need you to respect me the same way I do you."

Lupita peered at me shrewdly. I carried Ozzie to the other room without waiting for a response. I was hoping this visit would be fun. I didn't need another person to complicate my day. I needed to talk to Mauricio ASAP before things got messy. I laid Ozzie on the changing table then sent Mauricio a text. Almost instantly, my phone pinged. No way he had time to read what I typed that fast. To my surprise, it was Jabari. I hadn't heard from him since my last time babysitting for them in July. My heart skipped a few beats when I read the second sentence of his text.

-Hey there. I was just thinking about you. Hope all is well.

His message froze me in place. I forgot about my work issues momentarily. Jabari thought about me? Did he mean professionally?

Ozzie's cooing snapped me back to reality. As soon as I got his pajamas unzipped, he scrunched up his face and started letting it rip. Quick as a flash, I sat him up and removed the pajamas before they got dirty. I dared his poop to defy gravity that time. Lo and behold, a small amount of green poop bubbled to the top of his diaper. I held him up on the table until he finished then I completed his changing. As I fastened his clean diaper, my phone pinged again. It had to be Mauricio.

-*What happened?*

I could hear his desperation through text.

I need to talk to you when you get back home.

-*Is everything okay?*

Everyone is safe if that's what you mean.

In seconds, my phone rang.

"Hello?"

"What's going on?" Mauricio asked in a hurried tone.

"What is my role now with your mother visiting?" I cut to the chase.

"What do you mean?"

"Now that your mother is here, does my role as a nanny change in any way?"

"Why would it change?" Mauricio asked confused.

I walked back to the living room before continuing the conversation. "Your mother wants me to let her take over, so she can have personal time with her grandsons. I want to know what I should do." I put the phone on speaker before Mauricio answered.

"I still need you there as the boys' nanny. My mother is here to visit, not take on a full-time job."

"Cool. I just wanted to confirm." I did my best to sound diplomatic.

"What did she say to you?" Mauricio asked curiously.

"Do you want to ask her yourself?"

"Sure."

I handed my phone to Lupita, who had a mixture of anger and another emotion on her face. She took it off speaker and continued the conversation in Spanish. I wasn't able to understand everything, but I could hear her tone soften. She told Mauricio that there was no problem and that she was excited to spend time with her grandkids. While she talked, I laid Ozzie on the floor and took Oli from her to change his diaper. I sensed that she wanted to protest but wanting to seem agreeable with her son, she kept quiet.

I brought Oli back half-naked before she finished her conversation. I laid him next to his brother and changed his clothes before I could get the babies confused. Lupita finished the call apparently incensed. I immediately walked over, handed Ozzie to her and sat his clothes on the couch.

"You can change him. He always wears yellow or blue. Oli wears red or green. Christmas colors."

"Okay." She set to work dressing him, and an awkward silence fell over us. I picked up my phone from the arm of the couch intending to respond to Jabari's text, but a text from Aleyda distracted me.

-How are things going? Are you going to send a picture?

Instead of answering the question, I took a picture of Oli and sent it. Before I could get a picture of Ozzie, another text came through.

Where is Ozzie? Is he there too?

I rolled my eyes before I realized Lupita was watching me. I wanted to ask Aleyda where the hell else Ozzie would be. Sometimes her questions made me want to strangle her.

"Necesito tomar una foto," I informed Lupita holding up my phone.

The grandmother sat Ozzie up on her lap and straightened his clothes. I hurriedly snapped a picture and sent it without checking the quality. I was not in the mood to have both Aleyda and Lupita getting on my nerves. My phone pinged again.

-*How are things going with the boys and Lupita? Are you going to update the app?*

Of course. Things are fine.

-*Lupita is behaving okay?*

I found that question interesting enough to respond to.

Lupita is okay. But since you asked, should my role change at all now that she's here?

-*No, just let her help you a little.*

Good to know.

-*Why do you ask?*

I didn't want there to be any confusion. You know how new grandparents can be.

-*You don't even know the half of it.*

I'm going to give her some time alone with them. Let them bond. I'll sit in their room.

-*Okay. Good idea.*

My thoughts drifted back to Jabari. I wondered how life had been treating him. Before I could figure out how to reply, Lupita interrupted me. "What do you think about Aleyda?"

"Are you asking me?" I looked around confused.

"Yes."

"She's a great mom. Very attentive. Good communicator. Why?" I was sure to leave out any negative opinion.

"Was she the reason you rolled your eyes just now?" Lupita asked knowingly.

"I rolled my eyes?" I played dumb.

"Yes, when you got what I assume was a text."

"She did text me, but I don't remember rolling my eyes," I lied.

"It's okay, you don't have to say it." Lupita chuckled. "Mauricio already told me the excessive amount of communication she needs to be able to leave the boys home. I know she stresses him out. I just wanted to see if this extended to you as well."

"Oh okay." I did my best not to express an opinion.

"How do you think my son is doing as a dad so far?"

"Like I said, I think he's doing an excellent job. The twins have great parents. They love them a lot."

"Is my son a better parent than his wife?"

"That's a weird question," I said plainly.

"Sorry, I was just trying to gauge this situation." She paused for a second. "I have to be honest with you. I'm very protective of my son."

"I've gathered that."

"But I'm also not fond of Aleyda," Lupita continued. "So, I apologize if I say things about her that make you feel uncomfortable. I understand this is business for you."

"Thanks."

"She's just too controlling, too high maintenance, and too old for my son." Lupita openly showed her distaste.

"Is her being older than him that big of a problem though?" I asked.

"Well if she wasn't older, my son could have waited until he was done with his degree and then got married and had kids. But since Aleyda's clock was ticking, they sped up the process. Then they had to spend so much extra money on IVF. I guess it's a good thing that Aleyda's parents could help them financially." I remained quiet wondering if she was jealous of the kind of support Aleyda's family provided.

"Don't get me wrong. I help when I can!" she continued defensively. "But I have other children and things to take care of. Aleyda's parents don't have real responsibilities," she said with all the disapproval she could muster.

"I see," I said simply.

"She controls every aspect of their relationship: where they live, where they eat, when they have kids," Lupita insisted desperate for an ally.

"How does Mauricio feel about that?" I asked calmly.

"He complains to me about her! He doesn't seem to mind her taking the lead in everything, but the way she parents bothers him. He says she is very anxious. Her nervousness about anything that concerns the twins upsets him," Lupita huffed exasperatedly.

"Aleyda might be a little nervous, but I can somewhat understand why. She had two infants in her late 30's after struggling to conceive. She invested a lot of money in those babies before they even got here," I defended. "She doesn't have family here that she can trust with her kids, so she had to hire a stranger and hope for the best. We can't relate to her struggle. I'm not saying she shouldn't relax a bit, and eventually she probably will, but I understand at least why she is so stressed."

"I guess, but that doesn't account for her controlling nature before the kids," Lupita said clinging to her opinion.

"I can't comment because I didn't know her then. The good thing is, the issues you mentioned can be worked through. You have to let Mauricio handle his own problems though… if he sees them as problems."

"You don't have kids. You don't understand." Lupita waved me off.

"You're right. But that doesn't mean what I'm saying doesn't make sense…I have to feed the kids in a little while. If you want, I can leave you in here to play with them until then," I offered.

"I would love that," Lupita said sincerely.

"Okay, I'll be back." I took my phone and hurried off to the boy's room. As I walked down the short hallway, I could already feel myself blushing. I sat crisscross in the rocking chair and pulled up Jabari's messages.

-Hey there. I was just thinking about you. Hope all is well.

For five full minutes, I debated over an appropriate response. I didn't want to seem like I was flirting. I figured the best thing to do was to be as friendly as I was with any other client. After a few more moments, I finally landed on a response. My thumbs shook as I typed it.

Hey, I'm good. How have you guys been? How's Ethan?

A wave of nerves rushed over me even though I hadn't said anything significant. I felt like I was crossing an imaginary professional boundary. It didn't matter what I said to Jabari; it would always feel inappropriate and exhilarating at the same time. I didn't have time to overthink it because his reply was instant.

-He's great. He's grown a lot since I last saw you.

I'm sure he has.

-So how's work?

Good. The kids are great. The parents are cool. Mom is kind of hard to deal with though.

-How so?

She's a nervous first-time mom that's all, but she means well. How's work for you?

-Same old, same old.

And Emily?

-She's the same, too.

I hope that's a good thing.

-I suppose so.

-I enjoyed talking to you that day. I hope we can do that again some time.

Sure. Just let me know when you need a sitter.

-I guess I should keep this professional then.

What else would it be?

-Maybe we can go out and spend some time together outside of babysitting.

How would your wife feel about that?

-She doesn't have to know, does she?

-

"Girl! What did he mean his wife didn't have to know?!" Maakara screeched forcing Ms. Jones to give a stern look in the nearly empty library.

"I know right? I was shocked, too." Serena kept her voice low.

"But you weren't going for that were you?" Maakara asked cautiously.

-

At Jabari's question, the Cheshire like grin faded from my face and grew into a look of shock. I was flattered, offended, and fully disappointed. It was good to know that I didn't imagine the chemistry between us, but did he honestly think we could have an affair? What kind of girl did he think I was? What kind of guy was he? As many times as I had fantasized about us being together, I never thought the opportunity would present itself. That's what made Jabari attractive: being a smart sexy unattainable family man. On my end, not only was it unprofessional but unethical. I wasn't sure what to say to him, but I wanted to keep talking to him at the same time. How bad could his marriage be that he wanted to step outside of it for attention?

Those thoughts washed over me for a few moments until I remembered where I was. I shook them off and decided to distract myself with the twins. I walked back in the living room to find both of them sitting on Lupita's lap.

"Voy a tomar una foto. Okay?" I asked. Lupita nodded her head, and I snapped a picture of the three of them and showed it to her.

"Maravillosa! Gracias!" she exclaimed.

"De nada."

It was not quite 10:00 yet, but I decided to get the bottles warmed anyway. At 9:55, I handed Lupita a bottle for Ozzie. "I'll feed Oli," I said taking the infant away from her. I wanted her to feed Ozzie so she could witness how fast he pooped during mealtimes, since she was so interested in caring for them alone. I laughed out loud just thinking about it.

"What is funny?" she asked.

"Nothing." I smirked. The twins finished their six ounces in record time. As predicted, Ozzie started pooping up his back as Lupita burped him.

"Oh!" she shrieked.

"What is it?" I asked innocently.

"I think he's having a popo." She held the baby away from her body.

"Yeah, that happens when he eats. You should change him quickly. Or do you want me to?"

"I'll just watch you do it," she said clearly nauseated.

"Okay. You want to hold Oli while I do it?"

"Sure." She sounded eager to get the poopy baby out of her arms. We made the switch, and I rushed Ozzie to the changing table. His pants were fine, but his shirt was wet. Lupita hobbled over and watched me remove the shorts and top while I avoided getting poop in her grandson's hair. Once he was in a clean diaper, I picked him up and walked directly across the hall to drop his clothes in the sudsy water.

"Take him," I instructed then used both my hands to wash the clothes. Lupita observed me intently. I hoped at some point she would see that I was a valuable part of the family, but the look on her face was more displeased than anything.

After the boys were fed and changed, there was not much to do except play with them. I mindlessly engaged with them and Lupita, but Jabari kept crossing my mind. I wasn't sure if I should text him back or block his number. As soon as I picked up my phone to send a picture of the kids, I received another text.

-I guess I crossed a line. I didn't mean to offend you. I'm sorry.

I was paralyzed with conflicting emotions. I liked that he apologized, but it didn't make me feel better. After pausing for a few minutes, my curiosity got the best of me.

Can I ask you something?

-Anything

Why do you want to risk your marriage to see me?

-That's a good question. I have a lot to say. Can I call you?

I'm at work right now. And I have a grandmother hovering.

-I'll call you when you get off. What time?

4:00

-I look forward to talking to you.

Despite myself, I blushed.

-

   The rest of the day drug by as I thought about the looming conversation. I hated to admit it, but I was equally as excited as I was anxious. I looked forward to hearing the voice that made me weak. The tone that turned my cheeks red. Before I knew it, daydreaming got the best of me. I wondered if Lupita noticed. It didn't matter. I had more important things to worry about.

   At 4:02, I was on the elevator anticipating Jabari's phone call. I looked down at my cell which had no signal. I stepped off the elevator at 4:03 feeling anxious. What if he had called in the 60 seconds it took to get off the elevator? My anxiety clung to me as I walked the two blocks to my car. By the time I arrived home, it was 4:15. Still no phone calls or texts. To ebb my anxiety, I updated my friends on the latest.

Hey y'all! Okay so GUESS WHAT. The dad I have a crush on texted me earlier saying he wanted to hang out with me!

-He WHAT?

-OMG, are you going to go out with him?!

I'm not going anywhere with him. But I am going to talk to him on the phone. He's supposed to call me right now.

-What are y'all gonna talk about?

I asked him if his wife would be okay with us hanging out. You know he didn't want her to know about it.

-Oooh, shady.

-Def suspect

Right! Very. Then I asked him why he was willing to risk his marriage. He said he has a lot to say about that so that's what he's calling for.

-Did he give you a time?

No, I told him I get off at 4:00. It's 4:22. I'm scared he won't call!

-He's going to call. He wants you to like him.

-Girl, you know how fine you are? He's gonna call. He's probably shocked he even got this far.

I hope he does.

Oh shit, he's calling! I'll let y'all know how it goes.

-TTYL

-Keep us posted!

"Hello?" I answered on the third ring.

"Hey, Serena," Jabari greeted in a voice that heated up my insides.

"Hey, what's up?" I immediately regretted how childish that sounded.

"Nothing much. I had to work this morning. I came home to rest, and now I'm sitting outside my gym."

"Do you want to call me later?" I asked partly wanting a reason to get off the phone.

"Oh no! I've been wanting to talk to you all day. The gym can wait." I knew if I spoke, he'd hear the smile in my voice so I remained quiet. "It's nice hearing your voice again," Jabari continued.

"Is that so?" I asked not meaning to sound flirty.

"Yes. I like hearing you talk. You're pretty wise for your age," he complimented.

"I'm inclined to agree." I vowed at that moment not to let his age intimidate me.

"Oh really?" He chuckled. "I like the confidence."

"So, why did you want to talk on the phone?"

"Straight shooter. I like that… you asked me why I'm interested in you. I want to explain."

"Okay…"

"But first can I say that I did sincerely enjoy talking to you that day? I appreciated your perspective." The sincerity in his voice made his words all the more effective.

"I enjoyed the conversation too," I admitted weakly.

"But I also think you're beautiful. I felt like there was chemistry there. Was I mistaken?"

"…No, you weren't," I answered reluctantly, biting my lip until it hurt.

"You find me attractive too then?" Jabari pressed.

"Very much so." I strained to keep the longing out of my voice.

"I'm glad to hear it," he said audibly relieved.

"Yeah, well don't expect me to give you any more than that," I replied stubbornly.

"I wouldn't dream of it," Jabari said in a mock serious tone. "I guess now you want to know the status of my marriage?" He seemed to enjoy dragging it out.

"Yes. I do," I replied firmly.

"Well, it's a typical story. After Ethan was born, Emily seemed to lose interest in me. If I'm being completely honest, she never seemed that interested in Ethan either.

I've done my best to get her attention. I think she got pregnant because I wanted a child. I realize now she never wanted one. She had one to make me happy. Don't get me wrong, she tries. But this isn't what she wants... I'm not what she wants." He sounded pained to admit it.

"I'm sorry to hear that... How is she different now versus before she had Ethan?"

"Emily had more confidence in her physical appearance when we dated. Now she obsesses over the way she looks. She's insecure. It's weird to me because she looks exactly the same in my eyes, except for the boob job. Not sure if you noticed that."

"Yeah, I did wonder about that," I confessed

"She got those about three months before we met you. She was uncomfortable with the way her breasts looked postpartum. I thought she looked great, but she begged me to support her getting the surgery. It only helped her esteem a little bit. She pumped as much milk as she could before she got the procedure. She wasn't willing to risk ruining her investment so she didn't continue breastfeeding."

"I can understand that. It sucks she felt that way though. What did you do to make her feel better?"

"I mostly just tell her how beautiful she is. She doesn't believe me. I come behind her when she's changing her clothes and kiss her neck. She seems repulsed by it. We've only had sex a handful of times since Ethan was born, and she didn't enjoy it," Jabari disclosed.

"Oh wow!" I said genuinely surprised. "Have you tried to make big romantic gestures? Like a weekend getaway? Surprise her with flowers?"

"I've done it all."

"It sounds like y'all need counseling. Have you tried that?"

"No."

"Try it ASAP!" I ordered.

"I guess I could. She probably wouldn't be interested," Jabari said reluctantly.

"Listen, if you want your marriage to work, you have to try everything in your power to make it work." I sounded as if I had been married before.

"And if I do that and it doesn't work out, then will you go out with me?" he asked attempting to be cute.

"Let's just focus on your marriage for now *friend*. We don't need to see each other."

"Friend huh? We'll see about that."

The implication gave me chills.

-

"Whew! Well, you said he was dangerous. You weren't lying," Maakara interjected. "Did you actually believe him though? You know how married men don't do anything but lie." She peered at Serena carefully.

"I thought maybe he sprinkled in a little truth. I wasn't convinced he was completely honest though," Serena said.

"Good for you. I wouldn't want you getting hurt by some predatory ass dude."

-

Monday morning, I walked through the front door of the Apaza's apartment with a smile on my face, my conversations with Jabari still fresh on my mind. Before I could take my shoes off, the smirk was wiped off my face. There was tension in the air.

"Serena, can we talk to you for a second before Aleyda leaves?" Mauricio's voice called from another room.

"What's up?" I asked joining the family.

"Serena, my mother told us that you weren't paying attention to the twins at one point on Friday. Did you leave them in the living room while you were on your phone in their bedroom?"

"W-what? Of course not," I stuttered visibly taken aback. "I'm always attentive to the twins."

"My mother said otherwise."

"Forgive me, but your mother was not telling the truth," I said politely. I looked at Lupita and saw her feign a look of innocence. "I did leave the room, but I left in order to give your mother some time to spend with the boys. I know she doesn't want me around."

"Amor, Serena did text me that morning telling me she was going to do that," Aleyda cut in.

"Mama, is that true?" Mauricio turned to Lupita.

"It could be. But she didn't say that to me. All I know is that I was suddenly caring for my grandkids for such a long time when there was hired help in the home," Lupita boldly lied.

"Lupita, I was trying to give you all time alone. You complained about me intruding. We had a whole conversation about it. And it was only for 30 minutes," I asserted.

"Hmm, I guess it did slip my mind. Mijo, your mom is old. Forgive me." She turned to Mauricio and cupped his hands in hers.

"It's okay mama. Serena, I didn't mean to bombard you like that. I'm sorry." Mauricio reached out and touched my shoulder gently.

"It's fine." I couldn't even be mad at him. He was so nice in comparison to Kirsten and Raymond.

"Aleyda and I are going to head out. You two play nice," Mauricio warned.

"Wait," Aleyda interjected. "I think it's time Serena took the boys on a field trip outside the building. It's getting a little cramped in here don't you think?"

"I'd love to take them out!" I yelled excitedly.

"Great. We'll discuss the details later. But for now, go take a walk around the neighborhood when you need it. The keys are on the table." Aleyda snuck a wink at me.

"Thanks!" I beamed.

Freedom! Finally! I knew with her bad leg and cane Lupita would want to stay home. Aleyda had really shocked me. Her dislike of her mother-in-law must have been stronger than her anxiety about letting the twins go outside. Whatever it was, I was thankful for it.

-

"After four months, you got to take the kids out into the fresh air? I know you were ecstatic," Maakara intercepted.

"I needed it, girl. I never knew how important it was until I HAD to stay in," Serena said reliving the moment.

-

As I settled down next to the twins, I decided not to let Lupita bother me. I would ignore her as much as I could. My thoughts about Jabari kept my mood light. I still couldn't believe a man like him liked me. I knew I was pretty and smart, but he made me feel like a silly little girl again. I thought guys my own age were immature. I liked that Jabari was already settled in his career. He was interested in the same things as me. He was a great dad. All of his qualities made me wish he was single. He was perfect. Or at least he would be if he wasn't married. After our conversations over the weekend, my attraction to him reached new heights.

"Alright Serena, focus." I tapped my forehead hoping it would knock some sense back into me.

"What did you say?" Lupita asked me.

"Huh? What?" I didn't realize that I had spoken aloud.

"You said something."

"Oh, it was nothing." I checked the boys' diapers. "The twins don't need to be changed. We're going to go for a walk."

"Already?"

"Yep! We've been cooped up in this house together for months. We need some fresh air. It's too stuffy in here. Would you like to join us?" I asked knowing she wouldn't.

"Um, no I'll just see you later," she muttered.

"Okay." I jumped up to browse the twins' adorable coats and jackets we had never used before. I selected the adorable baby pea coats and put their arms in them. Before we left, I remembered to update the app and sent a pic of the twins in the stroller.

-

Walking down the streets of Hyde Park felt so refreshing. I had done this many times before, but being able to do it with the twins was freeing. Even though Lupita still had a couple of weeks to go before she left, Aleyda had assisted me in a small victory in the meantime. Luckily for me, it was a particularly warm November morning, so we were all able to enjoy the weather. With a smile on my face, I pushed the stroller with no destination in mind. My text alert stopped me in my tracks.

-*Good morning gorgeous.*

It was Jabari. Blood immediately rushed to my cheeks. I wanted to ignore him for a few minutes, but I responded in a millisecond.

Morning.

The chat ellipsis immediately popped up.

-How are you today?

Great. What about you?

-Same. Glad to be talking to you.

Don't do that.

-Don't do what?

Don't flirt with me. I don't want to be the girl who flirts with a married guy. And I don't want you to be the married guy who flirts with other women. I like talking to you. No flirting. FRIENDS. Got it? I felt oddly empowered by my words. They grounded me back in reality and reminded me to continue my walk with the twins.

-Loud and clear.

-So, we're friends?

Yes

-Perfect. I can deal with that.

Good

-You know friends hang out together right?

Jabari!

-Fine. How's your day going so far, friend?

Someone tried to ruin my morning, but they failed. I'm finally out on a walk with the twins so I'd say it's a pretty good day so far.

-Wow! Do you want to talk about it? Can I call you?

Sure.

I should have said no, but I didn't because the thought of hearing his voice made me feel tingly. His call came through in seconds. "What happened?" He asked without preamble.

"The grandmother tried to get me in trouble."

"Why would she try to do that? And if you're at work with her right now, how are you telling me this?" He sounded concerned.

"She's here from another country and doesn't like that I'm here. She wants to spend time with her grandkids uninterrupted. I can understand that, but she takes it out on me instead of being mad at her son. The mother gave me permission to leave the building, so I'm out with the kids right now without the grandmother. Lucky me."

"With the way she's acting, I'm surprised she didn't go with you," Jabari said as I heard people talking in his background.

"Well, she walks a cane so..."

"You're evil!" He laughed.

"What did I do? She does have a cane!"

"You're enjoying it though," he said in a fake stern voice.

"No honestly, I'm glad she can't join us, but I'm not happy about the cane. I'm happy because this is our first time leaving the house and nobody is bothering us! It's been exhausting the last few months."

"Wait, what do you mean?"

"I've never been out of the house with the boys before today. The parents are very protective so, I'm glad the grandmother can't come."

"Wow! What do you guys do all day?" Jabari asked stunned.

"Exactly. I've been with them like four months. It's the most repetitive boring thing I've ever done. But I do love the babies."

"Now I understand. So how exactly did the evil grandmother try to get you in trouble?"

"She told the parents that I neglected the kids. What happened was I left them with her in the living room. I went into their bedroom so she could have the time she wanted with them. This was for about 30 minutes," I informed.

"Interesting. I assume the parents didn't go for it?"

"Lucky for me, I had texted the mom saying what I was doing so she shut that down. The mom and grandma don't like each other."

"Wow, you have some real family drama on your end huh? Glad it's not just my household." Jabari laughed. "I'm happy it worked out in your favor too, though. You are good at your job," he complimented.

"Thanks. That's nice to hear sometimes."

"You could hear even more if you'd let me take you out," Jabari flirted.

"Watch it, sir."

"Fine. But I still would like to hang out with you… as friends." His tone made me reconsider.

"No thanks," I said flatly.

"So, I'll never get to see you again?"

"Only in a professional way," I reminded.

"Hmmm, do you work out? You look like you do."

"Why?" I asked suspiciously.

"I was thinking you'd be comfortable enough to be my gym buddy. We can just jog on the treadmill together. That's innocent enough right?"

"Why do you want to see me so badly?" I asked as if his persistence was annoying when in reality it made me want him even more.

"Because I like you, Serena."

The simplicity of his statement made me want to ditch the kids and meet him wherever he wanted. "You still there?" he asked after a moment passed.

"I'm here."

"Soooo is that a no?" he followed up out of breath.

"Why do you sound like that?" I asked.

"I'm on the treadmill."

"Do you want to get off the phone?"

"No, I want to talk to you. And I want to see you even if it's just at the gym," he pressed.

"I don't hang out with married men. Sorry, I think I should go. Bye." I mustered enough strength to hang up before I could change my mind. I tried to gain control of my hormones. The image of him in his work out gear was almost too much to bear. I walked a little faster to burn off some steam. I snapped another picture of the twins in the stroller, then my text alert chimed. I ignored it because I knew it wasn't Aleyda.

We continued our walk for 10 more minutes before turning back home. It was only 8:50 when we returned, and the twins had dozed off. I wasn't ready to go back to Lupita, so I decided to walk around the building to kill time. I checked my phone and was surprised that Aleyda was not drowning me in questions about our walk. As soon as I closed out of the baby app, my text alert chimed, and Jabari's name popped up.

-I didn't mean to make you uncomfortable. I apologize.

-It's going to be hard for me to keep our relationship platonic. Forgive me if I overstep. I'm human. I just want to have some good conversation and take you out to eat… if you'll have me.

The problem was, I did want to have him: at my house, at his house, in my car, in his car, at the gym, and anywhere else I could have him. I wanted this married man in every sense of the word. Less than a year ago, I was completely repulsed at Raymond coming on to me. I was offended at the idea of entertaining a married man, and there I was doing just that. My former client no less! I was better than that. I felt compelled to block his number, but I couldn't bring myself to. Instead, I deleted it, our call history, and the message thread. I had no way to reach out to him.

-

"Good for you girl!" Maakara cheered.

"I hated doing it so abruptly, but it had to be done."

-

"How did it go?" Lupita asked when I walked through the door. It looked as if she had been waiting for us.

"Fine," I responded tersely. Lupita wasn't the first person to lie on me at work. I wanted to limit what I said to her to keep it from happening again.

After leaving the babies in the stroller to warm up their bottles, I returned to the living room and laid them on the floor for a diaper change. "Where did you all go? Did the boys cry?" Lupita wondered.

"We walked up and down 51st and 53rd streets from Lake Shore Drive to Drexel. No, they didn't cry. They rarely ever do. Any other questions or can I grab their bottles and feed them now?" I asked with irritation in my voice.

"I-I-I was just asking because I didn't get to go," she replied visibly stung.

"To be honest, I'm scared to talk to you Lupita. I don't want you to lie about me again." I turned to grab the baby bottles, but not before catching the stunned look on her face. I handed a bottle to her then placed Oli on her lap. I was sitting on the floor with Ozzie before the grandmother spoke again.

"You know what?" Lupita's resolve melted. "That wasn't fair for me to do that to you. I do wish I could be alone with my grandsons, but you're just trying to do your job. If I have an issue with that, I should talk to my son. I am sorry."

"I accept your apology," I said plainly.

"Serena?"

"Yeah?" I replied still reluctant to engage.

"I'll talk with my son and be honest about what I did."

"That's not necessary."

"I'll call him now." She sat Oli on the floor and picked up her phone from under a throw pillow then dialed Mauricio and put him on speaker.

"Si mami?" he answered distractedly.

"Hola mijo." She continued in English, "I was calling to let you know that I wasn't completely honest with you about Serena. She did tell me she was giving me time with the boys. I've just been upset about her being here, but now I understand she's only doing what you've asked her to. I'm going to play nice from here on out." She looked at me to make sure I was listening.

"That's great mami. She's a nice girl. We'll talk later okay?" He hung up before Lupita could say more.

"Does that help?" she asked me taking Oli in her arms.

"It's a start."

-

"Wow, I'm glad that ended better than it did with Namrata. I couldn't deal with another liar," Maakara commented relieved.

"Yeah, it was hard working alone. I had nobody to back me up when someone lied."

"Shoot, sometimes you had coworkers, and they still chose not to speak up. A damn shame."

"Exactly. But luckily I didn't have to deal with that again after working with the Apaza's."

-

The atmosphere the next morning was drastically different from the day before. Everyone seemed to be in a better mood, especially Lupita. "Buenos días Serena." She gripped both of my hands as I walked through the door. "I have a surprise for you. It's small, and it's just an idea; tell me what you think."

"She's very excited about this." Aleyda scoffed rolling her eyes.

"Amor…" Mauricio warned Aleyda in a patronizing tone.

"What is the idea?" I cut in and looking from one adult to the other.

"Well, Mauricio told me that you usually work eight hours a day by yourself. I just thought that since I'll be here for three weeks, I could help give you a lunch break. Whenever you decide to take lunch, I'll stay up here with the twins. This way I get time with them, and you get time to yourself. What do you think?" The old lady trembled with excitement.

"I think it's a great idea. Thanks." Her enthusiasm was catching.

-

The next couple of weeks went by smoothly. Lupita and I didn't have any more petty encounters. She and I found our rhythm. I took the boys on walks without her, but she watched both of them while I took my lunch break. It was nice having a real break during the day. I hadn't thought that I needed one, but I was going to miss it when she was gone.

-

The twins were finally six months old. It felt like I had been working with their family for so much longer than that. Staying in the house for 40 hours a week and dealing with nervous first-time parents for four months straight had taken its toll. But things were finally taking a positive turn.

I dressed the twins in their corresponding six-month-old t-shirts and took a bunch of pictures. Even though Aleyda had reduced her texting throughout the day, I didn't press my luck. I still tried to text her every hour. In a way, I guess I should have been thankful to Lupita for the new changes. Aleyda had only relaxed around me knowing that it would annoy Lupita. I hoped she wouldn't revert back once her mother-in-law left.

As I laughed at the boys rolling around on the floor, grabbing their feet and cooing, my phone chimed. Without looking, I clicked the message assuming it was work-related. My heart skipped a beat when Jabari's number flashed on the screen.

-Still thinking of you. Hope all is well. And I am sincerely sorry about making you feel uncomfortable.

I had ignored all of his texts up until that point. I knew I should have blocked him; but if I was completely honest with myself, I liked his persistence. Maybe I wasn't just a fling for him. Maybe he wasn't a creep. The situation was hard for me because I wasn't sure if I should trust him. I planned to keep ignoring him, but what if he was the one? I wouldn't find out as long as he was married.

"Can you send me the pictures?" Lupita interrupted my thoughts from the doorway.

"Huh? Oh sure. Of course." I shook away my thoughts.

"Did I walk in on something?" she asked, reminding me how much I liked her accent.

"I was just thinking. A lot going on. Sorry about that."

"What were you thinking about?" She entered the room.

"I'd rather not share," I responded feeling guilty.

"Are you sure? I'm old. I might have some good advice for you."

"It's just that I worry I've met the person I'm supposed to be with. But we can't be together... at least not right now. I'm not sure it'll ever happen honestly," I blurted unsure where the desperation came from. It reminded me of the way Tessa opened up to me.

"You're so young; you have so much time to figure that out. You may not even be the same people in five years that you all are now. But why do you think the time isn't right?"

"I'd rather not say." I averted my eyes.

"Well, when the time is right, if it's meant to be, it will be. Don't waste time on unworthy men in the meantime."

"I won't. Thanks Lupita." I half smiled.

"You're welcome."

"Look at you being all sweet to me. Tried to get me fired two weeks ago though." I playfully rolled my eyes at her.

"Ay Dios mio! Let me live!" She laughed at herself.

"Does this mean things will get better between you and Aleyda too?" I asked hopefully.

"Look, I might have been wrong about you, but nothing can change how I feel about her," she stated stubbornly.

"Well excuse me. Let me mind my business."

"I like your sense of humor, chica." She smirked.

Lupita was opinionated and outspoken but also kind-hearted. She definitely was not the sweetheart Mauricio thought she was, but I liked her. I liked Aleyda too. She was hardworking and did not play about her kids in the same way that Lupita didn't play about Mauricio. They had more in common than they realized. Maybe one day the animosity would fade or at least diminish.

-

On Lupita's last day, I decided not to go out with the boys. I wanted to give her as much time with Ozzie and Oli as I could, but I encouraged her to bring the twins down to Maravillas during my lunch break so she could see the pool for the first time. To my surprise, (although I didn't understand why Chicago's unpredictable weather still shocked me) there were snow flurries melting on the glass ceiling. I looked over at Lupita whose face was awestruck.

"Why are you looking like that?" I asked her, scarfing down my fries.

"I have never seen snow before." She resembled a kid in a candy store.

"Are you serious?"

"It's so beautiful." She gaped at the sky not answering the question.

"Come on. Let's step outside for a second." I got up from the table.

"Won't it be cold?" she asked hesitantly.

"It's up to you if you want to go grab a coat. I'll put snowsuits on the twins too if you want."

"You know what? My sweater should be enough. Keep the twins inside. I'll step out alone." Lupita clearly didn't want anything slowing her down.

"Okay let's do it." I grinned, excitement growing inside my chest. Before that day, it would have been hard to imagine a woman in her 60's so excited about encountering snow for the first time. The innocence of it all was touching. We hiked to the lobby, and Lupita walked out of the revolving door without looking back. She drifted down the driveway to the sidewalk. I couldn't help pulling out my phone to record her. I zoomed in as much as I could to capture her catching snowflakes on her palms. I just knew that if enough snow had accumulated on the ground, she would have dived into it and made a snow angel, cane and all. Instead, she wore a look of pure bliss. If I could make the kids that I worked with feel even a fraction of that happiness, then I had done my part.

Bittersweet Goodbye

Hours later, Mauricio came through the door signaling the end of my shift. Lupita started smiling like a kid with a secret. She limped into Mauricio and Aleyda's room without her cane and came back with a gift bag swinging in her hand.

"Para ti, Serena." She handed it over.

"Para mi? Gracias." I took the bag and opened it to find a beautiful plush red winter scarf. "This is gorgeous, Lupita! Thanks!" I hugged her gratefully. "How did you know my favorite color was red?" I was impressed.

"I thought it was a safe choice since you wear a red hoodie and red pea coat every day. Your shoes are sometimes red. And correct me if I'm wrong, but I think I've seen you in red socks too!" She laughed heartily forcing me to join in.

"Yeah okay, maybe I do wear red a lot." I blushed at my stupid question. "But thank you for paying attention. You didn't have to. I feel bad for not getting you anything."

"Oh no, it's fine. Just keep taking care of mis nietos. You're doing a wonderful job. Maravillosa!" She kissed my cheek.

"It's been nice getting to know you. Have a safe flight. Come back soon okay?" I leaned down and gave her a long hug. "I'll miss you."

"Igualmente," she replied with a smile.

"You all have a good weekend. I'll see you Monday." I waved at everyone.

"See you, Serena. Thanks for putting up with my mom," Mauricio whispered then opened and closed the door behind me.

-

"Wow, that was such a peaceful way for her to leave," Maakara commented in shock.

"Yeah, I was surprised myself," Serena said. "It's funny how you make new friends. I never really thought about the fact that I would have to meet people of all ages from different cultures and backgrounds. I had only thought about the kids up until that point. I realize now there's so much more to it than that. I'm grateful for the exposure. Unfortunately, when it came to my experience working in childcare overall, the bad outweighed the good."

"Oh Lord. What now?" Maakara asked stuffing an Oreo into her mouth.

-

The next few months brought colds and cold weather with them. The twins' noses ran like faucets in the drafty apartment. Somehow their germs didn't affect me though. My new scarf must have been my good luck charm. I made sure to snap a picture of me wearing it so that Lupita could see. Sometimes she would text asking for pics of me and the kids. Aleyda and Mauricio were nervous about me leaving the building with the twins during winter, so we went back to only walking the perimeter of the building.

One thing that made my days more entertaining was the twins being mobile. Oli started crawling on Christmas day after a month of scooting across the floor in the most hilarious way. I was sure he would walk before his brother too, but Ozzie, not to be outdone, surprised me when he took his first steps at almost 10 months.

By March, Mauricio only had about three months until graduation. That gave me plenty of time to find another family to work with. Even with all their flaws, the Apaza's were the best family by far. I hoped my experiences would only improve from there. As I put the twins into their cribs for naps, my thoughts drifted to Anna, Rachel, and Tessa. I hadn't heard from them in months. I wondered how Tessa was doing. I felt apprehensive about reaching out, but my concern drove me to check in with her.

Hey, it's Serena. Just checking in.

As I bent over to pick up a teething toy, my phone rang. I checked the screen. Tessa. It was only 2:00 in the afternoon. I wondered what she was doing out of school.

"Hello?" I answered cautiously.

"Hey, how you been?" I froze at the sound of Raymond's creepy voice. "Serena? You there?" He paused waiting on a response. "I confiscated Tessa's phone because she did some stupid teenage crap again. I'm glad you called while I have it in my possession. I've been meaning to get in touch."

"What do you want?" I finally managed to ask with a quaver in my voice.

"Kirsten and I are over. Not only that but she's lost her parental rights due to an incident with Tessa."

"Is Tessa okay?" I asked forgetting who I was talking to.

"She's fine... I'd love to have you come back to work for us now that my marriage is over. Maybe we can take it a little further than those petty conversations we used to have."

"I hope you lose custody of your kids," I managed to say without vomiting then hung up.

-

"I cannot believe that creepy bastard did that," Maakara said with disdain.

"He was so damn repulsive. I never tried to contact Tessa again after that," Serena said solemnly.

-

For the rest of the afternoon, I couldn't help but worry about Tessa. My conversation with Raymond put me in a bad mood. I looked forward to leaving work so I could let off some steam at the gym. My mood didn't lighten until Mauricio came through the door.

"Hey! How's it going?" he asked happily.

"It's going well. I was just about to wake up the boys."

"Don't worry about it." He waved his hand as if it was of no importance to him. "I have some potentially good news for you."

"What's going on?"

"As you know, we're probably not going to be needing your services anymore once I find a job. You know Aleyda wants her chance to stay home with the boys, but a friend of mine is looking for someone to start full-time in the summer once his kids are out of school. I already gave him your information. I hope that was okay." He nervously bit his lip.

"Thanks! I appreciate it. How old are the kids?" I asked feeling better than I had in the last couple of hours.

"I'm not exactly sure. I think he said they are finishing up first and fourth grade. So how old does that make them?"

"About 7 and 10. Hm. That means they would only need me for the summer and possibly not at all in the fall. But it does buy me time to find something long term," I said mostly to myself.

"I don't know all the details, but I did tell him to text you and schedule a time to talk."

"Sounds good."

"You've been excellent with our boys. I appreciate it so much." He touched my shoulder, his signature. "Oh, my friend's name is Rohit Gupta."

"Thanks a lot." I almost hugged him but thought better of it. Not while Aleyda wasn't home. I didn't want anybody getting the wrong idea.

-

After an hour at the gym, I went home to enjoy a long relaxing shower. The hot water pelting on my back felt amazing. As soon as it started to get cold, I hopped out and toweled off when the cool air in the hallway hit my skin. Once in my pajamas, I looked forward to digging into the baked chicken, green beans, and mashed potatoes my mom had cooked. My stomach growled disrespectfully loudly as I watched the food swirl in the microwave. Just as I was digging into the first bite, my phone rang. *Unknown number.* I stared at my food longingly, but I knew I couldn't enjoy it while talking on the phone.

"Hello?" I answered begrudgingly.

"Hello, this is Rohit Gupta. I'm calling for Serena Davis," the man answered in a thick Indian accent.

"Hi, this is Serena." I adjusted my tone.

"I was calling in regards to a babysitting position that my colleague Mauricio Apaza recommended you for." His voice was robotic.

"Yes, he mentioned it earlier. Thanks for calling. What are you looking for?" I asked trying to sound professional.

"We are looking for someone to start full time for the summer," Rohit responded promptly. "It will be 45 hours a week. In the fall, it will be 15 hours a week with the kids in school. We would need you for their days out of school too. We can drop them off at school most days, but some mornings we might need you to take them as well."

"Can I meet you all before agreeing to anything? Where do you live? What do you want to know about me?

"We are willing to pay $20/hour. Mauricio has told us everything we need to know about you. We are ready to hire. But yes, we can meet if you want." Rohit obliged.

"Great, how soon can you meet?" I asked feeling confident.

"This weekend works. How's Saturday at eleven? I'll text you the address."

He ended the call.

A New Opportunity

Saturday morning dawned bright. It was almost April, but it still felt like winter. The high was supposed to be 40 degrees, but it felt colder with the brutal wind chill. I bared the cold earlier than I needed to in order to grab Burger King breakfast before I met the Guptas. I ate my croissant as I drove wondering what kind of house they had. They lived about 10 minutes away from me in Kenwood. I had never worked in the area before, but my old high school was nearby. The good thing about Kenwood was that the parking was better there than in Hyde Park or South Shore, so I wouldn't have a problem reporting to work on time in the mornings.

I searched each house on the block for the correct address then stopped in front of the right one. Only it wasn't a house so much as a mansion. It was breathtaking. There was a stunning white wrap around porch with white beams supporting the veranda's covering. The home was constructed out of a dull red brick on the first level and a pale gray on the upper level. The yard was enclosed in a tall brick gate. It seemed like the best place to raise kids and pets, exactly the kind of house I envisioned for my family growing up.

Curious to see the inside, I scrambled out of the car, stuffing the remnants from breakfast in my purse. I hoped they would give me a full tour. I suspected the rooms were humongous and imagined the backyard was twice the size of the front. For a moment, I forgot what my true purpose was. Abandoning my thoughts about the lavish home, I prepared to present my most professional self to this new opportunity. I pressed the button on the intercom and was met by a peppy female voice.

"Who is it?" she sang.

"Serena Davis. I'm here to see-"

The buzzing of the gate interrupted me before I could complete my sentence. I sauntered my way up the walkway leading to the porch. Before I arrived at the door, I was greeted by a friendly-looking middle-aged white woman with highlighted blonde hair. She was Amazonian in appearance with no curves from what I could see.

"Hi Serena! I'm Molly! How are you?" she called to me with a big toothy grin.

"Hi, I'm great. How are you?" I asked when I was close enough to greet her without yelling. I took in her full height. She was noticeably taller than me, maybe 6'0.

"It's good to meet you. Come on in!" She waved me inside.

"Thanks." I wondered if she was always that energetic.

She closed the door behind us. The inside of the home was remarkable. The dark hardwood floors were covered in neutral-colored rugs. The beige-colored couches with their blue decorative pillows complemented the pastel paintings on the pale blue walls. "Please take off your shoes," Molly instructed.

"Of course." I stepped out of my gym shoes expeditiously. "Even under the rugs, I can see your floors are beautiful. Why cover them?"

"We think the floors are beautiful too. We just want to reduce the amount of scuffing." She gave a girlish giggle then gestured. "This is our living room. We like to sit in here and let the natural light pour in from the big window. That's the kitchen. It's not much but it's home." She pointed to a stunning all-white kitchen with a charming island in the middle.

"This place is amazing. And it's spotless." I tried not to look overly impressed at the beautiful oak table and china cabinets.

"We had the cleaners come just for your visit. Usually, the place is a mess. Have a seat on the couch. Would you like a glass of water?"

"Sure," I said looking forward to seeing how comfortable the couch was.

"Honey!? Bring the kids inside! Serena is here!" Molly yelled. "They're out back with their dad."

Suddenly footsteps sounded in the back of the house. What I heard next was something running to the front at full speed. A cute white fluffy dog slid across the floor, nails scratching the exposed hardwood. It turned its attention to me. "Who is this?" I leaned back before the dog could lick my face.

"This is Maxwell. He's an American Eskimo. He's five years old and full of energy as you can see."

"Well hello, Maxwell." At the sound of his name, he enthusiastically sniffed my purse. I eagerly petted his head until he took a seat at my feet with his fluffy tail wagging in the air. "He's such a beautiful dog."

"I'm glad you two are off to such a good start. This is my husband Rohit and the kids." I glanced up as they stood in the doorway. The kids had their mother's narrow features and build. Their complexions were a mixture of their parents'.

"My son's name is Ronald Percy Gupta. My daughter is Wyandanch Amadeus Gupta." I was too taken aback by the girl's name to question why Molly used the kids' full names. Wyandanch was a mouthful.

"It's nice to meet you all." I waved at the kids. They shyly waved back.

"They aren't shy. Do not let them fool you." Rohit walked over and shook my free hand.

"I'm sorry. Did you say her name is Wyandanch?" I asked.

"I did," Molly stated proudly.

"She's named after the place in New York?"

"I'm surprised you caught that."

"I assume there's a story there."

"No, we just liked the name." Molly shrugged.

"Cool," I said weakly hiding my distaste. "I can't help but notice that your son's names are two characters from Harry Potter."

"Glad you picked up on that. You must be a big fan." Molly grinned.

"Fan would be an understatement. If I ever get a pet, I'm going to name it after one of my favorite characters, too. Something cool like Bellatrix or Hermione."

"Ronald is reading the series now. Hopefully, he still appreciates his name once he finishes. Maybe you all can play with his Harry Potter card game one day," Molly suggested.

"I'd love to." I directed a smile at Ronald.

"Let's get to the reason you're here. Kids, you can go play in the basement. Take a seat, honey." Molly patted the seat next to her for Rohit.

"I want to stay upstairs mom," Wyandanch whined.

"Okay honey, go sit in the study." Both kids left without another word.

"Serena what do you need to know about us?" Rohit asked in the same thick accent from our phone conversation.

"What do you all do for a living?"

"Rohit's in investment banking. I'm a professor at UIC," Molly answered placing her hand on top of her husband's.

"Oh cool. What do you teach?" I asked.

"European history."

"Nice. Tell me about the kids."

"Ronald is 12 finishing up 6th grade. Wyandanch is 9 finishing up 3rd."

"Mauricio totally butchered their ages." I laughed. "He thought they were in 1st and 4th grade for some reason."

"That's hilarious." Molly giggled girlishly again.

"If the kids are 12 and 9, how old does that make you guys? If you don't mind me asking of course. I'm always curious about the parents I work with."

"I'm 44. Rohit is 46," Molly answered.

Looking at them, I would have thought Rohit was older than he was with his serious demeanor. His wife was the exact opposite: bubbly and energetic. I wondered what brought them together. The physical contrast between the two was aggressively apparent. Molly was actually a few inches taller than her husband. She was starkly pale and thin; Rohit was brown and stocky; they weren't the most attractive couple aesthetically, but they must have had something that worked.

"Oh okay. I was just curious. I'll be 21 in a couple of months," I informed.

"Anything else you want to share with us?" Rohit asked moving the conversation along.

"Well, I'm CPR certified. I have a car to use for work. It's old but it runs well. I have plenty of references I can provide. I'm willing to get a background check if it's needed. Oh, what school do the kids go to? I meant to ask that before." I remembered.

"Lab school," Rohit answered concisely.

"Not far from here. Cool. What duties do you all expect me to perform while here?"

"Clean up after the kids. Make sure Max doesn't get out. Keep the kids occupied and safe. We have plenty of games for them to play during the day. We don't like a lot of TV. We'll give you a key and a credit card at a later date. During the school year, we just need you to pick them up and be available on their off days, fix their lunches, and help with homework. We also can pay you a salary to keep you on call. We know only working 15 hours a week is not enough… Since the kids are older, I don't feel the need to be overly specific about what they need. They can tell you. And we can learn as we go," Molly informed me comfortably.

"Any allergies I need to know about?" I inquired.

"No allergies," Molly said. "I know Rohit has already told you, but we are prepared to hire you today even though you won't be able to start until the summer. We can send you an advance to secure you if that makes you feel better about the offer."

"That's very generous of you guys. What do you all think is a fair salary?"

"Well," Rohit interjected "15 hours a week at $20/hour is $300/week. In order to secure your availability, how about we just do a salary of $500/week tax-free? We're open to paying more when the kids are out of school for winter break and spring break. We want to do what we can to make sure you're comfortable enough to stay with us when there are less hours."

"That sounds more than fair. And the advance is not necessary, but if you all feel like you really want to give one to me, I won't stop you." I laughed. "I've never had a family be so generous before. I'm not sure how to handle this, to be honest."

"We'll send you a little something," Molly said with a wink. "Can we send it through QuickPay using your phone number?"

"Yes. Thank you," I said humbly.

"I think that's enough information for now. Unless you have any other questions?" Molly concluded politely.

"I'm good. Thanks."

"We'll be in touch with an exact date. As of now, we think it'll be June 15. And we might have some babysitting opportunities for you on weekends if you're interested."

"Sure, just let me know." I stood up to make my exit realizing I'd been carrying my Burger King trash the whole time. No wonder Maxwell was sniffing my purse. "Oh… can I throw this away?"

"Is that fast food? Burger King?" Molly asked taking the trash from my hand looking fully prepared to vomit on her beautiful floors. "We don't eat this stuff. We hope you wouldn't feed it to the kids either."

"Not if you don't want me to." I was surprised at her reaction to my personal eating habits. "I look forward to hearing from you all." I headed for the door. Rohit followed me. "Have a good one," I muttered as I stuffed my feet into my shoes.

"You too. Thanks for meeting with us," Rohit said.

As I stepped over the threshold and Rohit closed the door behind me, I wondered what my future held. The family had money and no problem spending it on their kids. It was not as much as I was making with the Apaza's, but I'd have enough free time in the fall to pursue personal projects. The Gupta's confidence in me gave me a freeing feeling. I breathed a sigh of relief as I walked back to the car. By the time I was in the driver's seat, my phone pinged.

Rohit Gupta has sent you $500: Advance.

We were off to a great start.

-

The weeks leading up to Mauricio's graduation flew by in a bittersweet way. The twins perfected their toddling. Aleyda seemed to lighten up in direct correlation with the temperature change. I guessed the prospect of being a stay-at-home mom looming ahead made her feel more at ease.

Having a job lined up also relaxed me and allowed me to fully enjoy my last weeks with the twins. I was relieved that I didn't have to end a job on a bad note for once.

-

A month before I was scheduled to start with them, the Gupta's asked me to babysit one Saturday afternoon, and I happily obliged. When I approached the door, I heard Max's barking on the other side. He jumped on me when Molly opened it.

"Hey, boy. How are you?" I asked in a voice I only reserved for babies and puppies. "Hey, Molly."

"How are you Serena?" she smiled at Max's energetic greeting then pulled him off and let me in the door. "We're in a rush but I'll run everything down for you quickly."

As she made the finishing touches on her outfit, I took in her appearance. She was dressed casually in jeans, a fitted white t-shirt, clean white gym shoes, and a navy-blue blazer. Her clothes fit her perfectly. Her hair was freshly dyed and cut into a sharp shoulder-length bob. She wore minimal jewelry, two-carat diamond studs in her ears. There was something about her, a certain carefree vibe that was mostly reserved for people born into wealth. The house was just as polished as its owner. It made me want to skate across the floor in my socks and post pics on Instagram.

"What's funny?" Molly inquired after seeing the smirk on my face.

"Oh, I was just thinking about how silly I am for wanting to take pics in your house and pretend it's mine. Whoever did the interior decorating did an excellent job. The color scheme is fabulous."

"Make yourself at home. You haven't even seen the whole house yet. Feel free to explore," Molly said checking her makeup.

"Thanks! I will."

"I don't recommend you go into Ronald's room. It's a mess. He'll show it to you when he's ready." She made a disgusted face.

"Got it." I nodded my head in affirmation.

"For lunch you can make them grilled cheese with tomato sauce. Be sure to serve fruit as well. There's plenty of food for you too. They can have milk or water with lunch. Be sure to only give Ronald one sandwich. He can be greedy. We don't like too much screen time so please try to play board games. We'll only be gone for about four hours so there's no need to think about dinner. I'm going to leave labeled keys here in case you all take a ride or go for a walk. Be sure Maxwell is not in the backyard when you all leave. You have our numbers. Any questions just text me. K?" She flashed her professionally whitened teeth. "Honey!?! Let's go! The movie starts at 12:30!"

Immediately Rohit's feet hit the stairs. "Hello Serena," he greeted. "The kids are playing monopoly in the spare room upstairs if you want to join them."

"Sure. I'll be the banker." I made my way for the stairs curious about the rest of the house. "You guys have a good time."

"Thanks. We'll see you in a few hours," Molly said as they headed out the back door.

-

The winding staircase behind the kitchen lead me to the second-floor landing. I wanted to curl up with a blanket and go to sleep on the thick carpet in the hallways. I followed the sound of the kids' laughter, which lead me to a medium-sized room covered in the same white carpet. The interior decorator didn't spend much time there; the room housed a lonely queen-sized bed and a black wooden dresser. There were toys scattered all over the place.

"Hey, y'all. Can I be the banker?" I knocked on the cracked door.

"Did my parents leave?" Ronald asked jumping up excitedly.

"Just left." I stepped farther into the room.

"Can we have lunch now?" he asked eagerly.

"Sure. Grilled cheese coming up. Did you want to eat now too, Wyandanch?"

"No thank you. I'm okay." Her tone was inexplicably sad.

"I'll make you one anyway. If you don't finish it, your brother can have the rest so we don't waste anything."

"I'll take it!" Ronald piped up. "My mom doesn't let me have more than one."

"You're a boy going through puberty. I can understand why you have a big appetite, but I won't let you eat for the sake of eating either."

"Too bad my mom doesn't think like you," he retorted with a hint of bitterness. His words brought my attention to his thin frame.

"We'll get some meat on those bones. No worries."

-

Once I had everything I needed set out on the counter, Ronald entered the kitchen and took a seat at the island with his chin on his hands looking contemplative. "Did you just add two slices of cheese to my sandwich?"

"I did. Is that a problem?" I asked.

"No, my mom just never does that."

"How does Wyandanch like hers?"

"She doesn't care. I don't think it matters. She's weird about food," he said nonchalant.

"That explains why she's so tiny. You guys probably get it from your mom though."

"Yeah, I guess."

"Well once I'm done, let me know how you like your sandwich with the extra cheese. If you don't like it, I won't do it next time. I just wanted to be sure to cover the bread completely," I said as I twisted the tie back on the bread bag. "Did you want anything else with it? There's tomato soup, and I took out some grapes for you. Is that going to be enough?"

"Ummm." Ronald gave a mischievous look. "Are there any chips I could have?"

"I'm not sure. Does your mom keep chips in the house?"

"I was hoping you had some," he said slightly despondent.

"Maybe one day I'll bring you some. A few can't hurt, right?"

"Awesome." His tone brightened.

"But for now, let's stick to this amazing grilled cheese."

Once the sandwiches were done and the plates were prepared, Wyandanch took her time coming down the stairs. "I made this delicious sandwich especially for you. I want you to eat it all." I placed the plate in front of her.

"Thanks. Can you cut it in half for me?" she asked in the same melancholy tone.

"Sure." I cut the sandwich vertically in half. She immediately put one half on her brother's plate. He devoured it in seconds. "Aren't you going to try it Wyandanch?"

"Yeah, I'm just not super hungry." She nibbled the crust. "That's pretty tasty," she muttered dryly.

I had a feeling she didn't enjoy it, but instead of watching her eat, I focused on her brother. "How is it, Ronald?"

"Great," he mumbled with a mouthful. "I like it with extra cheese." He stuffed in his last bite before gulping down his soup then polished off his grapes in record time.

I admired his gusto for a few more seconds then turned back to Wyandanch. She hadn't even made it through a quarter of a sandwich. "I made it with extra butter too. Does it taste okay, Wyandanch?"

"Oh yes, I love grilled cheese. I'm just a slow eater."

As she ate, she gazed off into space, holding her sandwich in the air as if it was a cigarette. By the time she finished her entire meal, it was 45 minutes later. Watching her eat was like watching paint dry: dreadfully boring. I figured I could get her to speed things up if I made her meals extra tasty. I made a mental note to ask her parents their tricks to get her to eat.

-

After a couple more hours of playing games, it was almost time to go. I had a great time with the kids even though Wyandanch was very soft spoken. Ronald was rambunctious and warmed to me quickly.

"Hi, guys! How did it go?" Molly asked as soon as she returned with her husband.

"What do you think guys? How did it go?" I looked to the kids for an honest answer.

"Serena is awesome! She made a really good grilled cheese sandwich for me," Ronald asserted enthusiastically.

"She seems nice mom," Wyandanch added shyly. "She made our sandwiches with two slices of cheese instead of one, extra butter. It was tasty."

"Did she?" Molly turned to me. "Serena we only make their sandwiches with one slice of cheese and we don't drown them in butter. It's too unhealthy for them," she informed me visibly bothered.

"Not a problem. I added some extra butter, but I didn't drown them just so you know. I will say that Ronald seemed to enjoy them. He even ate what Wyandanch couldn't finish."

"He did?" She turned to him. "Honey, you know I don't want you eating too many fatty cheeses. It's not good for you." She stroked his face then turned my way. "If this boy could eat six grilled cheeses a day he would." She forced a laugh.

"Other than the food, we had a good time playing monopoly, connect four and some other games. The time flew by honestly," I told her.

"I'd say that's a nice way to start our working relationship. I'll send you some cash." Rohit pulled out his phone.

"I'll see you all next time." I gathered my belongings and petted Max on the head before opening the door.

"Have a good evening," Molly called as I skipped down the front stairs. Just before I made it to my car, my text alert chimed.

Rohit Gupta has sent you $100: Babysitting

I smiled to myself then unlocked my car and settled into the front seat. Rohit might have been a man of few words, but I respected how efficient he was. As I started the ignition, my phone rang. The number on the screen wiped the grin off my face.

"Hello?" I answered timidly.

"Hey, how have you been?" Jabari's tender voice greeted me.

"Uhhh," I responded stupidly, hating myself for letting him make me feel surprised, anxious, and excited all at the same time.

"Damn, you deleted my number huh? Was I that much of a creep?" he joked.

"What? Oh no, I- you just caught me off guard."

"So why didn't you know who I was then?" he teased.

"I was distracted. I thought you were someone else," I replied honestly, my heart fluttering.

"Another guy huh?" he asked with the audacity to sound disappointed.

"No." I rolled my eyes. "An employer. You caught me when I was leaving a job. I thought they were calling because I left something at their house." My tone was surprisingly hard.

"I'm sorry. I'm asking you questions, and it's not my business... Anyway, how have you been?" His communication skills were still on point.

"I've been great. Work has been good. No more crazy grandma troubles. We were on good terms by the time she went back home. The job is ending in a few weeks though," I concluded then remembered to pull out of the parking space.

"Why is that?" he asked, and I thought I detected a hint of relief.

"Because the dad will be finished with his Masters at the end of May. So mom is going to stay home with the kids when he starts working."

"Oh okay. Sounds like a nice arrangement for them. But where does that leave you?"

"It leaves me with another job already lined up. The family I currently work for referred me to another family. I'm leaving their house now." I gazed at the other mansions on the block as I drove.

"Wow, you're on it! That's good for you but not so good for me I guess," Jabari said pitifully.

"And why is that?" I asked.

"I was going to ask you to come back and work with Ethan full time until he starts school. We would be willing to pay $15/hour now if that sweetens the deal for you," Jabari offered.

"Thanks that sounds nice, but I think I'm okay for now. What made you all want to increase the hours?"

"Emily is pregnant. Due in July. It's a girl."

-

"How dare your future husband have a baby with his wife?" Maakara gasped.

"I know right?" I giggled at her sarcasm.

-

I felt weirdly betrayed. "So, she was pregnant when I last spoke to you."

"She was, but I didn't know then," he admitted.

"Yeah right," I spat at him.

"I swear!"

"Yeah well congrats. Is this a good thing? Are you all happy again?"

"No, we aren't happy. We tried to rekindle our sex life then this happened. Neither of us thought it made sense to have an abortion considering we're able to provide for another child, so here we are," Jabari disclosed.

"Have you all been to counseling since we last talked?"

"We have. She wasn't interested in continuing after a couple of months, but she tried."

"What's the game plan then?" I asked.

"We are going to try to stick it out while the baby is little, try to co-parent you know? But I think it's clear we aren't in love anymore, and we aren't going to be," Jabari concluded.

"Damn, that sucks."

"It is. But it would brighten my day if you would come back and work for us."

"I'm sure it would." I rolled my eyes but smiled despite myself.

"Is that a firm no?"

"It is… at least for now," I added reluctantly.

"So, you'd consider coming back? We did really like you," Jabari shamelessly complimented.

"If I'm desperate enough, sure."

"Damn, so you have to be desperate to ever see me again?"

"Yep! And it's not seeing you so much as working for you."

"I'll take that I guess." Jabari chuckled. After a moment he continued in a more serious tone, "Can I ask why you've ignored my texts all these months? How long has it been? Five months since we last talked? I just want to you to tell me."

"Tell you what?"

"Why did you cut me off?"

"Well…I was uncomfortably attracted to you. It was unprofessional. I felt like I was doing something wrong, and I didn't want you to ruin my perception of you. I didn't want you to be a cheater, and you kept trying to see me. I figured it was safer if I stayed away," I confessed

"I didn't see it as cheating knowing my marriage was over, but I understand and respect where you're coming from... Are you still attracted to me?" he asked audaciously.

"You must want me to hang up on you."

"Sorry!" He laughed. "I couldn't resist. Well, I still want to be friends. And if you need a job just let me know. Maybe I'll see you around?"

"Maybe."

"Can I call you some time?"

"No." I was happy he couldn't see the toothy smile spreading across my face. "But you can text."

Adios

Mauricio found a job as a postsecondary education administrator at UC Berkley. They gave him six weeks to move his entire life to California. "How are you guys feeling about everything?" I asked Aleyda and Mauricio. They were both home early to see me off.

"I'm excited and so thankful that this all worked out. I worked hard, and it's finally paying off." he said with emotion.

"What about you Aleyda? How are you?"

"I'm excited to celebrate the twins' 1st birthday. And I'm happy for Mauricio, but I'm nervous about the move. You know how high strung I am," she half-joked.

"We're acknowledging that now?" I widened my eyes.

"I mean I always knew I was." Aleyda rolled her eyes playfully.

"I would be nervous, too. I love Chicago so much. The move might be exactly what your family needs though and luckily, you'll get to spend more time with your babies. You won't even need winter coats."

"You're right. Thanks." She smiled genuinely. I hadn't seen her do that in a long time.

"It's nice to see you happy, Aleyda. I wish you all the best on this new journey."

"No, thank you," Mauricio cut in. He took my hands in his. "We appreciate it so much. It's been great having such a good experience with our first caregiver." His voice cracked with his last words. "We've heard horror stories, and we were fortunate enough to get it right the first time." He hugged me.

"Yes, thank you." Aleyda hugged me and added, "I know it was hard to deal with first-time parents like us, but you were always a joy to have in our home. We have a gift for you."

She retrieved something rectangular from behind a throw pillow. "Remember that picture we took of you holding the twins?" She turned the object over in her hands. It was a 5x7 picture frame encasing the beautiful picture of the boys and me.

"Thank you! The picture turned out perfectly! I usually hate how I look in photos."

"We thought you'd like it," Aleyda responded full of pride. Of course, she'd make sure I'd always keep her babies with me.

"I won't keep you all any longer. Let me hug the kids and let you all pack." I picked up Oli, took one long look at his face, squeezed him and kissed his cheek. I repeated the process with his brother. It didn't feel right to just hold one. I had to hold the both of them one last time. I picked up the other twin and nuzzled their faces. They still had that newborn smell.

"Alright you two, don't let your parents get too wild in Cali okay? Keep them in line. Los amo chiquitos." I kissed their cheeks again, stood them up on their feet then turned to their parents. "Again, I say good luck. You all stay in touch. Send me pics. And please tell Lupita I said hi. Mauricio, congrats again." I gave them my warmest smile and headed for the door.

-

"I love that it ended on such a good note." Maakara smiled happily.

"Me too. It was long overdue."

Moving on

Once my job with the Apaza's ended, I had a couple of weeks to myself before my new one started. I decided to go to the gym in the mornings to avoid the after-work crowd. The place was mostly empty. After a good stretch, I hopped on the stair master, which was nothing but pure torture as usual. I mindlessly watched the gym's TV screens as I climbed. After 10 minutes I'd had enough. I could barely breathe, and I was sweating in places I didn't know I could sweat in. As I started my two- minute warm down, another member stepped onto the machine next to mine. Good time for me to get off. I liked having my space. I saw the stranger's hands reach out to pull himself higher onto the machine. I couldn't help noticing how amazing he smelled. I glanced at him out of my peripheral and my jaw dropped.

"Jabari?!" I took in all his beautiful darkness in total shock.

"Oh my God, Serena?" Happy recognition spread across his face. "What a surprise! What are you doing here?" He awkwardly reached out and hugged me across the machines. "Man, it's good to see you."

"Ew, I wish you hadn't hugged me. You see how sweaty I am." I wiped my forehead with my towel.

"Pshh! You look and smell fine." He turned on his machine.

"This is so weird," I said decreasing my speed again. "This is the gym you go to? I've never seen you here." I was more than a bit flustered and self-conscious.

"I have memberships at a couple of gyms. I joined this one recently. Are you not happy to see me? I'm happy to see you." He gave me sexy puppy dog eyes.

"You just caught me off guard that's all. What a coincidence. How is Ethan? How's everyone?" I asked finally gathering myself.

"They're fine. I'm doing great too. Thanks for asking." He smirked, reminding me how charming he could be.

"Great…" I trailed off awkwardly. We'd been texting consistently, but I had no intention of ever seeing him again. I wasn't sure how to behave.

"Is this really that awkward for you? Is seeing me so hard?" he asked picking up on my discomfort.

"I just wasn't expecting this at all. I come here all the time. The one time I switch my schedule, I run into you. It's crazy."

"Yeah okay. I see what you mean."

"But yes, it is nice to see you. You're still looking healthy I see." I turned down my speed again, wishing I could turn down my hormones too.

"You're not looking bad yourself." His suggestive tone made me want to burn calories in a different way.

"Yeah, I know." I faked cockiness, hoping to keep things playful and not flirty.

"Still don't know how to take a compliment huh?"

"I only get this way with married men." I shrugged.

"Are you ever going to stop throwing that in my face?"

"Are you ever going to get a divorce?" I lobbed back at him.

"Ouch! So, if I get divorced, you'll give me a chance?" He challenged.

"Hmmm, I'm not sure I'd ever date a guy who tried to date me while he was married to someone else. Would you date a woman who did the same?"

"Well considering what I've gone through with Emily, yeah I would be open to it. Marriage can be very complex. Couples go through phases. Sometimes they explore to see if they want to stay married or not. You wouldn't understand."

"You're right. I've never been married, but I did witness my mother's marriage go through some ups and downs. She ended up reconciling with her husband after they separated and dated other people, then they got divorced a year later. It depends on the relationship. I'm just not sure about yours considering you have another kid due in less two months, right? What kind of man seeks out other women while he has a pregnant wife at home?" I folded my arms and gave him a fierce look.

"Damn, you don't play! That's a fair question. Well, as I said we were not planning for this baby-"

"You didn't use a condom, and she wasn't on birth control but you all didn't want another kid? Make it make sense," I demanded and stopped my machine completely.

"Well, we didn't want another kid, but we didn't take the necessary precautions either. Emily was worried birth control would make her gain weight, so she was never on it. We didn't think when we had that pathetic attempt at sex that it would lead to this pregnancy. Maybe we thought we had to like each other for it to work." He scoffed. "I don't know, man. Honestly, I think we were so disinterested in each other by that point that I'm not sure we thought the sex would be successful."

"I do not envy you." I shook my head actually feeling sympathy for him.

"Gee, thanks."

"Sorry, it's such a messy situation. How does Emily feel?"

"She's miserable! She's gaining weight, which she hates, although she could stand to gain a few pounds. She's just waiting to drop her load. She plans to be just as good to this baby as she was to Ethan. I also think it's easier for us financially to live together at the moment. It's easier to co-parent this way as well. I'm not opposed to it for now," Jabari admitted.

"So, why are you interested in seeing me? Seems like you should be repulsed at the idea of being with another woman so fast," I quipped

"How old are you again?"

"Just turned 21. Why?"

"I'd swear you were older."

"So I've been told," I smiled slyly.

"To answer your question, I realize Emily and I made a mistake in getting married. We are too different. We both know that now. We try to treat each other with respect, but we don't like each other at all romantically. And that's okay. We'll give it until the new baby's 1st birthday and start the divorce proceedings after that. Emily is free to see other men. Unfortunately for her, she's the one who has to carry the baby, so it might prevent her from exploring new relationships, but she is welcome to. I want her to be happy, and I don't want you to let my marriage get in the way of you taking me seriously."

"Who says I want anything serious from you?" I asked sassily putting my hands on my hips.

"I don't know. What do you want from me? Surely you want something." He gave me a daring smoldering gaze, and I almost told him exactly what I wanted.

"All we can be is friends." The longing in my voice betrayed me.

"I know that's not all you want from me." He turned off his machine and fully faced me. "If I wasn't married and didn't have a baby on the way, would you allow anything to happen between us?"

"I'm sure I'd allow a lot to happen if that was the situation." My heartbeat quickened, even though I was no longer climbing the machine. "But considering that isn't the case, it doesn't matter what I'd do, does it?"

"It matters to me. I'd like to hear about it in great detail if you're willing to share." He flashed a naughty smile that made me want to jump on him.

"You have no shame, do you?" I tried to be angry at him, but he was almost irresistible. Almost.

"Look, I like you. I want to spend time with you in whatever way you'll allow me to. I will not deny that I want you, but I don't want to make you feel uncomfortable like I did last time either." He took a deep breath. "If you don't want to deal with me, I get it. You're young and don't need all my baggage. If I'm too much for you, then I understand. You should leave me alone. Go back to ignoring me. Block me because I won't stop reaching out until I think you mean it. Our chemistry is strong, something I've never had before. I want to explore it while we have the chance to. I can't risk you finding someone your own age and forgetting all about me, can I? I see something I like, and I have to go after it. When you know something is right, you just know."

"I-I didn't realize you felt so strongly about it." His earnest declaration disarmed me momentarily. "I don't know what to say or where we go from here."

"You could let me take you out on a date. You pick the place. Totally innocent." He put his hands up defensively.

"I don't know about that. I'll just settle for catching you at the gym on occasion for now."

"Is that all I get?" he asked disappointed.

"I mean I could just cancel my membership instead," I suggested.

"Please don't do that," he begged.

"Then yeah that's all you get... for now."

"I'll take it." He smiled brightly.

"You're very persistent. It's annoying." I rolled my eyes at him.

"I'm nothing if not persistent."

"I'm going to leave you to your work out." I jumped off the machine.

"Don't leave on account of me."

"I'm not. I accomplished a lot today. I don't want to get in the way of your routine. Got to keep that beautiful body sculpted right?"

"You're not doing bad yourself. Your thighs look amazing in those pants." He gawked at me lasciviously.

"Thank you." I managed to mumble before looking away to hide the blush spreading across my cheeks. "See you later, Jabari."

"I'll text you," he said to my back. I could feel him watching me walk away. I was so thankful I wore the leggings that accentuated my butt that day. I considered running to Target and grabbing a few more pairs.

The Guptas

Kenwood

After a couple more run-ins with Jabari at the gym, my two-week vacation was over. Wyandanch and Ronald were expecting a summer full of fun, and I was ready to give it to them. Stepping foot into the mansion, I expected the same tidy interior that I had seen on other occasions, but was met with the opposite. The house was in total disarray. There were clothes scattered everywhere. Dishes all over the counter and toys on the floor. I could smell that Max had had an accident somewhere too.

"Please excuse the mess. Our housekeeper hasn't been here in weeks," Molly said in a hurried tone. "The kids are upstairs getting dressed. Rohit is already gone. I left the credit card and keys on the counter. Food's in the fridge. Anything you need from me?"

"Anything in particular you want me to do with the kids today?" I asked trying to hide the face I was making from the stench.

"Nope! Just see what the kids want to do. We'll come up with some other ideas later... I'm late for my lecture. Text me if you need me!" Molly rushed out of the back door with her gray stilettos in hand. Max clambered inside soon after.

"Hey, Maxie. What's going on today?" I sniffed around the room. "Did you pee around here somewhere?" The dog whimpered in response.

"Let's see what we can straighten up." I focused on picking up clothes and putting them into kid and adult piles. I had them sorted and all the dishes in the sink when Wyandanch entered the room.

"Morning Serena."

"Hey, Wyandanch. How are you?"

"I'm okay. You?"

"I'm great. Happy to be hanging with you guys. Are you ready to eat?" I took a peek in the fridge.

"I can wait."

"Are you sure you're okay?" I peered at the little girl intently.

"Yep. Fine."

It was then that I noticed her gaunt like face and the way her stretchy shorts and t-shirt highlighted her narrow figure. "What do you want for breakfast?" I asked ignoring her previous statement.

"I can have whatever you make for my brother," Wyandanch replied uninterested.

"Cool… Hey, do you have a nickname?" I faced her with an idea forming in my mind.

"Sometimes Ron calls me 'Wy'. That's it. Why?"

"Well, your name is kind of long. I was wondering if we could shorten it."

"That might be cool," she said brightening for the first time.

"Hmm let's think of a new one…Your initials are W-A-G. We could call you just Wyan? Nah that sounds like when little kids can't say their r's. Danch? Danny? Chichi?" I made her laugh at the last suggestion.

"What about just Wag? It's weird, but I like it. Only you can call me that though," Wyandanch advised me.

"It would be my pleasure Wag." I bowed wanting her to feel at ease. "You are the most mature little girl I've ever met. You sure you're only nine? I can check your birth certificate," I joked hoping we could bond.

"Yes, I'm sure." She giggled.

"Cool. For now, let's just focus on breakfast." I clapped my hands together.

"Can I just have cereal? No need to cook," she said faintly.

"Cereal works. What kind?"

"We only buy one kind. Honey nut cheerios."

"Only one kind?" I asked in disbelief. "You've never had Froot Loops or Frosted Flakes or even corn flakes with sugar?"

"No, my mom says honey nut cheerios are the healthiest. Sometimes we get regular cheerios if they run out."

"Maybe one day I'll bring you a small box of a different brand so you can taste something different." I whispered behind my hand, "What kind would you like?"

"It doesn't matter," Wag said indifferently.

"I'd like to try Cookie crisps!" interrupted Ronald, bursting into the kitchen. "And Froot Loops and Fruity Pebbles and Cap'n Crunch!"

"That's good to know!" I laughed at the boy's appetite. "But what do you want to eat right now?"

"Pancakes?" he asked hopefully.

"Pancakes coming right up. Can someone get me the mix? I just need water, mix, and butter." Wag obediently grabbed the mix from the pantry. I retrieved the butter from the fridge. Fifteen minutes later, we had beautiful buttery pancakes. I couldn't resist having one for myself.

"Can I have another one?" Ronald asked between mouthfuls.

"Sure, babe. Slow down though, and make sure you're chewing all the way." I used the spatula to slide another pancake on his plate when I noticed Wag struggling to get through her small one. "What's going on? You don't like them?" I asked her.

"Oh no, they taste great. Better than when mom makes them. I just don't eat a lot." Wag shrugged.

"You don't have to eat a lot. But you're not even eating enough!" I laughed. "If you don't like the pancakes, it's cool."

"They really do taste good," she said unconvincingly.

"I'll believe you when you finish it." I looked at her suspiciously. "I want you to look forward to meals, so I'm going to figure out what you like to eat."

"Okay." She gave me a genuine smile.

"I think I'm done. Can I show you something?" Ronald asked.

"Of course. Can I wash the dishes first?"

"I want you to see it now," he spoke with a seriousness in his voice then jumped off of his stool and ventured up the staircase. I stood up to follow him and stepped in something wet. Max's pee. How the hell didn't anybody see it before I did?

"Hold on Ron. Let me get this off the floor."

"What is it?" Ron inquired, descending the staircase.

"I think Max peed right here." I looked down at my foot in disgust. "Let me get a paper towel."

"No, I'll get it." He raced passed me to grab a napkin and cleaning spray. "I let Maxie out too late this morning. That's my fault."

"It's okay. Thanks. Now, what did you want to show me?" I asked wiping my foot off.

"Follow me." He took off up the stairs again. I did as he suggested then realized I had yet to see their rooms. Most of the doors were closed on the second floor.

"What do you want to show me, Ron?" I asked apprehensively. He stopped at a closed-door once Wag caught up to us.

"Here's my room."

The room behind the door was medium-sized with its own bathroom. It was painted dark blue with spaceships all over the walls and junk on the floor. There was a wooden bunk bed against the far-right wall. Ronald walked right up to it, reached beneath it and pulled out a small suitcase. Without words, he revealed its contents. I was underwhelmed at what I saw.

-

"What was it? You're creeping me out!" Maakara exclaimed.

-

"Snacks? Why are you showing me this? Why do you have these?" The truth loomed just ahead, and I did my best to brace myself for it.

"I want to tell you…because you care about what me and Wy eat." Ron took a deep breath. "We aren't allowed to have snacks like these."

I took a closer look at all the different types of wrappers: chocolate bars, fruity candy, chips, and cookies. The boy was a hoarder. "Why aren't you allowed to have these?" I asked already knowing the answer.

"Mom says it's unhealthy."

"So, how did you get them?" I sifted through the treats finding a bag off Skittles.

"Because it's hard not being able to have snacks like a normal kid!" he yelled in frustration. "I ask my friends from school to sneak me stuff when they can. It took me months to fill up this suitcase. We always have to eat veggie straws or fruit, rarely ever chips. Nasty multigrain bread instead of the plain kind. I don't want to eat bread with grain and nuts in it! My mom is not a good cook either. One time she made some macaroni and cheese, and I couldn't even tell what it was! It looked like it was 2 weeks old!" he raged.

"Let me cut in for just one sec," I said trying to keep from laughing "First of all, you're hilarious for describing the food like that. But if you've never had good food, how do you know what good mac and cheese tastes like?"

"Going to grandma's house. She married a guy who's a really good cook. Mom doesn't like for us to eat his food too often though."

"Why is that?"

"She says he makes it too fattening. So when we go visit, I eat as much as I can. Mom doesn't listen to anybody when it comes to food. She makes this soup with greens and noodles that she says is yummy, but I've yet to taste the yummy part!" He flailed his hands dramatically. "She puts all this extra healthy stuff in our oatmeal too. We can't just add syrup or brown sugar; it has to be her way. She likes to make healthy pancakes from scratch but sometimes she uses the mix because it's quicker. They are so gross. Serena, the pancakes you made were so good! You didn't even add fruit or milk or anything!" Ron concluded out of breath.

"The secret is butter. Nothing special. As far as oatmeal, all I add is brown sugar. I can't comment on how your mom's tastes, but what I can do is try to get you to enjoy eating as much as possible when we're together. I told Wag the same thing this morning. Y'all really can't afford to lose any weight."

"Wy definitely needs to eat more, but she won't admit it. She doesn't like to go against mom," Ron said pointedly.

I turned to Wag realizing the younger of the two children had been completely silent the entire time. "Are you not eating because the food isn't good? Are you hungry? Or you really don't have an appetite?"

"Um..."

"It's okay Wy. Tell her," Ronald encouraged.

"I used to get really hungry, but I didn't like the food that we had. Now I don't care about eating," Wag confessed.

"We'll fix that."

"It would be nice to have store-bought cookies sometimes," she admitted shyly.

"Maybe I'll sneak you a couple Oreos one day." I winked at her. "But I have one question."

"What is it?" Wag asked cautiously.

"Does mom worry about your eating habits even on holidays? Like Thanksgiving or Christmas?"

"She counts our candy on Halloween and Easter. And last year she told our grandma we had eaten too much on Thanksgiving. Grandma asked her how that was possible. Oh, and one Halloween, mom told grandma we had too much candy. Grandma told her that was okay and turned to us asking if we saved her any." He chuckled to himself. "I don't know why mom thinks grandma agrees with her. She knows we're too skinny. We're both the smallest kids in our classes."

"I can try to do something about that. Ronald, I'll dispose of the empty wrappers for you. Just give me a plastic bag."

-

"Oh Lord!" Maakara threw her hands up in frustration. "Damn kids were being starved to death. I can't imagine how skinny they were."

"That is not something you would have wanted to see in person," Serena remarked.

-

After a long day of playing board games and hanging out in the backyard, it was almost time for me to go home. Working 8:00-5:00 without a nap was going to be tough, but I enjoyed being around the kids. Interestingly, Wag was haunted by the same issue that affected her brother, but it affected her so much more differently. I'm glad they trusted me enough to open up, and I hoped I didn't lose their trust when I talked to their mother about buying them more food options.

"Hey, guys? I need to talk to you before your mom gets here."

"What's up Serena?" They both looked up from the books they were reading.

"I'm going to talk to your mom about the food issue."

"Please don't," Wag uttered quickly as if she had already adjusted to the idea of getting some sweet treats.

"Why are you going to talk to her? I already told you she doesn't listen," Ronald chimed in.

"I hear you guys, but I just want to be careful. I have an idea though. How about regardless of what she says, if you are well behaved, I'll sneak you treats at the end of the week?"

"Deal!" the kids agreed in unison.

"You're not allergic to anything are you? I asked your parents already, but I just want to be sure."

"Nope, Wy's appetite isn't as big as mine, but we can eat anything. Trust me, I've tried."

-

Five minutes later, Molly breezed through the door just as fabulous as she was that morning. The kids tried to scurry away, but she caught them just in time. "How was your day, kids?"

"It was great, mom! Serena's the best," Ronald answered with alacrity.

"I agree," Wag added in her usual timid voice.

"What did you all do?" Molly asked more to me than to them. The kids took the moment to sequester themselves somewhere upstairs.

"It was a pretty chill day. We played here most of the time. I like working with them."

"Well, isn't that great to hear?" Molly beamed.

"How was your day?"

"Busy. I had meetings all day. I needed to prep for summer courses as well."

"I don't envy you. Did you get everything done?" I asked genuinely curious.

"I wish. Lucky me, I brought my work home. Yay!" she cheered sarcastically, setting her purse down on the counter. "I see you cleaned up in here. Thanks. You're a doll... What did the kids eat today?"

"For breakfast, we did pancake-"

"You didn't use a lot of butter, did you?" She suddenly panicked and checked the fridge. "Serena, please don't use a lot of butter when cooking. It's not good for the kids. What else did they eat?"

"They had sandwiches for lunch…They liked the pancakes, but I can reduce the butter more if that makes you feel better. I didn't try to use a lot though."

"Thank you." She looked genuinely relieved.

"What do you consider a lot of butter though? Just so there's no issue."

"Just a thin sliver is enough. I can cut the butter into appropriately sized squares if you need me to. Maybe using cooking spray would be healthier," she spoke to herself.

"But that is a good segue into my next question."

"What is it?" she asked instantly stressed.

"Can I buy some fun snacks for the kids? They told me they've never tried Froot Loops. I can get them some Scooby Doo graham crackers, potato chips, maybe some Capri Suns. It doesn't have to be a daily thing. I can reward them with candy when they have really good days. Just to spice up the variety."

"I don't want them coming to depend on candy at the end of the day. I also don't want them consuming so much sugar, butter either. They have Honest juices in the cupboard. I think they're fine with what they have. Thanks though," she replied without thinking about it.

"Those juices taste like when ice melts in your pop. Have you tried them?" I made a repulsed face. "I just wanted them to have some tastier options. I didn't mean to overstep. It was something the kids brought to my attention, so I told them I'd run it by you. Now that we talked, I'm going to head out. I'll see you tomorrow."

"See you later," Molly said from her seat at the island in the kitchen. She didn't bother to walk me to the door. Ever so faithful Max came running from his hiding spot in the house and barked at me before I could leave.

"See you, Maxie." I petted his head and closed the door behind me. A wave of anxiety followed me. I thought maybe it would subside once I threw the bag of empty candy wrappers away.

-

"What does the lady have against Capri Suns though?" Maakara asked defensively.

"She was just very weird about sugar."

"And butter obviously. I'm not saying the kids should have eaten that stuff all the time, but damn they deserved SOMETHING that tasted good," Maakara continued.

"Yeah, I think if they were on the heavier side I would have felt better, but they were clearly underweight. Something in their diet needed to change."

"But even if they were chubby kids, I don't think that means they could never have chips or sweets."

"I totally agree. But their mother felt the way she felt." Serena shrugged.

"What did you do about it?"

Revelation

The next day with the Guptas brought a more optimistic attitude from Molly. "I thought about what you said yesterday, and I let the kids have some chips and salsa as a snack."

"That's great!" I exclaimed.

"I know but it's so bad for them!" she said regretfully.

"Is it?"

"Oh my god, the salt! You wouldn't believe it," she replied theatrically.

"I guess I had never viewed tortilla chips as unhealthy but okay."

"Trust me."

"If the kids can't have that because it's unhealthy then what can they have?" I asked.

"Veggie straws are their favorite, but they aren't healthy either, just not as bad as chips. They like carrots, applesauce, dehydrated mangos, or raisins," she rattled off the snacks while counting on her fingers.

"Do they like them? Or do they eat what they're offered?" I couldn't resist asking.

"What do you mean?"

"I'm curious to know when the last time was you saw them excited about food. Wyandanch hasn't seemed interested when I've made her meals. I'm worried she's not eating enough."

"They eat just fine. They need to learn to eat for nourishment, not for happiness," Molly said firmly.

"Nourishment is important for sure," I agreed. "I just don't think it would be horrible for them to try sugary or salty foods on occasion... if it would help with Wyandanch's appetite, I mean. Or maybe there's another option I'm not aware of. I can look into it," I offered. "This isn't the first kid I've worked with that refused to eat, so I do want to help in any way I can. I think I get that from my grandmother. She loved feeding people."

"It's just so bad for them!" Molly whined ignoring everything else I said.

"Speaking of the kids, is there anything they want to do today?" I changed the subject.

"Maybe check out a museum. But I do need you to go through their clothes and make a pile of what doesn't fit anymore."

"I can do that."

"Oh, and the kids should be doing this, but could you just make sure they feed Max in the evenings? He only needs to be fed enough hard food to cover the bottom of the bowl," Molly mentioned.

"Okay. Anything else?"

"No. Museum membership stuff is in the drawer by the garbage."

"Great. See you later."

As Molly headed out of the back door, I climbed the stairs to go through the kids' old clothes while they were upstairs, just in case they needed to try anything on. "Morning Serena," Ron greeted with a toothbrush in his mouth.

"Hey, how are you?"

"I'm great. What's for breakfast today?"

"First you need to sort through your clothes. Make a pile of what doesn't fit. Then you can eat. I need to help your sister. Which room is hers?" He pointed to another door in his bathroom. I knocked on it and entered. The other side was a room fit for a princess. It was sky blue with clouds and stars on every wall and the ceiling. There was a gorgeous white canopy bed that any woman would be envious of. Wag's room was spotless unlike her brother's. She came out of her closet half-naked with her outfit of the day in her hands. I couldn't help noticing how apparent her clavicle was.

"Hey, Wag."

"Oh!" She jumped. "Hey! You scared me." She covered her chest with her clothes but not before I saw her pronounced ribs.

"Sorry, your brother told me you were in here. You want me to step out for a second?"

"No, it's okay," she said preparing to put her shirt on.

"Before you get dressed, let me quickly go through your clothes to see what still fits."

I walked to her dresser and started with her t-shirts in the top drawer; the size of them confused me. They had to be mismarked.

-

Wag was nine. There was no way she should still have been able to fit 5T shirts. Holding them up, I could tell they still fit her slight frame. I didn't bother to make her try them on. Next were the pants. Wag should have been wearing about a size 7/8 in pants since she was small for her age. Unfortunately, most of her jeans were a size 6 slim.

"These are my favorites!" Wag announced happily grabbing her black jeans with white glitter all over.

"Can you still fit into them?" I held them up to her.

"I hope so!"

"Okay, try them on." I hoped they were too small.

Wag slipped her slight legs in the pants effortlessly. The only problem with them was that they weren't long enough. "I'm sorry Wag. Those are way too short. I can see your ankles."

"Nooo," she pouted.

"I won't throw them out, but your mom might not want you wearing them."

"Hmmm let's see if we can turn them into shorts," Wag suggested.

"Yeah, that's a good idea."

After 10 minutes of trying on clothes, it was clear that 5T shorts fit her the best. Her one pair of size 6X jeans were too big around her waist, but they were long enough around the ankles. I wasn't sure if I should have been as worried about Wag's size as I was. She wasn't being deprived of food. I knew her parents cared about her. Even with heartier meals, she could still be naturally thin like her mother so maybe I was overreacting.

"Alright. Let me go check on your brother."

-

"I'm almost done. I'm ready to eat Serena!" Ron informed as soon as I entered his room. He threw on a new pair of jeans that fit him similarly to Wag's. The ultra-skinny fit emphasized his scrawny thighs.

"What size are those pants?" I asked hesitantly.

He took them off in the bathroom and inspected the tag.

"Ummm it says nine."

"Nine?"

"Yeah," he replied unconcerned.

Then I was worried. At age 12, he should have been wearing a size 12 or at least a 10.

-

"Wait, so the kids could fit clothes 3 sizes too small for them?" Maakara asked for clarity.

"Yes. It scared the hell out of me. Anybody could see how small they were without knowing their sizes."

"And their parents weren't phased by it?" Maakara asked.

"Honestly, I started to think the mom preferred the kids to be thin whether they were healthy or not."

-

The kids enjoyed another breakfast consisting of pancakes. I make a few turkey sausages to go with them. "How do you like them Wag?" I checked in.

"They're good. Thanks." She smiled and looked down at her plate like Max had pooped on it. Ron's cheeks were stuffed with way too much food.

"Ron, clearly I don't need to ask you if you like it or not. What do you guys want to do today?"

-

The kids and I journeyed to Harold Washington Park to enjoy the weather. There was plenty of grass, a big jungle gym, and a water feature, which immediately caught the kids' attention in the sweltering heat. Luckily, I was proactive and brought towels and spare clothes just in case they needed them. Both kids ran right for the water feature, abandoning their original desire to play catch. I slipped off my sandals to cool off my feet in the water.

"I'm still hot!" Ron shouted and snatched off his shirt revealing his bird chest. His ribcage was not quite as apparent as his sister's, but it was enough for me to want to talk to Molly about their diet again. If she didn't listen, I'd just have to do what I could to help the kids gain weight. I was uncomfortable having the conversation so quickly after the last one, but I felt I had good reason to broach the subject.

"How hot do you guys think it is today?" I squinted up at the sun.

"300 degrees!" Ron yelled as he ran through the sprinklers.

"Ronald, don't be silly. It's probably in the nineties," Wag remarked sounding like the older sister.

"But it does feel like it's about 300 though, Wy!" Ron griped as the water pelted his skin.

"It is pretty hot!" Wag shrieked and zoomed through the sprinklers as Ron tried to head-butt her.

"You guys are so silly. I'm going to get on the swings for a little while. I'll be over there." I pointed in the general direction.

"Okay!" The kids yelled in unison chasing each other in a circle.

Walking away, I looked forward to drying off just to get back in the sprinklers. I could already tell I was going to get an awesome tan in that weather. If I could get the kids to soak up just as much food as they did sun then it might have been the perfect summer.

Just as I swung high enough to rattle the swing set, my phone buzzed. A message from Jabari.

-*This marriage is not going to work.*

What's going on?

I typed awkwardly as I maneuvered on the swing so I wouldn't fall off. My phone rang instantly.

"What's going on?" I asked again.

"Can you talk?" Jabari sounded frazzled.

"Yeah, what's up?" I asked trying to reduce my speed.

"Emily wants to move out after her six-week check-up. She wants to leave the kids with me and see them on weekends. She doesn't want to raise them together for the first year anymore," Jabari finished aggravated.

"What changed?"

"She hates my guts. That's what."

"According to you, she hasn't been feeling you for a long time. What made her conclude this all of a sudden? Nothing?" I wanted the full truth.

"Honestly, I think it's dawning on her that our marriage is ending. She became a mother for me. So now that the marriage is over, she's ready to start fresh. I wanted the kids, so I have to raise them in her mind," Jabari analyzed.

"I understand she needs her space," I sympathized. "But I'd hope you all could do joint custody at some point."

"She's not interested. How can I be married to a woman who pulls this?" Jabari asked hopelessly.

"Sounds like you won't be married for long unfortunately. But I do hope that she co-parents with you longer than six weeks. It's a such a precious time for infants."

"I'm not sure I can get through to her," Jabari said apparently defeated.

"You have to try. It could just be her hormones talking. But if not, you are capable of doing it on your own. Single mothers do it all the time. Luckily for you, you have the finances to hire help and pay for daycare."

"I guess so. If I need you to help out a single dad with two kids, will you?"

"You just won't quit." I shook my head through the phone. "But I'm not opposed to helping out if I'm needed."

"That's good to hear. This won't be so bad then huh?" I could hear him smiling.

-

"That man was using every tactic to get you girl." Maakara raised her eyebrow at Serena.

"Gee, you think?" Serena asked sarcastically.

-

After two and a half hours at the scorching hot playground, Wag, Ronald and I got into my car with huge appetites. As I drove, I had an idea. Instead of driving back home immediately, I stopped at the McDonald's in Hyde Park.

"What do you all want?" I asked in the drive-thru.

"We've never been here before," Wag said in a nervously.

"I'll order for you all," I replied keeping the shock out of my voice. I ordered Wag a happy meal with nuggets and Ron a Big Mac. It wasn't so bad if they had fast food every now and then, was it? I handed the kids their food, and they wasted no time digging in as I drove them home.

"How do you guys like it?" I asked peering in the rearview mirror.

"It's delicious," Wag mumbled stuffing fries into her mouth.

"Yeah, McDonald's has amazing fries. I don't eat anything else on the menu. I knew you'd like them." I grinned.

"I love burgers. I'm starving," Ron added in between bites.

The Secret

The kids were done with their lunch by the time we arrived at their house. I thought it would be best if they left their trash in my car. No need to freak out their mother. "Guys, leave your garbage in here. Your mom doesn't need to see this, does she?"

"Nope," Ron pronounced happily.

"I'm not going to tell her anything!" Wag said energetically.

"Guys we can't make a habit out of it, but sometimes we can eat at places that are much better than McDonald's. It'll be our little secret okay?" They nodded in silent agreement.

"I'll eventually get you all some snacks for the car too. Cool?"

"Perfect!"

"Awesome!"

"Alright, let's head inside. We'll wash up then relax for a while." I unlocked the car doors.

Once inside, the kids went right up to their bedrooms. I laid on the couch while I had a moment to myself. Before I knew it, Wag was shaking me awake. "I didn't even realize I was sleepy." I sat up groggily. "How long were you upstairs? What's wrong?"

"Only for like five minutes."

"Good. Um Wag," I paused confused by her appearance. "Why are you still wearing the same clothes?"

"I washed up first, and they didn't look dirty, so I put them back on."

"When you shower, you should put fresh clothes on, baby. Otherwise, you're just putting dirty clothes on a clean body," I told her.

"But I put clean clothes on all the time even when I haven't showered. What's the difference?"

"Why would you put clean clothes on a dirty body?" I asked puzzled.

"Mom says we don't need to shower every day," she admitted plainly.

"When was the last time you showered before today?"

"Saturday, I think?"

"You think? For three days you've been putting new clothes on your unwashed body?" I was bewildered.

"Mom doesn't care." Wag shrugged.

"Had I known that, I would've told you all to shower yesterday! You have to bathe every day especially when you leave the house and get dirty," I informed her taken aback by her nonchalance.

"I didn't know." She looked wounded by my tone.

"I know. I just needed you to," I said softly.

"You shower every day, Serena?"

"Of course. Every morning before I come to work. Imagine if I didn't, how stinky I would be." I held up my arm pit then sniffed and made a face.

"Well..." she hesitated in deep thought. "You were right about the food, so if you say I need to shower and put on clean clothes, then I'll do it."

"I'm a sucker for compliments. You might just get all the snacks you want out of me, little girl," I playfully warned.

"Good to know." Wag giggled. "I'm going to change my clothes."

"Okay wash up again then change your clothes!" I called to her back as Ron made his way down the stairs. "Hold it! You have on new clothes which is good. But did you shower first?"

"Um no..." he faltered.

"When you want to get clean, you have to wash your body with soap and warm water then put clean clothes on. Got it?" I instructed assertively.

"Got it," he said looking confused at the sudden lecture.

"Sorry. I just had the same conversation with your sister. Y'all should be practicing good hygiene. I'll talk to your mom about it later. I didn't mean to snap at you."

"It's okay." He looked relieved.

"Go wash up then come back down with clean clothes on."

"Okay."

"Hey, Ron?" I called out, a thought occurring to me.

"Yeah?" he turned around.

"Do I need to tell you to brush your teeth EVERY morning too? Or you got that?"

-

After what seemed like forever, Molly came home. Max ran to greet her like he hadn't seen her in centuries. "Hey, Maxie. How was your day, boy?" She reached down and stroked his ear.

"He had a good day. We all did. Didn't we guys?" I faced the kids.

"Yeah, mom. We went to the park and got soaking wet," Wag chimed in sounding more her own age.

"It was fun," Ron added for good measure.

"Excellent. I'm glad things are going so well. What did you guys eat today?" Molly tried to ask casually.

"Serena made us sandwiches. Nothing major," Ron answered mimicking his mother's casual tone. Molly hustled over to the fridge to check.

"Hey Molly, before I go, I want to mention a couple of things." I changed the subject.

"What is it?" Worry spread across her face.

"Nothing bad. I wanted to follow up about the kid's clothes."

"Oh okay!" she said clearly relieved.

"I sorted them. But I did notice something. And I'm not sure if I should be worried about it or not."

"What's that?"

"Hey guys, can I talk to your mom alone for a minute?" Without a word, the kids obeyed.

"The kids seem to be able to fit clothes that should be too small for them. Wyandanch can still fit size 6 pants and 5T shorts and shirts. Ronald can somehow get into size nine pants even though they're too short." I took a breath before continuing. "At the park today, when the kids ran through the sprinklers, their clothes clung to their bodies, so you could really see how slim they are. When Ronald took his shirt off, I could see his ribs. The same happened when I saw Wyandanch change her clothes this morning. I could see her clavicle. Is their weight something I should be concerned about?"

"Oh, I wouldn't worry about it. They're just picky eaters and thin like me." Molly brushed it off a little too easily.

"Okay... The next thing is hygiene. Was I supposed to be making sure the kids bathed and brushed teeth every day? I assumed when they came downstairs in the mornings that they were already clean."

"We're pretty lax about bathing. They don't smell. They aren't that dirty. We usually make them bathe every few days or so unless they are filthy. But they should be brushing their teeth every day for sure."

"Okay, I did see Ron brushing his teeth, but I just wanted to be sure that he knew to do it everyday." I made a mental note to make sure they bathed more often. "Oh, and they haven't fed the dog yet," I informed gathering my belongings.

"Thanks. We'll see you tomorrow."

"See you." I headed out of the door feeling a little less weighed down.

-

By the end of my first week; I had fed the kids fast food three times, and I didn't feel as guilty as I should have. To cover our tracks, the kids and I are rationed food from the refrigerator for me to take to the homeless people under the viaduct on 51st street. I wondered how long we could keep it up. My fear was one of the kids getting sick, which would force me to admit what we'd been doing.

The excitement on their faces showed me that they had been missing out. They needed to know there was more to life than tasteless low-fat food. One day, I planned to bring them fried chicken, greens and cornbread, and my grandma's famous spaghetti. I believed there were a lot of ways I could introduce them to delicious foods that also had the fats they needed. Balancing those foods with their mom's healthy ones should have helped them gain weight and stay healthy.

"Hey, you guys want to check out the Shedd aquarium Monday?" I asked during a game of Connect Four.

"As long as we get a treat, I'll do anything you say," Ron answered just before he made the exact wrong move in the game.

"You're addicted to sugar little boy. I'm cutting you off," I told him as I connected four red pieces.

"No! Please don't cut me off!" He hopped up, knocking over our game and grabbing my arm in a desperately playful way.

"Then stop acting like a mad man." I shook him off.

"I will. I swear!"

"We have an ant problem!" Molly announced Monday morning in a total frenzy.

"Oh okay. Where?" I asked unsettled by her demeanor.

"In Ron's room. Mostly under his bed. Apparently, he had an old candy bar under there for God knows how long. Exactly why he doesn't need sweets."

"All you found was a candy bar?" I asked worried Ron's cover was blown.

"Yep. I guess the crumbs attracted the ants. For now, I put down ant traps. I also sprayed vinegar and water under there. Let me know if you see anymore anywhere else, k?"

"Sure will. I'm glad it's only ants and not..." My voice trailed off thinking of roaches and rats. I shuddered at the thought.

"Yeah, I know." Molly blanched. "I'm going to get out of here. Rohit will be the one relieving you tonight."

"Okay. Have a good one." I realized I hadn't seen her husband since I started.

"You too." She left appearing to have the weight of the world on her bony shoulders.

"Ron?!" I called as soon as Molly closed the door. He ran down the stairs immediately like he had been waiting at the top. "What happened in your room?" I asked urgently.

"I woke up this morning and went to get a snack from my suitcase stash." He looked at his feet as he spoke. "That's when I noticed the ants. I called my mom before thinking of a way to explain them; I put a bar and some crumbs on the floor under the bed then moved the suitcase so she wouldn't look inside."

"That was clever of you," I reluctantly admitted.

"I thought so too," he said looking pleased with himself. "I told mom that I can't remember how the bar got there, but of course she was suspicious anyway."

"At least you covered yourself well."

"She's totally flipping out."

"Maybe if you guys could have treats more often, you wouldn't hoard food the way you do," I retorted. "Listen, you have to be careful. Don't leave open food out. If you don't finish it, then give it to me, and I'll toss it. Keep this up and your mom is going to find your stash."

"You're right," Ron said disappointed in himself.

"And why are you waking up eating Kit Kats? You can't wait until the afternoon?"

"It wasn't a Kit Kat. It was a Snickers."

"That explains it then," I quipped sarcastically. "Little boy, be careful or I'm going to confiscate it myself," I scolded.

"Okay, okay. Fine. I'll do better." Ron huffed.

"Snickers are my favorite too though." I smirked at him. "Go finish getting ready."

-

Later in the afternoon, the kids and I lounged in the living room after a busy day at the Shedd Aquarium. Just as I closed my eyes in an attempt to get comfortable, I detected the smell of poop. I opened them to find the source of the smell. "Ron, what's that?" I pointed to the small pile under an end table.

"Looks like dog poop." He peered underneath to get a closer look.

"Clean it up then," I ordered.

"Gross. No way," Ron refused.

"Wag? Can you come and clean this up?"

"Ew," she mimicked her brother's sentiments.

"This is you all's dog. Who's going to get this up?"

"Not me!" the kids yelled in unison.

"Okay fine. I'll just let your mom know it's there." I snapped a picture and sent it to Molly.

Max pooped on the floor. The kids refuse to clean it up. Just letting you know.

-Oh my gosh! Serena, can you pick it up?

No, but I'll bribe one of the kids to do it.

-And if they don't, can you do it? They aren't comfortable so we don't always make them.

If it was kid poop, of course I would do it. Seeing as though we're talking about a dog, this is out of my job description.

-Please? I'm worried about the floors.

The floors? This dog belongs to your kids. If you don't make them clean up after it, then why would I? I'm an adult and the dog is not my responsibility.

-I know, but there are going to be things that you have to do that you aren't comfortable doing sometimes.

Should I have the kids call you so you can tell them this?

Molly didn't respond, so the poop was left there until Rohit got home to deal with it. I wished Molly was coming home so we could discuss it face to face. I wasn't going to force the kids to pick up their own dog's poop if she wasn't even forcing them to herself. I especially didn't care if she respected her kids' discomfort for their own dog over mine.

-

"Hello?! Did anyone pick up the poop?!" Molly shrilled neurotically, walking in the door at 5:00.

"No, the kids wouldn't do it." I took in their shameful expressions. "I thought Rohit was relieving me today."

"I rushed home. I was anxious...I asked you to clean it if they refused, Serena."

"And I told you I don't clean up dog poop, Molly. Especially poop that the owners themselves refuse to clean up. It's not my job. It never will be," I concluded firmly.

"I just wish you would work with me."

"I just wish your kids knew that the dog is their responsibility when you're not here."

"Uh! Fine!" She threw her hands up in frustration as Rohit walked through the door.

"Hey, what's going on? What was so urgent?" he asked.

"Well apparently Maxie pooped on the floor, and Serena wouldn't clean it up. The kids wouldn't either. I'm worried it'll ruin the floors." Molly groaned on the verge of tears.

"Did you clean it up when you got home? I'm confused. What did you expect me to do?" Rohit asked his wife.

"I wanted Serena to understand that she might have to clean it up sometimes. She refuses to, even though she knows the kids won't do it."

"And I'm letting both of you know now that I don't clean up dog poop. I'm willing to clean up anything relevant to the kids, but I draw the line at dogs."

"And you shouldn't have to do that, Serena." Rohit turned to Molly. "The kids need to clean up after their dog. That is not a part of Serena's job. You're so concerned about the floors, but you didn't clean up the poop." He went to the counter to get paper towels and handed a few to both kids. "Clean it up. Don't give your mother or Serena a hard time about this again. Got it?" Without a word, the kids scurried to do as they were told.

"I'm sorry... she wanted you to clean dog shit for a dog that wasn't your responsibility?" Maakara asked dumbfounded.

"Yeah, her entitlement rubbed me the absolute wrong way that day," Serena admitted.

"A dog that belonged to her children who she didn't force to clean up?" Maakara asked.

"You understood correctly," Serena told her.

"She was bold as hell and way too comfortable." Maakara rolled her eyes.

-

Molly gave me an unusually terse greeting the following morning. "Good morning Serena."

"Good morning Molly." I matched her energy. "Is there anything you want me to do with the kids today?"

"Nope. You can do what you want," she replied tartly before leaving out of the back door.

-

"Do you all want me to add cheese to your eggs?" I asked when the kids finally came down fully dressed

"No," Wag answered taking a seat at the island.

"Yeah sure," Ron said less enthusiastically than usual. "We have something to tell you." He joined his sister.

"What is it?" I asked pouring the eggs in the skillet.

"We want to say sorry for being difficult yesterday. We should have cleaned up Max's poop," Wag stated.

"And I'm sorry we made things awkward between you and our parents." Ron walked to the stove and hugged me from the side.

"I guess I can forgive you two." I hugged him back. "You guys can make this right by eating all your food this morning. And if you're good, I'll take you to Harold's for lunch."

"Who is Harold?" they asked in unison.

"Excuse me?"

"Who is Harold?" Wag repeated.

"Harold's is a famous Chicago chicken joint! Known for it's mild sauce, duh! Were you guys born in Chicago or not?" I was frustrated that they didn't know what I was talking about.

"Never heard of it," Ron confirmed.

"I assume you guys also never had Nick's? Italian fiesta? Portillos?"

"No, but can we try those too?" Ron asked greedily.

"You can count on it." I smiled and ruffled his hair.

"Serena?" called Wag.

"Yeah?" I turned sausages over in the skillet without looking up.

"Thank you."

"For what babe?" I turned to face her.

"For letting me try different food."

"You're welcome. I know you still might not eat a lot, but I at least want to expose you to new things, not get you hooked like your brother." I jerked my head in Ron's direction. Wag giggled and hugged me from behind.

-

The Museum of Science and Industry was the field trip selection for the day. The cool interior was a reprieve from the unbearable heat. The first stop was my favorite display: the Swiss Jolly Ball. Watching that metallic ball roll from the hotel to the bank to the phone booth had fascinated me since I was a kid. Wag and Ron seem to enjoy it but not as much as me. I had to pull myself away before it restarted.

"Okay, guys. What do you want to check out next?"

"I need to see the princess castle," Wag stated as if her life depended on it.

"I want to see the airplane," Ron followed up.

"Princess castle first then the airplane. Let's go."

Colleen Moore's fairy castle was more impressive every time I saw it. The intricate details in each room were unmatched. As grand as the dining room artwork and furniture resembling King Arthur's round table were, it was nowhere near as breathtaking as the Great Hall. The spiral staircase, high ceilings, and chandeliers highlighted the exquisite room. I wasn't a fairy princess kind of girl, but it was hard not to appreciate the artwork in the dollhouse-sized castle.

"This is the most beautiful thing I've ever seen," Wag openly marveled.

"How many times have you seen this before?"

"A bunch, but it's just so pretty." She dreamily stared at the tiny kitchen.

"I understand. I love the pinball machine. There's just something about it that draws me to it."

"Can we go to the airplane now?" Ron interrupted impatiently.

"We're going to stay here until Wag is ready to peel herself away," I told him.

"Fine." He pouted.

Twenty minutes later, we boarded the United Airlines Boeing 727. It took me back to when my three-year-old self saw it for the first time. The cockpit, the technology, the seats were all the same. The difference that time was that an actual pilot was answering all of the visitor's questions. He was a white man in his 60s with a gray beard and pilot's uniform.

"I want to be a pilot when I grow up!" Ron exclaimed. His enthusiasm almost rivaled his love for sweets.

"You would make an excellent pilot. You want to ask him any questions?" He hesitated a moment then marched over to the pilot and asked a question I thought I knew the answer to.

"If I wear glasses, can I still be a pilot?"

"You sure can. But you should always bring back up contacts or glasses when you need to fly," the pilot told us pedagogically.

"How long have you been a pilot?" Ronald followed up.

"A long time. 30 years. I'm retired now."

"Wicked!" Ronald complimented reminding me of his namesake. "Maybe one day I'll be standing in the same spot as you."

"Good luck, son." The pilot patted Ron's shoulder and walked away.

After an eventful morning, I decided to take a trip to Nick's Gyros on 63rd and Damen. It was way past time for the kids to try a pizza puff for the first time. They needed to try the true delicacies of Chicago.

"What's this place?" Wag asked as we walked through the doors.

"Nick's, best fries and sauce in town. I've been eating here since I was little. It used to be in that small place across the street." I pointed towards the building on the corner. "But they expanded. Luckily the quality of the food wasn't compromised. You guys have never had pizza puffs, right?"

"No. What are those?" Ron asked, and I rolled my eyes in frustration.

"You guys can be so annoying sometimes." I pretended to strangle him. "Never mind. I'll order for you. I want you to try their pizza too."

-

The car ride home was cloaked in silence. The kids inhaled their food even though it burned their tongues. "I loved the sauce on the fries. It's different," Wag said once we pulled up to the house.

"It's my favorite. I'm glad you liked it." I turned to watch them from the driver's seat.

"The pizza puff was good. My mom would never let me have one of those," Ron piped up.

"Yeah, they're pretty good. Next time you'll have to try it with mild sauce. And you can buy eight frozen pizza puffs from the grocery store and make your own at home."

"When I have my own money, I'm going to buy all the food I want. But for now, I'll just eat whatever you get me."

"Me too," Wag chimed in.

"You guys are just using me for food!" I shook my head in faux disappointment.

"No! We really do like you!" they screamed in unison.

The Oversight

Days later on a particularly warm Friday, the late June breeze blew in, bringing a heated Molly along with it. "Serena? I just walked by your car and saw food wrappers inside. Have you been feeding that junk to my kids the last two weeks?" She checked the fridge for the amount of groceries leftover.

"We had burgers and fries today," I admitted deciding the best thing to do was tell the truth.

"And other days?" Her face reddened.

"This was their first time going to that place." I looked at the sad, shocked faces of Ron and Wag. The truth was we ate out every day that week; we just hadn't tried Portillo's until that specific afternoon.

"WHAT ELSE HAVE YOU GUYS HAD?" She paused after every word glaring at her kids. The kids responded with silence.

"What else?" She looked back at me.

"Nothing else," Ron cut in.

"I don't believe you. Serena, I suspect you're the one who gave him that candy in his room," Molly accused.

"I didn't give him that!" I defended guiltily.

"What did you give him?"

"She didn't give us anything mom!" Wag interjected.

"We begged her to give us some different food, so she treated us Portillo's. And we loved it!" Ron screeched. "Mom you never let us have good food! Serena told me you can buy packs of frozen pizza puffs. Please buy them for us and try one! I know you'll like it. I know you want us to eat healthily, but we're hungry! Your food is not good!" Ron's voice broke.

"I'm not buying you all pizza puffs. Whatever those are." Molly was repulsed at the idea.

"Mom, we are underweight." Ron gained control of his voice and spoke slowly as if to a child. "Serena is worried about us. She tried to hide it last week when she checked to see if our clothes still fit, but she didn't do a good job. Sorry, Serena." He chanced a look in my direction. "Mom, she made us happy letting us get those burgers. Please don't be mad at her. We love you, but we want to eat more stuff than you let us. Your food is always so healthy. The bread has grains in it. There's no way you think that tastes good. I think you like being able to say we're thin like you. But maybe we're supposed to be a little heavier like dad. Is that so bad?"

"No! Your father agrees with me on this." At those words, Rohit came through the back door.

"What's going on here?" He set his briefcase on the kitchen counter.

"Serena has been giving the kids unhealthy foods. They only admit to doing it today, but there's no telling how many times this has happened in the last two weeks. I only found out because something told me to check her car. I had a feeling that something was off."

"If the kids ate then I don't have a problem with that," Rohit responded patronizingly calm.

"Really honey!?" Molly looked around for some support. "That stuff is not good for them! I should have installed a camera! The food in the kitchen is depleted just enough for me not to suspect anything. Rohit, don't you see? She's been feeding our kids unknown foods! She put them in danger."

"I wouldn't do that Molly. The kids don't have allergies," I weakly offered.

"Serena likes us, mom! She's not trying to hurt us!" Ronald said in a shrill voice.

"I don't think Serena intends to put them in danger Molly. What is the harm in them having fast food occasionally?" Rohit asked.

"I said they couldn't have it. She gave it to them anyway. She disobeyed my instructions. She disregarded my wishes. She has to go. Serena let's make this your last day. Rohit, send her payment now. Serena, please leave," Molly dismissed me.

"Not a problem. It's been nice knowing you all. I'm sorry for upsetting you." I picked up my bag and headed for the door. Wag beat me to it.

"Thank you for everything," she said with tears in her eyes.

"Thank you," Ron added in a somber tone. Both kids hugged me.

"Good luck guys. Goodbye." I shut the door behind me tightly.

Before I made it to the front gate, I whipped out my phone to text Jabari.

Are you all still looking for a nanny?

-I was hoping you'd change your mind

-

"Damn girl. You really got fired? At least you had good intentions for the kids though." Maakara opened a pack of Starburst.

"I did. I would have kept it up had she never found out."

"Maybe it wasn't the best decision to make on your part, but I totally understand why you did it. Those kids were way too small. I wish you had stayed long enough to feed the whole family some of your grandma's cooking! I know that would have changed Molly's mind." Maakara chewed the lemon flavor.

"It most definitely would have."

"Now back to you and this married guy…"

Playing with Matches

Once home, I ran a hot bath and replayed the day's events in my mind as I undressed. Maybe I was wrong for feeding the kids junk food. I knew it was against Molly's wishes, but the kids needed it. If she was concerned about health like she claimed to be, then she would have been worried about their weight. At least they got to try some popular foods from their hometown… even if that meant not seeing the kids again. I wished them the best.

Easing into the steaming bath, I closed my eyes intending to relax until dinner time. I had about two minutes to myself before the silence was shattered by the sound of my ringtone. "Hello?" I put the caller on speaker.

"Hey," Jabari's deep voice greeted me warmly, relieving some of my stress.

"Hey there." I sank deeper into the tub.

"How are you?"

"A little stressed, to be honest."

"What's going on?"

"I got fired today," I confessed.

"What the hell? Are you serious?" He sounded stunned.

"Yep."

"What happened?"

"The mother found out I gave the kids fast food," I answered simply.

"Why did you get fired though?" Jabari asked confused.

"She is very weird about their diet. They aren't allergic to anything, but she felt everything was unhealthy for them. The kids are underweight, so I fed them treats when she wasn't around. They had never had a pizza puff before. Can you believe that?"

"When you say underweight, how bad is it?" Jabari asked fearfully.

"I could see the girl's rib cage. She's nine and could fit size 6 pants and 5T shorts and shirts. The boy is 12 and can fit into size nine jeans. The pants are too short on them, but they fit around the waist."

"Shouldn't five-year-olds wear 5T shorts?"

"Something like that. I can understand a six-year-old wearing them too, but nine is pushing it. I'm not trying to say the kids are being starved, but they do need to gain some weight. Their mom is on this extreme health kick, and she's not a good cook according to the kids. They were tired of her cooking, so I introduced them to some different foods. I just wanted them to gain weight, honestly. I know it was wrong, but I don't regret it. Do you know they had never had Harold's or Portillo's before? Like how the hell are they even from Chicago and had never had mild sauce? It's blasphemy!" I screamed dramatically.

"I'm inclined to agree with you there," Jabari said flatly.

"Thank you! I knew I wasn't overreacting. It was worth it. I hope they have healthy relationships with food in the future though."

"You're ready to come over to the dark side then huh?" Jabari asked with a laugh.

"Jabari..."

"I admit that was pretty corny. Let me rephrase. So, you're finally ready to give me a chance?"

"I'm ready to give working for your family another chance," I said emphasizing the word family.

"That's what I meant," he lied.

"Well, I need a job. I've been struggling for way too long to find a good long-term family. Maybe it can be you all."

"We'd love to have you start with us. How does July 13 sound? Emily is due in two weeks. We're going to need someone to help us around the house. I'd love to have you."

"I'm sure you would." I rolled my eyes but felt turned on at the same time. "Should I call Emily myself and talk to her about my start date?"

"There's no need. Emily is... feeling cranky these days. I'll handle it," he answered suspiciously.

"I want to talk to her about this," I pressed.

"Why? You didn't feel the need to talk to me when you first met Emily, did you?"

"I did not. But I didn't have access to you then. I have access to both parents now. And I'm always more comfortable talking to the mothers. I think they're more thorough and not usually attracted to me if you know what I mean."

"You thought I was attracted to you this whole time? I was just being friendly," he joked.

"Oh, is that what that was?"

"Maybe I flirted a little. Can you blame me?"

"You're married with a small kid and another on the way, so yeah I can blame you. Look," I took a deep breath and shifted in the tub. "Are we going to be able to do this without crossing any lines?" I attempted to shake away the unprofessional thoughts creeping in.

"I can't speak for you, but I will do my best. I know it's been difficult for you to control yourself all this time," Jabari answered.

"Really?" I laughed. "You play too much. I'll be on my best behavior as always."

"Good. I don't need anything distracting me," he responded in a mock-serious tone.

"You are crazy. You know that?" My grin was wide enough to touch both of my ears.

"I try to keep things fun."

"Hey listen, thank you for this opportunity. I know I texted you last minute. I could have called you guys and done this in a more professional way. I feel like I'm already showing that I'm too comfortable with you... Maybe we shouldn't do this." I hesitated.

"It's not a problem. It'll be fine," Jabari reassured.

"I appreciate that, but I'm going to text Emily tomorrow to see if she wants to talk to me in detail. I need to start this out the right way, and I need you to be okay with that."

"I understand. To be honest with you, Emily may not care about any of this. She doesn't want to be a mom. But please do reach out to her if that will make you feel better."

"I will. Thank you. I'm going to go now before my bathwater gets too cold."

"You've been in the tub this whole time?" Jabari asked sounding intrigued.

"Goodnight Jabari!"

"Goodnight Serena." Silence filled the bathroom as I closed my eyes and replayed his voice in my head. Suddenly the water was steaming again.

-

Two important text messages welcomed me the next morning.

-Morning Serena! I told Emily to reach out to you to confirm that we both want you to start with us full-time. She said she would text you. Hope that makes you feel more at ease.

-Hey Serena. Jabari told me you want to work for us full-time. The 13th is fine. Call him to hammer out pay details.

Emily's early morning text was what I needed to see. Since I was attracted to her husband, I thought it was only fair to do everything by the book. I needed to communicate with her directly so there was no uncertainty or suspicion.

Hey Emily! Good to hear from you. Will do. Can't wait to see you all.

Hey Jabari. I talked to Emily. She raised an interesting point…

-What's that?

What are my new hours? She only said that I'd be full time.

-I'm not sure exactly. Let's try for 8:00-4:00. Cool?

That's fine. Is the rate still $15/hour?

-What would you like it to be?

Don't play with me.

-Lol, what? I was just asking.

Answer the question.

-Let's see. Before we paid you 12.50/hour. Now there will be two kids. Does $16 sound fair?

Throw in an extra $1.

-Lol, and why should I do that?

Consider it compensatory damages.

-For what???

For all the inappropriate behavior I'm going to experience daily on account of you.

-Better yet, let's make it $18/hour

That's what I thought.

"Were you sure you could handle working with him again?" Maakara asked apprehensively. "Definitely doesn't seem like you should have."

"Exactly." Serena pointed at her old friend knowingly. "But I still needed to move out of my mom's house. The rent was hard for us to manage, and I didn't want to move in with her boyfriend. I felt like I had already taken too long, so I did what I had to do."

The Atkinses... Again

The morning of July 13th dawned hot and bright. I wasn't sure if it was because I was excited to see Jabari or because it was just an unseasonably hot summer. Either way, it should have been a good day in spite of my conflicting emotions. I was thankful to have secured a new job so quickly, but a large part of me couldn't help but wonder if it was a bad idea. Could I be exclusively professional with Jabari? Should I take a break from work and move in with my mom and her boyfriend? During my commute to work that morning, I made a promise to myself that I would quit at the first hint of impropriety. If I didn't have my integrity, what did I have?

As I pulled up to the Atkins' condo building, the urge to glance in the rearview mirror overwhelmed me. I parked the car then checked my hair, which was in sleek cornrows so I knew it looked fine, but I still couldn't resist looking myself over completely. My nose, eyes, and teeth were clean. Skin was clear. I looked presentable. I nervously stuffed a stick of gum in my mouth as I rang the bell.

I took a deep breath to calm my nerves before pressing the buzzer. The trek to the third floor only made me more uneasy. A few more deep breaths and I was standing at the apartment door. Before I could knock, Jabari opened it shirtless, with a t-shirt draped over his shoulder. You'd think I would have been used to it by then, but the sight of him half-naked affected me more at that moment than it did the first time. His lips were moving, but I couldn't hear him.

"I'm sorry what?" I asked shaking the thoughts of out my mind.

"Emily's in labor," he stated plainly and walked away from the door, throwing his shirt over his head.

-

"What can I do to help?" I asked stepping inside the door taking my shoes off.

"As of now, just keep Ethan busy and calm," Jabari said assertively. "Emily's been in labor for about four hours. We're going to head to the hospital now."

"Got it." I nodded my head.

"Thanks." He walked away.

"I have one more question," I called to his back.

"What's up?" He turned around.

"How are you?" I met his eyes, which I always tried to avoid. To my surprise, he smiled at me causing heat to rush to my face.

"I'm okay. Thanks for asking." He walked towards me, squeezed my shoulder and hurried away. The scent of his light cologne lingered behind him. The beautiful vision that welcomed me at the door had distracted me from little Ethan who was sitting quietly on the floor of the living room. He was two by then, taller and thinner than he was the year before. Aside from his skin being shades lighter, his face mirrored his father's more than ever.

"Hey, Ethan! It's been a while. How have you been big boy?! Did you forget about me?"

"Hi," he mumbled quietly from the rug.

"Dang, you forgot about me already. That's okay. We'll just have to have a lot of fun today. What do you want to do?" I asked.

"Puzzle."

"Okay, where is it?" I squatted down to his level, and he pointed to the top of the bookshelf.

"I'll pick you up so you can get it. Stand up," I instructed.

Ethan got to his feet, and I grabbed him by the waist, hoisting him up. He giggled at his newfound height and grabbed the box from the bookcase. "MY puzzle! MY face!" he exclaimed.

I glanced down at the puzzle's lid. It showed a beautiful picture of his smiling parents holding an infant Ethan. "That is such a nice puzzle! It's only 50 pieces. I bet we can do this really fast. Let's try!" I encouraged.

"Yeah!" Ethan cheered as he dumped out all of the puzzle pieces and spread them out on the floor.

"Okay get ready. Set. Go!" I yelled.

Five minutes later, the puzzle was complete. Sadly, the picture didn't reflect how the family was in real life. They looked so happy just two years before. It was too bad the marriage had taken a turn for the worst.

Emily's sudden scream of anguish shattered my thoughts.

"Oh no," I said under my breath.

"What's wrong with mama?" Ethan asked, his eyes wide and fearful.

"Mama's stomach hurts. She's about to go to the hospital to have your little sister. Daddy is going to take her to the doctor to help her feel better. She'll be fine." I tried to soothe the little guy by sitting him on my lap.

I heard a sound in the hall and looked up. The unfortunate image of Emily struggling toward us undermined my previous statement. She was sweating profusely, and her limp brown hair was pulled back in a loose ponytail. Her gray t-shirt dress hung loosely over her large belly, and her face was contorted in pain. Jabari gingerly escorted her and her packed bags down the long hallway.

"Hey, Emily. Sorry to see you again under these circumstances, but at least you'll have a gorgeous baby girl when you get back home," I offered weakly.

"I hate this," she said uninterested in small talk. "Jabari, let's go. I need drugs, either that or someone is going to have to hit me over the head with a sledgehammer."

Jabari grimaced then said, "Serena, I'll be back at some point to pick up Ethan so he can meet his little sister. If anything happens, would you be willing to stay later?"

"Sure. No problem. Keep me posted."

"Oh, and we're potty-training Ethan so please make him use the bathroom often."

"Good luck Emily. You guys need any help?" I asked wanting to feel useful.

"No, just lock the door behind us please," Jabari requested as he ushered his wife through the door. I watched them walk down the stairs, and Jabari looked up with a tired smile.

-

Four hours later, while serving Ethan lunch, I received a picture of a pale wrinkly newborn covered in vernix. She didn't resemble her parents at all. I wasn't sure what to say about her appearance so I texted, *Congrats Poppa!*

-Thanks. Our new edition's name is Eden. Emily named Ethan so she left it up to me to name her.

Congrats. How's Emily?

-She's fine. Everything went smoothly. No stitches. She's napping now.

Who do you think Eden looks like?

-Neither of us Lol. But time will tell.

I thought the same thing. I'll send you a picture of Ethan in a second.

-Thanks. TTYL

I sent Jabari a picture of a sleepy Ethan eating his chicken nuggets. The little guy couldn't even finish his meal for nodding off so much. "Take another sip of your milk then we'll take a nap." The toddler obediently nodded his head and did as he was told.

"Let's go sit on the potty." I took his hand and guided him to the bathroom. He slid down his pull up, and I sat him on the toilet. He peed with his eyes closed. I wanted to celebrate his achievement, but he was much too tired, so I washed his little hands then carried him down the hall to his room. It had been updated since the last time I was there. He had a new racecar bed, but the rest of the room was the same. Once the little guy was under the covers, I closed the door behind myself.

Looking for something to do, I inspected the small kitchen. It was clean but cluttered with dishes. I put some of the plates and silverware back in their rightful places then I washed the ones I had used. Once the kitchen was in order, I moved to the living room to do the same, but curiosity got the best of me. Some invisible force pushed me to the master bedroom. I had never thought to check it out before. It was smaller than I expected it to be but neat nonetheless. Everything except the floor was completely white. The comforter on the bed was so full and soft looking that I was tempted to lay across it. I resisted then wandered over to the dressers. There were a couple of combs and brushes laying amongst a glasses case and loose coins. A bunch of miscellaneous bobby pins and earrings were scattered across both dressers. I wondered which bottle of cologne Jabari wore that morning.

The one thing that stood out was the wedding photo in a picture frame. I picked it up to take in the details. Jabari looked breathtaking in a black and white tuxedo. It highlighted his broad muscular shoulders and minimized his trim waist. Immediately to his left was Emily in a huge princess ball gown that swallowed her tiny frame. The dress was lovely, but it would have looked better on someone who wasn't so petite. Her hair was styled fittingly in a curly up-do accented with ivory flower petals. At closer inspection, I wasn't sure how happy they actually looked. They resembled a cake topper couple: strained smiles and forced poses.

I sat the frame down then glided over to the master bath. It was vastly spacious considering the size of the bedroom. The off-white tiling on the floors and walls complemented the white tub, his and her sinks, and see-through shower. It was the most remarkable room in the house by far. Jabari's red du-rag, Murray's wave grease, and razor were housed on his side of the sink. The same went for Emily's blow dryer, contact solution and hair spray on her side. I found no obvious signs of an unhappy couple. Having my fill of being super sleuth for the day, I left their room exactly as it was and decided to take a short nap with Ethan. I grabbed a throw blanket and pillow from the couch and settled on the floor next to the racecar bed. Before drifting off, I wondered what it would be like if my things were strewn along the countertops instead of Emily's.

-

"Crackers please," Ethan's small voice requested two hours later.

"Let's sit you on the potty first." I reached out for his hand.

Once Ethan was seated, I kneeled down to check his pull up, which was completely dry. "Yay! Check you out, big boy! Good job!"

"Hooray!" he shouted. In his excitement, he forgot to point his penis into the potty. His pee landed directly on my t-shirt.

"Ahh!" I screamed and leapt to avoid the urine.

"Sorry," Ethan replied laughing at my screech.

"It's okay. Are you done?" I asked squeezing my shirt.

"All done!" He hopped off the potty.

"Wash your hands."

After he cleaned his hands remarkably thoroughly for a two-year-old, I stripped down to my bra and used the hand soap to wash my soaked t-shirt in the sink. "I need to throw this in the dryer for a little while. I wonder if your dad has a shirt I could borrow." I tossed my shirt in the dryer. "Let's get you a snack. I'm not sure what time your dad is coming back, but you'll get to meet your little sister later on today! Isn't that exciting?!"

"Yay!" Ethan sat down at his kiddie table.

"How about graham crackers?" I asked grabbing them off the counter and pouring them on a plate. As I placed it on the table, I heard a key turning in the front door. I froze not knowing what to cover myself with. Unfortunately, I hesitated a second too long. Jabari walked through the door and halted awkwardly. My body language mirrored his, and silence consumed the air.

-

"Please tell me you're making that up!" Maakara cracked up laughing.

"Don't laugh at me!" Serena whined but couldn't help chuckling at herself.

"What did Jabari do when he came in?" Maakara asked when she composed herself.

-

"Daddy!" Ethan cried running towards Jabari. "I pee-pee on Rena shirt."

"Oh, is that what happened?" Jabari asked scooping his son into his arms.

"I am so sorry!" I shielded my nudity with my arms. "My shirt is in the dryer. If you have an extra one, I'll throw it on."

"Of course. Let me get that for you." He placed his son back on the floor and swiftly marched towards the back of the condo. I stood in the dining room unable to escape the uncomfortable situation. Seconds later, Jabari came back with a clean white shirt.

"Here you go." He handed it to me and turned his back.

"Thank you." I pulled the shirt on; it smelled like him: cologne and fabric softener.

"Good?" Jabari asked with his back still turned.

"Good." I let out a deep breath.

He turned around, and I blushed. "Again, I'm so sorry you walked in on that. That was inappropriate. I'll have to bring extra shirts in the future."

"Or you can always grab one of mine," he offered politely.

"What are you doing home? How are Emily and the baby?" I changed the subject.

"Em is good. Her mother is there with her, so I stepped away to get food and a change of clothes. The labor didn't last long. And she got the drugs she wanted. Eden is great, too." The dad beamed proudly for the first time. "She's beautiful. She weighs nine pounds and didn't even tear her mother."

"Wow! She's a big girl. It's always funny when tiny women have big babies," I commented.

"Yeah, it's fascinating."

"Did you eat already? I'm sure Ethan wouldn't mind sharing his crackers with you." I gestured towards the kiddie table.

"I would love to share a few crackers with my son." He took a seat on the floor next to Ethan's chair.

I sat cross-legged across from him and handed over the cracker box. We all sat nibbling in silence before Jabari's mood abruptly shifted. "Are you okay?" I asked.

"To be honest? No. There are some things going on that I wish I could change." He looked at me pointedly.

"Like what?" I asked resisting the urge to tilt my head downward and sniff the shirt he gave me.

"I'm going to do my best here, but it's really over this time. Emily didn't even want me in the room with her once her mom got there. The situation is going to be tough for a while, but I want out before it makes me hateful and resentful. I wouldn't want to take that out on my kids or you. I want to be happy. I should be happy at the birth of my beautiful healthy daughter and in a way, I am, but in other ways I feel imprisoned. I'm going to do my best to get out of this funk. I have to," he concluded.

"You will definitely get through this. Today is just a hard day. I'm here to make things easier on all of you. And Ethan is here to brighten your day. Everything will be fine."

"I hope so." Jabari sounded unconvinced. "Let me go grab some clothes. I'm going to take Ethan with me. Did he nap well?"

"He slept for two hours. No accidents all day. Besides on me." I paused and looked down at my shirt. "But he was sitting on the potty when that happened!"

Jabari laughed loudly then said, "Great. I'll give you the spare key. You can lock up behind yourself once your shirt is dry."

"Thanks."

"Or... you know you could just keep my shirt and sleep in it tonight," he added with a sly grin.

"Such a creep," I said with faux disgust.

"Just trying to find some happiness. That's all."

-

The next few months were eventful to say the least. Eden grew to be the bubbliest little ball of fat I had ever worked with. She fussed only when she needed to be changed and smiled most of the day. The amazing thing was she was not super clingy. I could put her on the floor for tummy time and play with Ethan at the same time. Ethan was an exceptional big brother. He tried to help me as much as possible. The two of them were a breeze to work with so I never felt overwhelmed.

Unfortunately, I couldn't say the same for their parents. Emily said as little to her husband as she possibly could. Truthfully, she didn't seem particularly interested in talking to me much either. Any questions I had she directed them to Jabari. She was present with her children physically but mentally distant. I didn't know much about postpartum depression, but sometimes I wondered if she was suffering from it. Jabari functioned at his best around the kids, but when Emily was around, it was like a dark cloud on a sunny day.

Emily also didn't move out like she wanted to, but she went back to work about two months after Eden was born. I assumed staying home longer than that was too much for her. When that happened, my hours changed to 8:30-5:00. The kids and I usually took walks, went to the library and went to free days at the museum. The highlight of my day was Jabari doing surprise drop-ins for lunch. Sometimes he brought food, other times he ate what Ethan did. It was nice to have him there keeping Ethan company when I fed Eden. I imagined that was what his life would be like if he had a happy wife.

The Shift

"Ethan needs to go to daycare," I told Jabari during naptime after an unusually quiet lunch.

"You think so?" he asked surprised.

"Yes. He likes being with Eden and me, but he's so smart. He should be playing with kids closer to his age. Maybe part-time daycare could be good for him. Prepare him for preschool you know?" I walked to the kitchen to wash the dishes.

"I'll mention that to Emily," Jabari replied distantly.

"So how are things?" I asked tentatively waiting on the faucet water to warm.

"Fine."

"Doesn't seem fine," I pressed.

"My acting is that bad huh?" He scoffed.

"You and Emily seem miserable," I blurted.

"We are," he stated plainly.

"Has she changed at all since going back to work?" I asked hopefully.

"I think it's a distraction for her, but she still dreads coming home. She's already started coming home later than she needs to. She likes drinking with friends after work," Jabari reluctantly admitted.

"Well, I'm glad to hear she's being social," I said running a dish under the hot water.

"Yeah well, that's not the whole story."

"What am I missing?" I asked confused.

"I think she's ready to see other people, so I wonder if sometimes these are actually dates that she's going on," he speculated.

"Seems soon after a baby to be dating. But I guess she's been ready to move on for a while, so I can definitely see why she's hanging out. What's the next step for you?" I asked adding dish soap to the water.

"I don't think she wants to leave just yet. I think living together is convenient for now. I imagine that will change once we separate. She's also way too financially comfortable to leave." Jabari rolled his eyes.

"So, it's back to the original plan of co-parenting for the first year and then signing divorce papers?"

"It's going to be a long nine months." He sighed.

"Sorry, this is so difficult for you all."

"Luckily I have you," he said with a look that make me blush.

"As an employee," I reinforced.

"We aren't friends?" he asked mischievously.

"I guess."

"Do I ever have a chance with you, Serena?" His question caught me off guard.

"I don't give married men chances, sir. Sorry." I shrugged.

"And what about miserable lonely married men whose wives haven't been interested in them in over a year?" he asked pitifully.

"It's gonna be a no for me dawg," I rejected playfully.

"Dang!" He laughed. "When I'm divorced then can we give us a shot?" He insisted.

"Not a second before then."

"Then I do have a chance!?" He perked up.

"It gets smaller by the second," I lied. The truth was I was dying to find out if his lips were as soft as they looked.

"Fine, let me leave before I ruin it." He left the kitchen expeditiously.

Three months of me rejecting his advances. Every day I liked him even more. And every day my lust grew stronger, while I got weaker.

-

"Girl," Maakara drug out the word slowly. "I don't know how you lasted as long as you did working with him."

"Me either to be honest with you," Serena admitted.

"Did they ever end up getting divorced?"

-

Apparently, Jabari trusted my opinion. He immediately enrolled Ethan in the daycare down the street from the house called Tots and Cots. "I didn't expect you to follow up so fast. Didn't I just mention this last week?" I asked one morning.

"We had already looked into this place before we hired you. Luckily, they had space for him. He can start next week."

"What will his new schedule be?"

"He'll go Monday, Wednesday, and Friday for a full day. He'll be home the other days," Jabari informed.

"You'll drop him off and pick him up?"

"Yep."

"What was Emily's response when you asked her about it?" I asked carefully.

"I didn't ask her. I told her what I was going to do. She was fine with it. I think she'd be fine with anything that keeps them safe, anything that gives her a break from home life," Jabari confessed.

"I understand needing a break from kids, but Emily might need a real vacation. Or maybe she has PPD. Maybe she needs meds. I don't know, but I want her to be okay," I said sincerely.

"She's miserable. Maybe even depressed. But I don't think it's post-partum. I think she's bitter about becoming a mom to kids she never wanted. Bitter about having kids with a man she doesn't love. She married for security. I realize that now. Maybe I got married for the wrong reasons too," Jabari considered.

"What do you think your reason was for marrying her?"

"I cared about her. Don't get me wrong. I still do. But I wasn't in love with her. I married her because I wanted to be married by the time I was 30. She was just the woman I was with at the time. I've been happier with other women. Shoot, I feel happier just talking to you!" he proclaimed desperately.

"Maybe you guys should consider getting divorced sooner," I suggested softly. "I know Eden is young, but staying married is not the solution for anybody involved."

"You're right. I know that. A part of me wants us to be able to make this work though. I'm scared of failing. What kind of husband was I? Was I a bad partner? Is marriage pointless?" Jabari wondered sadly.

"I understand being scared of failing, but your kids should get to see both of you happy. You'll fail them if you don't show them that."

"You're right," Jabari admitted.

"I really do wish you both the best. I just want y'all to be able to parent to the best of your abilities."

"It's so condescending when you say that," Jabari said with a chuckle. "Like you're happy it's not you who's dealing with this."

"That's because I am happy it's not me!" I laughed. "These are old people problems. I'm never getting married. No, thank you."

"You never want to get married?" Jabari asked shocked.

"I'm not interested at this point. Maybe it'll change when I'm 30."

"Please take your time," he begged.

"With Ethan going to daycare what does this mean for-"

"For our lunch dates?" he asked with hope in his eyes.

"Um no, for my pay." I rolled my eyes at his presumptuousness.

"Oh! Duh. I'll just keep it the same. Cool?"

"Perfect," I paused awkwardly. "But, about the lunch dates..."

"I'll be here if you'll have me milady." He bowed goofily.

"I would love to have y-" I stopped the words from tumbling out of my mouth. "It would be nice to see you. I like our talks."

"It's a date then." He smiled at my awkwardness.

"I know this ruins the moment, but it would be nice to talk to Emily sometimes. She can be so distant. It's weird not talking to the mom I work for. I feel like I only get your side of things. I'd like to know her better, but I'm thankful that you're willing to share with me. I know that's weird for me to say considering..."

"I can understand why you're curious about her, but I like that talking is just our thing."

"Speaking of...you should get to work. We've been talking way too long." I hoped he couldn't sense what I was really thinking. I wanted him to stay. I wanted him.

"You're right. I'll go. See you later." Jabari made his way for the door.

I didn't think I'd ever get tired of watching him go to work.

Temptation

Ethan's first day of daycare came a week later. I thought he would be excited about going to school, but he was not pleased. "Don't want to go!" He pouted.

"I know little man, but school will be fun," Jabari reassured him.

"Want to stay with Rena and Eden!" Ethan wailed with tears streaming down his face.

"They will be here when you get back," Jabari soothed.

"We'll be bored all day without you, just waiting on you to come home," I added bending down to hug him with Eden in my arms. "You go be a good boy for me okay?"

"Okay." He stifled a sob.

"And guess what? You only have to go three days a week. You're so smart and so nice that you need more kids your age to play with. You need some friends," I assured him.

"And if you don't like school after the first week, you don't have to stay. Okay little man?" Jabari was eager to keep his son happy.

"Okay, daddy." Ethan held back tears.

"Cool, let's go." Jabari reached for his son's tiny hand.

"See you, Ethan! Have a good day. Eden and I already miss you." I kissed him on the cheek.

"Bye Rena!" Ethan's voice quivered.

"Bye Ethan." I closed the door behind them.

I looked around the apartment realizing how bored I really would be without him there. It made me reflect on the months of being stuck in the house with the twins. The good thing was Eden and I would not only be playing lots of music and doing tummy time, but we could take walks. It would be fun watching her grow and learning her personality one on one. I was glad she was so little. She napped frequently, so I could nap with her, one perk of the job that I didn't have to feel guilty about.

After a warm bottle and burping, I laid Eden down on her Boppy pillow on the floor next to the couch. She stared up at me with droopy eyes. In seconds, she was asleep. I planned to read my new book next to her on the couch, but just as I got settled, I heard the apartment stairs creaking outside the door. I sat on the floor next to Eden's pillow to make myself look useful just as a key turned in the lock.

"Hey," Jabari greeted stepping inside the apartment. "I called off work. I hate to do that, but I'm not feeling it today. My son's first day of school. His mother not being interested in her family. It's getting to me," he confessed.

"You want to talk about it?" I asked noticing Eden stirring on her pillow.

"No. Are you hungry? Can I make you some breakfast?" Jabari offered clearly needing something to do.

"I could eat."

"You want some eggs? Pancakes? Sausage?" Jabari offered on the verge of desperation.

"Wow, I take it you're a stress eater?" I raised an eyebrow.

"That I am." He blushed bashfully.

"Don't be trying to fatten me up just because you're stressed out," I scolded wanting to lighten the mood.

"I'm not," he laughed. "I just thought it would be rude if I ate in front of you."

"Fine, let's move to the kitchen before we wake her up." I motioned towards Eden.

"You're the boss." Jabari extended his hand and pulled me off of the floor.

I felt the same jolt of electricity that I did that day at Dunkin Donuts, but I brushed it off. Jabari followed me to the kitchen. I hoped I wasn't doing that awkward walk people do when they're aware of someone watching them. Luckily the kitchen was just a short distance from the living room. Once there, he busied himself getting the ingredients he needed while I took a seat on one of the stools. While his back was turned, I took the opportunity to fully check him out. His body was flawless regardless of what he wore. Almost as if he could feel my eyes on his back, Jabari took off his suit jacket revealing his broad shoulders in a yellow shirt. He really could have been an underwear model. Somehow, he managed to look perfect even when cooking. His facial hair and lining were always fresh, and he always smelled like heaven. In that moment, I was convinced he wanted other women's attention because he was just entirely too attractive for his own good.

My invasive thoughts got the best of me. I hadn't heard a word Jabari said. "I'm sorry. What?"

"You weren't listening?" He turned away from the stove to face me.

"I was in my own world," I confessed.

"What were you thinking about?"

"Nothing." I suddenly found my feet extremely interesting as I avoided eye contact.

"Nothing huh?" he asked knowingly.

"Nothing," I asserted stubbornly.

"How do you like your eggs?"

"Scrambled hard with cheese preferably cheddar," I answered promptly.

"A woman who knows what she wants. I like that." Jabari admired.

"There's no reason for me to act like I don't know what I like."

"Is that so?" Jabari asked intrigued.

"Yes, it is."

"I think that's probably true for you most of the time," he said wisely.

"Why only most?"

"I don't think you're as direct with me as you'd like to be," he admitted.

"Why do you say that?" I asked fake innocently.

"I think you're very attracted to me. You do your best not to show it," he said simply.

"That's not something I feel comfortable showing. What else am I supposed to do about it?" I asked.

"Say that you like me. I see the way you look at me. Your face says you want me to take my shirt off. Your words say you're just here to do your job."

"You're wrong."

"Am I?"

"Most times I want you to strip completely if I'm honest. I've already seen you without a shirt on…twice." I held up two fingers.

"I can do that now if you want." He reached for the buttons on his shirt.

"You're going to burn the food," I stated weakly.

"Forget the food." He turned off the burners. "I want you, Serena." His eyes burned into mine.

"You are married Jabari. I work for you. This isn't right." I reminded him while my resolve melted away completely.

"I know." He decreased the space between us. One more step and our bodies would touch.

"This isn't right," I repeated breathlessly. I wanted to touch him.

"So, what if I just want to be close to you then?" He looked down at me, fingering my long braids.

"Jabari…" I whispered as he brought his face down to mine.

"Hm?" He gently kissed my right cheek then my left before pecking my lips. I nearly fainted.

"Nothing," I mumbled as his lips met mine once more. He eagerly picked me up and sat me on the counter. Our lips touched over and over again sending waves of pleasure all over my body. I never knew kissing could be so intense. I couldn't breathe, and I didn't want to. For a split second, I was able to when he nuzzled his face in my neck. I threw my head back and bit my bottom lip. Our faces met again, and he slid his tongue in my mouth. I was certain I would pass out at any second. I attempted to reciprocate the energy he gave me, but his passion was unmatched. I was totally lost in the moment until his hands ventured under my shirt to caress my boobs. It snapped me back to reality, and I pulled away.

"We can't." I wiped off my mouth and jumped down from the counter. "I have to go."

"No, you don't." He grabbed my hand reminding me of my past experiences at work. "Serena, I haven't had anything that felt this right in so long." He was so vulnerable that I almost surrendered. Almost.

"I'm going to go." I pulled away heading back to the living room.

"I hope I didn't push you too far." Jabari followed me.

"I didn't do anything I haven't wanted to do for a long time. You just made it easy for me to do it. I need to go, so I can think straight." I hurried to the door.

"Are you coming back?" he asked pathetically.

"I don't know." I retrieved my things and left the defeated man in the doorway. My last thought as I approached the second floor was gratitude. I didn't wear a bra that day.

-

"You have GOT to me kidding me! I know you're lying!" Maakara screamed.

"Wish I was lying."

"You kissed a married a man who you WORKED for?" Maakara grinned in spite of her attempt to be self-righteous. "You said you'd never do that!"

"I did."

"You might as well tell me everything now." Maakara pulled a Super Donut from her purse and ate half in one bite without caring if Ms. Jones saw her.

-

Thirty minutes later, as I was soaking in the tub, I received a phone call from my living, breathing predicament.

"Sorry," Jabari muttered with no greeting.

"I'm sorry too. Please tell Emily I got sick or something. Don't tell her about this." I was drenched in embarrassment.

"I won't. I'm so sorry. I- I don't know what to say," Jabari faltered.

"I can't say it's okay because it's not. I should have been stronger. I blame myself. I knew this would be tough when I accepted the job."

"I could have tried harder too. I should have been more respectful of your wishes." Jabari paused. "Are you going to come back tomorrow?"

The question left me uncertain. I knew it would be stupid to go back. I vowed to quit under the circumstances. The situation was not worth losing my dignity over. It wasn't worth hurting Emily over. Not worth the kids finding out what their father and I did.

"...I guess that's a no," Jabari added dejectedly.

"Um, I'll be back. We'll act like it never happened. I need to find another job before quitting for good. We'll be cordial until then. Nothing inappropriate. Deal?" I asked.

"Deal!" Jabari exclaimed sounding relieved.

"I'll see you tomorrow," I said feeling so disappointed in myself that I didn't want to see my reflection in the bath water.

"So sorry and thank you so much, Serena." Jabari hung up.

-

The following day shined brightly, unlike my mood. I was nervous. I was embarrassed. I was angry at myself for getting in that situation. But it was a new day. Things would be different because I was determined for them to be. Walking into the Atkins household appeared to be the same as usual. Ethan was waiting on me to lead his day. Eden was laying on her back on the floor with her tiny feet in the air.

"Good morning Serena," Jabari greeted in a platonic tone. "How are you today?" His attempt at being professional seemed unnatural.

"Better. Thanks for asking. I think today is going to be a great day." I performed along with him.

"I'm inclined to agree with you. I'm so glad you're doing better. And I'm so sorry if I did anything to make you feel bad."

"All is forgiven. I hope you have a great day at work." I turned towards Ethan. "How was your first day of school big boy? Did you like it?" I asked forcing some alacrity into my voice.

"Yeah!" he cheered.

"You want to go back tomorrow?" I asked positively.

"Yes!"

"Great but today you're going to hang with us okay?"

"Okay." He had the audacity to sound disappointed.

"I'm going to head out. I'll see you all later," Jabari called from the door.

"Have a great day at work," I said without looking up.

"You too." He closed the door behind himself. The mock cordiality would only last so long. I needed a new job.

-

For the next four weeks, almost as if by magic, Jabari and I acted strictly as professionals. He stopped coming home in the middle of the day. Eden was still one of the coolest babies I had ever worked with. Ethan loved school so much that he should have been there full time. The only issue was Jabari was obviously bothered by the situations with me and his wife. He did well with being friendly, but his eyes were sad. I didn't want to see him that way. I still hadn't found a job, but it was time for me to go. Maybe that would make things easier for him.

-

Friday, November 20 was different than any other day in the month prior. Jabari came home during lunchtime, barely spoke to me, and went straight to his room. I knew something was wrong. I had never seen him like that. After a bottle and burping, Eden was ready for her nap. I laid her inside the Pack N Play then straightened up the living room. After my stomach growled loudly a few times, I decided to make a grilled cheese. Since Jabari was home, I considered making him one too. I figured offering him food was a great way to break the ice. I trekked down the hall and knocked gently on his door.

"Yes?" called an unrecognizable voice.

"I was won-"

"You can open the door," the same voice called out.

"I was wondering if you wanted a grilled cheese." I opened the door to find Jabari on his back with his hands folded behind him on a pillow.

"No thank you," he declined politely.

"Are you okay?" I asked hovering awkwardly the doorway.

"I'm a little upset, to be honest."

"Why?"

"Emily is seeing someone else. There's been some nights when she didn't come home. It bothers me even though I knew we were over, even though I'm not happy and haven't been for a long time," Jabari admitted in a wounded voice.

"I'm sorry," I said weakly. It was all I could manage. I pitied him.

"And not being able to be with you makes it harder," he stated angrily.

"You've been doing good being friendly this past month. Let's not go there." I pulled my eyes off of him when I felt a familiar stirring in my groan.

"You know how I feel about you," he continued.

"I do know," I muttered faintly. "And I hope you know how I feel about you too." I stepped into the room.

"Yeah, I know. I'm just tired." He brooded, making me feel for him even more.

"Me too." My heart thundered in my chest as I closed the door behind me.

"What are you doing?" He sat up looking directly at me for the first time.

"I'm tired of being tired, and I don't want you to be tired anymore either. Emily found some happiness. We can too." I took off my shirt and walked to the edge of the bed. Jabari scooted over, throwing his legs over the side. "Can I take this off you?" I asked. He nodded and stood up. I slowly unbuttoned his shirt and removed it from his shoulders.

"You sure you want to do this?" Jabari finally found words after a few moments of silence.

"Absolutely. Do you want to?" I almost burst at the question.

"I want you so bad it hurts, but I don't want to do something that you'll regret. Don't do this because you feel bad for me."

Instead of responding verbally, I reached for his pants. He allowed me to undo the belt buckle and then the button and zipper. His pants fell to the floor, and he stepped out of them. He gently tossed me on the bed and climbed over me gazing down, making me feel self-conscious. I fought the urge to close my eyes because I needed to see and feel everything. He leaned down and kissed my lips making my entire body tremble. That's all I needed. I was ready. His kisses trailed down my chin then neck and eventually breasts. He nuzzled them until my body was on the verge of exploding. I wondered if anyone had ever died from pleasure before. The kissing suddenly stopped when he leaned over to pull down my yoga pants. Then for a second, he stood on the floor to remove his briefs. I looked down the length of my body and was surprised to see how well-endowed he was. My face must have revealed my thoughts because in a second he was on top of me again.

"You have done this before right?" he asked.

"Of course. Just not with someone your size," I admitted.

"I'm not going to hurt you. Don't worry."

"I was more excited than worried." I smirked.

Without words, Jabari quickly pecked my lips before gingerly taking off my soaking panties. I unhooked my bra then he took my breath away with his kisses once more. When his wet mouth met my bare breasts, I shivered with pleasure, and my back arched in anticipation. He took the hint and reached to his dresser drawer for a condom, slipping it on before I could blink.

"You ready?" His voice was thick with desire.

"Yes," I managed to gasp breathlessly. Jabari French kissed me before slowly pushing in his entire fullness causing us both to groan in pleasure. His thrusts gradually accelerated, and I gripped his sweaty back to make sure he was real.

"I love you," he moaned breathily in my ear. "Oh God!" Jabari eventually grunted his last words as he collapsed next to me on the bed, our naked bodies tainting the comforter. "You're amazing," he said once he caught his breath. "I'm going to marry you one day."

"No need for false promises, sir."

"You wouldn't want to marry me?" he asked as he propped himself up on his elbow.

"No. You're just hurting right now. You don't mean anything you're saying."

"Watch. I'll show you." He laid on his back.

"But to know that you genuinely care about me and aren't just using me would make this feel less wrong. The wait was worth it though." I smiled and looked in his eyes comfortably for the first time. "You need to wash this blanket though."

"I will," he said contently.

"It's literally the least we could do," I pressed.

"So, we can do this again? You don't regret it?" he asked hopefully.

"I'd love to do it again, but we have to be careful... Only on the days Ethan is at school," I said trying to maintain some type of respect.

"You're reading my mind. Damn, I love that about you." He punctuated the statement with a kiss.

"I'm going to get back to Eden." I sat up to put my clothes on, but Jabari hugged my waist and pulled me towards him.

"One more time before she wakes up?" He snuggled my neck.

"Okay, but this time I'm getting on top."

-

"Serena..." was all Maakara could manage.

"Huh?" Serena played dumb.

"No, you did not."

"Yes, I did. And I was just as shocked as you are."

Indiscretion

I was sleeping with a married man, a client no less. The very idea of jeopardizing my integrity was ludicrous when the client was Raymond, but with Jabari it was different. He made me question my morals. He was smart, sexy, and sweet. He genuinely cared about me unlike Raymond who was just a complete creep. And Emily didn't even care about her husband. She was barely home and had a new boyfriend who she was spending most of her time with. Was what I was doing really so bad?

Jabari and I continued our trysts for the next few Fridays. To spice it up, we had sex on the floor in his room, the counter, and the shower while Eden slept. Being with him made me happy enough to burst. I hadn't experienced love before, but I thought what I had with him was the real thing.

When he walked through the door with lunch for the both of us, I wasn't hungry for anything but him. I pulled him to one of the dining room chairs as soon as he put the food on the table. "Take your pants off," I demanded attempting to take charge. Then I straddled and rode him until we both climaxed, a first for me.

"I think I had an orgasm." I felt confused and proud.

"We'll have to recreate that when there are no kids around," he flirted.

"Now that I've had my appetizer, I'm ready to eat. I'm starving." I made a beeline for the food.

"You're the one that had to have me first," Jabari teased.

"You're right. And I might want some dessert too."

Growth

Three months after our affair started, it was way past time for me to have found another job. I had gotten comfortable seeing Jabari every day, and my paychecks were enough for me to save money and pay my own rent. I wouldn't continue sneaking behind Emily's back. Before telling her my intentions, I told Jabari.

"What will you do now?" he asked quietly.

"I found another nanny gig. And you'll give me a glowing recommendation when they call you." I kissed his cheek.

"Yeah, but the only client you sleep with is me. Got it?" he said jealously.

"Of course." I hugged him. "But I have to do this. And we can find other ways to see each other."

"That could be fun," he admitted reluctantly.

"This is my two weeks' notice. You'll have to tell Emily in person since I never get to see her. It's almost like she wants me with you. How she could pass you up I'll never understand." I squeezed him around the waist and inhaled his scent.

"I'll enroll Eden in Ethan's daycare ASAP. I should have known this day was coming. I was too happy to think straight," Jabari said dispirited.

"It's not the end of us. Only the beginning. As soon as you get divorced, I could move in. Or maybe you can visit me when I get my own place. I've been dragging my feet anyway. My mom can't wait to move in with her boyfriend."

"I can help you with your finances if you want," Jabari offered.

"I love that about you." I kissed his forehead. "But I want to do this myself."

"You enhanced my life so much. The least I can do is get you settled into a new place and a new job. Then I'm going to talk to Emily. I think it's time we all made a change," Jabari said resolutely.

"You know what? You're right. My mom needs her own space and so do I. I've been trying to be independent for so long. Maybe I don't know how to accept help when it slaps me right in the face. If the man I love wants to take care of me, who am I to say no?"

-

It was hard leaving little Ethan and Eden. But what was the alternative? Staying on and providing good childcare while disrespecting someone's marriage and home? What kind of woman would I be if I didn't leave?

"Bye Ethan!" I hugged the little guy on my last day.

"Bye Rena!" He squeezed me back.

"Be a good boy in school okay?"

"Okay!" he agreed excitedly not understanding he wouldn't be seeing me anymore.

"Bye Eden!" I walked over to the infant crawling along the rug and kissed her on the forehead.

"I guess I'll see you around then?" Jabari asked leaning against the front door.

"I guess you will," I flirted not caring if the kids were present. "Bye Jabari. It was nice working for you."

Dream Come True

Months later, on my 22nd birthday, I was in my first apartment surrounded by the love and gifts my boyfriend showered me with, laying in the bed he bought for us, and eating food and drinking alcohol that he splurged on. He provided me with great sex and money whenever I needed them. I had gotten used to being pampered. I no longer cared if Jabari divorced Emily or not. I was lavishly comfortable and could trust him with my life. It couldn't get any better.

"You enjoying your birthday babe?" my love asked me while checking his phone.

"Best birthday ever. Thank you." I leaned over to hug him, catching a glimpse of his cell. *Cleaning lady/Sasha* had just sent him a text.

-*Last night was fun. Can't wait to see you again.*

Epilogue

"Do you have anything to say?" Serena asked Maakara after a full minute of silence.

"I'm just…" Maakara trailed off. "I'm honestly disgusted with men in general but especially him. Let me make sure I was keeping up. The man went out of his way to pursue you while he was married while his wife was pregnant just to have a side chick for the side chick? Two women wasn't enough. It just had to be three huh? Assuming the text meant what I think it did."

"Oh yeah. The argument we had ruined my birthday. I raised hell. He swore all he did was talk to Sasha."

"Don't tell me you believed that."

"I didn't! But I hoped he would do better. I ended up staying for two whole years. The only thing he didn't lie about was divorcing Emily. I realized he never respected me or her. And he certainly never cared about all the other women he dealt with. Nobody could satisfy that man," Serena remarked bitterly. "Anyway, I finally got tired of the lies. I stayed longer than I should have because he was supporting me," Serena concluded.

"So, when did you finally leave him?"

"Late last night. I packed my shit up and moved in with my mom and her boyfriend, as hard as I tried to keep that from happening. The problem is I don't know what to do with myself now. I haven't worked in so long."

After thinking for a moment, both girls were stumped.

"Well, you got a knack for storytelling," Ms. Jones called from the circulation desk. "Ever considered writing a book?"

Acknowledgements

I would like to thank Ericka Ballard, Antonette Kierra, and Darronte Matthews for being more excited about this book than I was. Special thanks to Gloria "Gloski" Parker for listening to every boring detail and doubt in my mind for nearly two years. I'm particularly thankful that you read through that pitiful first draft. My editor Nicole Lauria and graphic designer Gabby Gaston were extremely professional, which made the book writing process flow smoothly. Lastly, thank you to my unnamed friends and family who encouraged me during this new experience.

About the author

Arika Brittany was born and raised in Chicago, Illinois. After an eight year long career in childcare and the suggestions of a few friends and family members, Arika finally got the idea to write about her personal work experiences in a fun, fictional way. While she has no background in writing, she hopes her readers can overlook the inexperience and sink their teeth into the drama.

CPSIA information can be obtained
at www.ICGtesting.com
Printed in the USA
LVHW041934130123
736976LV00011B/448

9 798506 820741